No More into the Garden

BY DAVID WATMOUGH

Fiction

NO MORE INTO THE GARDEN

LOVE AND THE WAITING GAME

FROM A CORNISH LANDSCAPE

ASHES FOR EASTER

Nonfiction

NAMES FOR THE NUMBERED YEARS (*Plays*)

A CHURCH RENASCENT

No More into the Garden

The Chronicles of Davey Bryant

DAVID WATMOUGH

Doubleday Canada Limited, Toronto, Ontario
DOUBLEDAY & COMPANY, INC., GARDEN CITY, NEW YORK
1978

Chapter Eight first appeared in *Canadian Fiction Magazine* under the title "Charlie Is My Darlin'." Chapter Ten first appeared in *Saturday Night* under the title "Terminus Victoria."

ISBN: 0-385-13452-5
Library of Congress Catalog Card Number 77–12886
PRINTED IN THE UNITED STATES OF AMERICA
First Edition

For Michael Mercer
Friend and Comrade in Arms

No More into the Garden

. . . INTO THE GARDEN

Oh, Davey Bryant, if the artist in me had not created you, the coward in me would have had to invent you. How grateful I am for the fictional fact of you and your world, for only you allow me to return to that Cornish garden by the sea where innocence lived and where, in the anodyne of my recounting your living and growing, I can also face the future. It was there, Davey, in your Celtic womb, where you learned to love and play the waiting game, that you acquired the identity which still holds the exiled me in good stead . . .

Chapter One

By one o'clock on Christmas Day we were full up with food and fed up with visiting relatives. Full up with turnips and parsnips, potatoes and batter pudding. Almost brimming over from a huge, goose dinner.

But the biggest hunks of food weren't devoured at that table in the front kitchen. It was with the clearing up that my Cousin Jan and I crammed food into bulging, hamster-like cheeks, as we took the goose carcass out to the dairy where there were supposed to be enough cold leftovers to complement the home-cured ham on Boxing Day.

It was there, standing on the cold slate floor of that severely whitewashed room, with broad slate shelves stomach-height on all three sides of us, that we grabbed whole slivers of uncarved goose, handfuls of remaining roast potatoes, and even unwieldy lumps of sausage meat stuffing, before placing the demolished bird under the huge meat safe, to keep off the odd fly which had mysteriously forgotten to disappear with summer.

We had to be quick, as a mother's suspicious timing of exits and entrances lurked menacingly in the background.

"What you boys doing? Don't need *both* on 'ee in there at the same toime. Now come on, Davey. Come and get these other things."

"Here, Jan. Here's a bit of the bugger's breast, you! I can't take that in wi' me."

"Do 'ee think she've counted all these roast spuds?"

"Davey, come on out and taike this trifle. And there's still these mincepies. I want this table cleared afore we settle down. Come *on* now!"

Jan, his mouth full as his eyes roved over tomorrow's ham all studded with cloves and glazed sugar, could only mumble.

"Best go. I could do with another of they mincepies, you. An' there's saffron buns left out there too."

So back and forth we went from the front kitchen, filmy with smoke-wreathed air made heavier yet with the somnolent murmurings of satiated adults, to that crisp and fresh-aired dairy where delicious combinations had to be swiftly invented—a finger in a crust of thick Cornish cream, the other hand busy as a buzzard's beak, stripping off slivers from the remains of the goose.

But the womenfolk finally began to collect in the back kitchen for the washing up (we boys were excused that chore on Christmas Day), we felt we wanted freedom from that crowded farmhouse, and some exercise, too, to relieve that groaning sense of surfeit.

I may say that apart from the grub, and the fact that there were now eleven adults instead of two under our roof, a stranger might not have thought it was Christmastide at all. For one thing, we never had a tree nor decorated the house. This was not, I think, a conscious matter but related largely to the fact that our farmhouse in the Amble Valley was surrounded on all sides by a dense array of trees, for the most part massive elms. Red-berried holly grew everywhere, and there was scarcely an apple tree in either orchard which wasn't festooned with mistletoe. Our lush Cornish valley had no need of vegetation *inside* the house when the foam of greenery surged to our very windows and often sent vigorous tendrils through the various slits and holes in the centuries-old cob walls.

As we slipped outdoors through the linney and wheeled our bicycles out to the lane I realized that Jan was as aware as I was of how different our December world was from that of traditional Christmas cards. It was a mild and windless afternoon in our valley, and the sun breaking through the leafless trees to make sharp shadows at the foot of the hedge was pleasantly warm to the skin. "I know, let's go down on the beach. There b'aint many upcountry people what can say they did that on Christmas Day, you!"

The idea appealed to me too. "Let's go down to Ephaven, then. There'll be no one there."

Jan gave me a funny look and I pushed forward on my bike. I knew that he was thinking about stupid Doctor Menhenniot's remarks to Mother that because I was so short for my age and maybe not as strong as some of the other kids my age at school, I had to be treated something special, like.

"Got to get down all they bloody rocks, Davey. Sure you can manage?"

With a couple of hard pushes on his pedals he had already managed to catch me up. But I didn't look in his direction, just stared ahead as I lowered my three-speed for the approaching hill.

"Cos I can bloody manage. I'm no bloody cripple, you! You can give me a bit of a hand, can't you?" I added, relenting somewhat, "Or you just too full of goose and Christmas pud?"

With one hand brushing his black forelock away from his face, Jan had the other at the center of his handlebars. Something I had not yet learned to do.

"You silly bugger! Who always goes off at half-cock if anyone ever mentions giving you a bit of a hand? You blowed up soon enough at Aunt Ellen when she started to help 'ee with that new puzzle game you got for Christmas." I colored at that, but hoped Jan thought it was merely from the flush of exertion as he knew I always had difficulty in pedaling up that first steep incline in the curving lane. "Aunt Ellen is a silly old cow, and you know it. Always interferin'. An' if Mother do say anythin' to her, tis allus her weepin' and hollerin' and sayin' her'll never visit agin for Christmas. I dunno why Mother do put up wi' her, year arter year. I really don't, you!"

"She's still frettin' over her Harry goin' down on that ole battle-wagon—H.M.S. What's-her-name. That were only two Christmases ago, don't forget."

"I s'pose," I agreed. Glad that the talk had shifted from me to Aunt Ellen.

When we reached the Celtic cross at Treveare Turn and

started to speed up along the flat of the ridge, I tried to think of Cousin Harry—dead, drowned, food for fishes—somewhere out there in that gray-blue expanse we could now see behind the tower of Endellion church. But all I could conjure up was a freckled face under a shock of red hair, and a summer's day in the harvest field when he'd come home to St. Tudy on his last leave. He'd taken off his naval jumper and worked in that white shirt-thing sailors wore: with a square collar and short sleeves. Three years older than Jan so five years older than me, he'd not paid either of us much attention, but talked only to Father and Uncle Jan, or old Jim Treharrock who was stacking up the sheaves.

But the Cornish coast, snaking away below the silvery Camel Estuary, with its pea-green clifftop and black rocks abruptly scissoring a blue and sun-tamed sea, pushed a fragile memory of a drowned cousin right out of mind. As we started the final descent down the cliff lane to where we would have to leave our bicycles and continue on foot for the long climb down, the breeze from the sea suddenly brushed our faces, excited us, so that we yelled in glee, took our feet off pedals, and played Spitfires in a dive, down that unmade, bumpily dangerous track.

It is true that my head ached a bit and I suspected the exertion may well have made me pale, by the time we let the bikes flop against the leeside of the hedge, but I managed to screen my face from Jan's scrutiny by walking just behind him. In a short while I knew I'd be safe from solicitude as the path we walked degenerated into a single-file track where it wound between the already visible clumps of enormously high gorse which were as flamingly yellow in their December flowering as I could ever remember them.

But once beyond the giant bushes of prickly furze, (as we called gorse in Cornwall) Jan turned, looked hard at me, and suggested we *both* have a rest before making the final steep descent to the cove. So to the tune of a still invisible surf and the desolate cry of gulls, we lay on our backs and, smelling the sun-warmed turf, watched the great clouds sail by.

"They look strong enough to hold your weight, don' 'em?" said Jan. "How'd you like to be a captain of a cloud, Davey?"

4

"I'd rather—"

"Rather what?"

I'd been going to say "grow a few inches and not feel pooped so fast," but quickly decided not to. "Go roight up there in the blue. Between they two clouds, there. Be a hawk or something."

From the corner of my eye I watched Jan roll over onto his stomach, then raise himself so that he could prop his head on his cupped hands.

"Oi reckon Oi'd like to be out there. Not one of they ships in a convoy, though. A destroyer, maybe. Or a frigate."

"Funny to think of people out there, somewhere, sitting down to Christmas dinner. Think they have turkey and Christmas pudding, Jan? Or goose like us?"

"Ham or corn-beef," he said firmly. "If 'tis in tins, that is. And if they'm not at Action Stations."

Somewhere behind us, away in the distance that is, a dog started to bark. Probably rounding up the cows for milking, I thought. It vaguely bothered me. I didn't want to hear farm sounds just then. It reminded me of work, and that was what we'd just cycled away from. I stood up. "Let's go on down, Jan. I expect 'tis bravun warm down there. I want to lie flat out on they rocks."

By the time I'd finished speaking I had already started down the rabbit-cropped turf, toward the winding brown stream, half-choked with watercress, which spilled through the rocky crevice of the cliff to reach the water's edge.

"Ack-ack-ack-ack-ack—I'm dive bombing, Boy-o!" I ducked as Jan sped past me, his long legs flying over that grassy slope, the smoothness of which was such an invitation to run pell-mell. I prayed for the day when I could race him right from the top—and win. But realizing what lay ahead I only walked as fast as I dared, to preserve my breath; telling myself at the same time that it was I, after all, who had suggested the place, wasn't it?

Jan was waiting for me as I reached the upcurled lip of the cliff and peered over and down at the tiny cove, its piled rocks and frothy breakers spending themselves in time to leave a narrow strip of glistening sand.

"Is the tide coming in or out?" I shouted, having to raise my voice over the screaming gulls as well as the periodic crash of surf.

"In, I think. Want me to give you a hand? 'Tis bloody slippery where that green weed is, you."

"I can manage," I said firmly. "I'll tell 'ee, if I need a bit of a tug later on." Teeth clenched, I moved determinedly past him and started the sharp descent between the boulders, the noisy waters of the fanning stream about my feet.

Right opposite, somber in shadow, was a huge cave. The tide *thundered* in there and I could see gray jackdaws flying about its mouth. It looked so big and dark in contrast to the sparkle and warmth of the sun that I turned right around and faced the rock-face down which I was gingerly climbing.

"That's roight," Jan called, "Better facing inward loike that."

"Of course," I called back up. "You know I've climbed Everest, don't 'ee?"

I even smiled to myself for holding back the real reason I'd turned around. I decided to say a little ditty to myself—partly in honor of the time of year, partly because such things helped when I had to concentrate on something physical which I found hard to do:

"I am Marley's ghost, feed me on bread and toast . . ." (That rock there looks a bit like the knocker old Scrooge had to bang . . . Careful now . . . Musn't get frightened . . . Musn't panic . . .)

"Swing round a bit this way," Jan shouted. Somehow he must have passed me because he was obviously already far below.

"I'm just resting a moment. Looking at this slate. It's loike they round the fireplace in the front parlour at home."

I could smell the seaweed and kelp, now, which the tide had pushed to the top of the beach. It was so strong it made my eyes water and I was nervous again about climbing down.

"It's lovely down here, Davey. Breeze is all gone. We can sunbathe, youl"

That settled it. I was going right down and I was getting there under my own steam. With beads of sweat forming on my upper lip as I gave myself to the task, I climbed, slithered, jumped, and almost fell, but in a few minutes I was there with Jan on the coarse, dark-flecked sand at the very top of the beach, sinking in it almost over my ankles.

"Where?" I said, trying unsuccessfully to hide the fact I was panting. "Where shall we lie? Gosh! 'Tis bravun warm down here, idn' it you! You'd not know it from on top."

"Warm enough to bathe, if 'ee loikes."

"But we didn't bring our things."

"Think they gulls and jackdaws is g'in fret? There b'aint no other buggers comin' down here, I'll tell 'ee that."

But my objection was the merest formality. The words were hardly out of my cousin's mouth before I had accepted them as the most wonderful idea in the world. There ahead of us was not only that clear green swell beyond the sparse waves (even climbing down I'd noticed you could see the smooth sand on the bottom), but in that water I could be even superior to Jan because I was a better swimmer than he was. In there I could squirm like a seal, be as agile as a mackerel. I drew a deep breath, tearing off my pullover as I did so. "Let's go," I said.

But Jan wasn't having everything as quick, as instantaneous as I wanted.

"We'll get undressed over there. On that big flat one." He pointed to a smooth slab of rock which grew out of the beach and rose two feet or so out of the water at its far end. "Leave your clothes roight up on 'un. Jest in case the tide's still coming in a bit. And remember that barbed wire on the other side, Davey. Keep well this side of it, you hear?"

I nodded, but as a matter of fact I'd quite forgotten. Ever since the danger of invasion—whenever that was—the beaches of North Cornwall had been festooned with barbed wire, and in some places, cement fortifications too. But a couple of winters of Atlantic storms, plus the aid that several of us boys had given during summer holidays, had broken down those rusty entanglements. And here at Ephaven most of it had by now been carried out to sea—or maybe taken by some farmer to use in lieu of a hedge.

But now I could see what Jan meant. There was a pile of it in the shadows by the cave's mouth. Looking over there I thought I could also see a smudge of cement on an occasionally exposed

7

rock, and an iron stanchion welded to it. I turned away. I didn't like that side of our little bay. Mind you, the sea is often like that. In sunshine it is a place to play. In darkness or shadow all sorts of cruel things spring to mind . . . I suppose that's because although we can learn to swim, we really belong to the land.

I fairly scampered in Jan's wake, and didn't get far up the slope of that rock before I began peeling off my shirt and unbuckling the silver clasp of the belt that held up my gray flannel shorts. It was after that I paused, though. "You mean take *everything* off? Before we get in the water?" But Jan was already down to stripping off his socks; his trousers and Aertex shirt already strewn across the rock's surface. "Well, you b'aint going in there to do your laundry, idiot! You'm not ashamed of your birthday suit, be 'ee?"

It was obvious that *he* wasn't. He stood up and swung his arms as if he was doing gym at school. I couldn't help noticing the faint line around his waist: the fading heritage of last summer's tan. I could also see he had some body hairs growing where they were not on me . . . Perhaps when I could grow taller . . . Splash! And Jan was in—right off the rock at its highest point. I got up and marched over to stand just where he had.

"Merry Christmas!" I called to the water-chuckling cove. And dove in after my adored cousin.

It was like a cool, cellophane skin enclosing me. Not cold, harsh, but velvety smooth to body and limbs. I had never felt so buoyant, so free, as I did on swimming for the first time on Christmas Day, and for the first time in the nude. For a while I played my secret games. First I was a gamboling dolphin, then Tarzan's son as I swam along the bottom, opened my eyes, fought the smarting, and wished I had a dagger or something, to defend me from crocs and alligators. Then seeing Jan's legs, an arch of invitation, I swam quickly between them. Rose swiftly, and clung to his unsuspecting back.

He yells: "Aaaaaah!" It echoes around the confines of the bay.

"Weren't expecting that, were you?" I laugh, as I bob in front of him, both of us treading water.

"Know what I thought it was?"

8

"No. What?"

"A corpse. A dead-un, you!"

"What 'ee mean?"

"Didn't you hear that explosion a little whiles ago?"

My ears are full of water. I can hardly hear him! "No. Why? What were it?"

"Depth charge, I reckon."

I stop treading water. My feet find a submerged rock. If I tiptoe I can keep my balance on it. Just . . .

"Way out at sea, of course. There's a Jerry, a U-boat out there."

"You don't think 'tis coming in 'ere, do 'ee?" I can't hide my anxiety.

"Don't be maze! As if 'er could! This idn' Padstow in the Great War, you know! No, what Oi were thinking were about what might have 'appened earlier."

"Like—like what?"

"If 'twere following a convoy it moight have got one of 'em. Last night. Yesterday. Last week for that matter."

"Well, we do know that there were that one back a whiles when Jim Pengelly's dad told as 'ow he saw them Coastal Command Wellingtons flying up and down, looking for 'un. *They* was dropping depth charges, too."

Jan must have also found a rock to stand on. He wasn't bobbing up and down any more either. "Corpses get washed ashore, then, don' 'em?"

I looked quickly beyond his head. There's the mouth of that damn cave again! The water swirling there looks black. And—and what's that rising up and down in the mass of seaweed?

"Let's get out," I say. "I'm getting cold."

"Jest cause I mention bodies floating in 'ere on the tide? Don't be so stupid, Davey! I was only 'aving of 'ee on."

"I—I baint feeling so well, if 'ee must know. Feelin' proper poorly as a matter of fact."

"Thought you allus felt better than anyone when you was in the water."

"Well, tidn' so now! Not that there's anything the matter with Oi moind. Jest a bit of spell, you understand, Jan?"

"All right, then. But let's have a look for bounty on the way in. How about that, eh?"

"Bounty?"

"Fred Trethewey found a crate of oranges washed up. They was proper soggy with seawater, though. Couldn't eat the buggers."

Anything, I think, is better than being here in the water where, any second, I expect something cold and slimy to brush against me. I kick off from the submerged rock and swim overarm (my fastest stroke) toward the slope of the beach. I hear a splashing and realize that Jan is swiming just behind me. I reach the shallows just in front of him, and even pause so that we can leave the water together. Now I feel safe again. The shingle includes fragments of mussel shell which are sharp to my feet, and when our bottoms are fully out of the water the funny sense of being nude comes over me again. But I am walking with my older cousin whom I have just beaten in that short race from the rock, and I am certain that we are the only two boys in the whole of the British Isles who are walking naked out of the sea on Christmas Day.

Up at the top where the seaweed is piled, lots of it bright yellow bundles of what looks like a giant's bootlaces, we start to search for treasure.

"Look out for that bloody barbed wire," Jan cautions for the second time. "Mind where you walk now."

But he need not worry. I pick my way very carefully indeed.

"There's a dead bird here, Jan. A cormorant. It's got oil over 'un."

"Well, come over here, boy-o, and see what I foun'. 'Tis better than a bloody dead jackie, you!"

I look up sharply at that and see he is almost at the rock where our clothes are lying. I hurry over. "What is it then? Cripes! Don' this seaweed stink!"

"How 'bout this, then?" Jan is standing, legs apart, holding up something dark and dripping, by a strap. As my sight flits swiftly down the strap I fleetingly notice how shriveled his thing is now, from all that time in the water. But it's still so much bigger than mine . . . "Well, what is it?" I can't keep the irritation out of my voice. (Why does he have to find something and not me?)

"It's a binocular case, that's what it is."

"Anything in it?"

"Dunno. 'Avn't opened the bugger yet."

(I knew he had held back doing that just for me. But I couldn't rid myself of the spurt of spite that his finding the case had generated in me.)

"Well, 'twont be no good, will it? I mean all that soakin' in the sea . . ."

Jan shrugged, even as his fingers fiddled with the buckles and strap.

"Your friend Wesley Jago picked up that German jackknife on Polzeath beach. 'Tweren't a bit rusty. Hey! What you'm frownin' for? 'Tidn' a hand grenade, you! 'Tis Christmas Day, remember?"

I forced a grin I didn't feel. "'Tis just that you'm such a butterfingers wi' that buckle."

But I spoke too soon. Jan was already lifting the flap. I caught a glimpse of the inside lid. It looked like velvet. Then into the sunshine he pulled a perfect-looking pair of binoculars. The glass in them glinted and I grew aware of my blood pounding as I noticed how marvelously complicated they seemed, with several focus rings between the lenses, and small white markings here and there.

"Are they"—I cleared my throat of accumulated excitement—"are they ours, or Jerry's?"

Jan turned them upside down, looking for lettering. Nothing dripped from them and I knew then that they were bone dry. "Well, if this is English, I'm no Cornishman."

"If—if it says 'Deutschland,' that's Germany all roight." I was tingling with excitement and felt quite flushed. I may even have been dancing up and down but, if so, was unaware of it. "Can I?"

"Here." Jan's arm jerked out toward me, and the strap of the binoculars suddenly unfurled and dangled there. I took them with both hands; feverishly tried to read the tiny, indented words.

"Happy Christmas."

I looked up. "What—what you mean?"

"What I say. They'm for you. Christmas present, you silly bugger."

"But you give Oi that aircraft recognition book I wanted."

"So here's present number two. You'm lucky, that's all. Well, you'd better see they do work, don' 'ee think?" I glance at Jan, glance at the binoculars, and then look about me. "On the rock, up there where our clothes is. Let's try 'em out up there, Jan."

He's smiling at me, which makes me feel kind of daft. "Lead the way then, skipper. Maybe *you'll* see something floating in this toime."

But I only have eyes for the precision instrument clutched in my hands. The flat slab of rock proves warmly comfortable to my stomach as I spread-eagle there, propped on elbows, turning all the sight adjustment rings to achieve proper focus.

"Well, do 'em work? See any Jerry subs?"

They were as clear as I could desire and marvelously powerful. As I focused on the meeting place of dove-gray sky and charcoal distant sea I started to talk, knowing that Jan was lying there on his side watching me. I also sensed he was rather happy.

"I—I can see land . . . A bravun big place . . . Hold on, I got to focus better. There . . . 'Tis a town . . . a big city . . . lots of ships tied up there in the harbor."

"That 'ud be Halifax, Nova Scotia, would it. That's roight, opposite here, they say."

"Well, they'm roight! 'Cos I can see trappers—and that stuff Cousin Leslie brought home last toime?"

"Maple syrup."

"Maple syrup. And bananas and oranges. And real milk chocolate. Whip cream walnuts. And Oi can see Grey Owl and his beavers. And—"

"Get on wi' the food, Davey. Is there any coconuts, you?"

"Don't be daft! 'Tis Canada I'm looking at, idn' 'er? There's the St. Lawrence . . . And buffalo . . . hundreds on 'em."

"I'm getting bloody hungry."

"If Oi 'old 'em higher I can see further and further. There's wheat growing—must be summertoime out there. And the Rockies! I can see the Rocky Mountains, you!"

"What about Cadbury's milkflake. Oi'm bravun fond of they!"

"There's another big city. That's Vancouver cos we did that last week with Miss Trewelyn. Then water—that's, that's the Pacific Ocean!"

"Water? We got enough of that bloody stuff here!"

I lowered my magic eyes. "I love the Atlantic—look what it brought me today! But when the war's over and we'm grown up and Oi'm taller an' that, I'm g'in' cross it. Oi'm g'in' go where the binoculars jest took Oi."

"Let's have a go, then, can Oi?" I handed them over to my cousin.

"What can 'ee see, Jan?"

"Wait a sec'. That's it! I can see a convoy. Escorts is corvettes and destroyers. God dammee!"

"What's the matter?"

"There's me. Sublieutenant. On the bridge. Drinking a cup of hot cocoa I am. Kai, they calls it in the Navy. I got the second dog watch. We just sank two subs and is depth-charging for a third bugger. Here, they'm pretty good, b'aint 'um? Trust they ole Jerries, you! Got to admit they'm bravun' smart when it come to things loike this."

On the warm, slate rock in the sun-gilded afternoon, I lie content. "They're quite the nicest Christmas present Oi've ever had, Jan."

"Here, you'd better look some more. But don't look up at the sun, moind, or 'twill bloind 'ee for life!"

Taking them from him I trace the low flying of a cormorant heading out to sea. It's so *close* I feel it might hit my nose if I'm not careful. "I think I can see a seal playing out there, Jan. I'm sure 'tis a seal."

"You hear that?"

"Hear what?" I ask, searching now for a rare Cornish chough and its bright red regs, but prepared to accept even a jackdaw.

"Listen hard. Towards me."

"You farted again?"

13

"'Tis me *stomach*, Matey! Oi tell 'ee, Oi'm starvin! That's a stomach rumbling from hunger, that is."

Reluctantly I lower the binoculars and turn toward him. He's already putting on his singlet. "Toime we was started back, Davey. You got they cliffs to climb, remember? Don't want to be late for supper, do us?"

I remembered. The cliffs, that is, and my sweating fear when descending them. But the binoculars were a stronger thought. With them I had more powerful eyes than anyone in our school . . . "All roight," I say, putting them carefully back in the sea-blackened leather case. "I reckon I could do with a bit more goose, meself. And there's that stuff she didn't bring out at all at dinnertoime."

At the top of the cliff face we stopped for breath, and took a look back. I took out my binoculars again and looked right up that cave opposite. It didn't look half as dark and mysterious with everything so close up . . .

. . . Perhaps only child-molesters refuse to accept that our sexuality lies outside the garden. Though, Davey, when you were seventeen, you were unaware of it. But when the knowledge settled in you, as chill as the Cornish mist, there were intimations of madness in your response. And even now, in 1977, David Watmough needs the psychic wounds muted through my beloved scapegoat. You can speak of my shame, can burn in the humiliation of a publicly revealed erotic bias and show the futility of a blind retreat toward a Christ whose crucified arms could not cover, could not conceal . . .

Chapter Two

Even after a year in the Royal Navy I had never seen so much gold braid on an officer's arm—at least at such close quarters. I was very frightened. I stood there trembling in my sailor's bell-bottom uniform signifying the very lowest rank imaginable, while this tall Admiral (I thought that's what he was) paced the length of his posh cabin, occasionally throwing my quaking figure a glance but more often examining his long fingers, especially the nicotined one.

"Well, Bryant. Let's try again. Why did you do it?"

"I—I don't know. I think it was to do with the metal, though. The steel, that is."

How could I explain to him that my seventeen-year-old heart ached for the sight of green elms in a Cornish lane; for the sun-warmed hush of my native valley and soothing granite (whether outcroppings in a sea of golden bracken, or as stout posts on which mossy old wooden gates could swing)? How could I tell this handsome, silver-haired Englishman that under the rough blue serge of my uniform was a farmboy's body? Or that suddenly, up there on deck at Morning Divisions that gusty May morning, under joyously free clouds scudding quickly over the River Tamar to shadow soon the far Cornish shore, Davey Bryant had abruptly split in half?

My body had been there at attention as the Chaplain droned on in prayer to his nautical god for "those who go down to the sea in ships and occupy themselves in great waters." But my mind and feelings had slid out of that hated uniform and hurried

back to that womb-farm I had fretted to leave just twelve
months earlier.

". . . Roight then, Davey. You just milk Blacky and the
Ayrshire, will 'ee? An Oi'll take the three heifers to the lower
shed."

"Right, Dad. Then we'm taking the sheep down to Tretawn for
dipping after breakfast, b'aint us?"

Standing there in line with hundreds of other sailors I imagined the acrid tang of the flock and the tattered ropes of turds
adorning the back flanks of the ewes. And when order for Ship's
Company to march off was bellowed by the Chief Petty Officer,
fierce in his white gaiters and belt, I heard instead the thud of
small cloven hoofs as those ewes, lambs, and the black-faced ram
panicked and baa'd their way between the high stone hedges of
the winding lane.

"Steel? What the hell has steel to do with it? You were given
an order and refused to obey it."

"I—I didn't hear it, sir."

"Didn't hear it? Well, the Master-at-Arms yelled loudly
enough. I could hear it up on the quarter-deck—and the wind
was the other way. In any case, you were given at least a dozen
orders after that—including one from the C.O. himself. Now
what about this steel business, eh?"

"I suddenly wanted trees and grass. Here it's always metal un-
derfoot."

"I'm sorry, Bryant, but the days of wooden ships are over.
There's little one can do about that."

"All this cold steel, sir. It's getting me down. I want to go
home. Back to our farm. I—I'm not well. But Mother can look
after me."

"Do you know what the Service thinks of mutiny? Even one-
man mutiny, son?"

I knew he was trying to be kind, but it only allowed the anguish to well more in me.

"I shouldn't have volunteered for this lot. It was a terrible mistake."

He stiffened at that. "There's just the little matter of a war
going on which seems to have escaped you, Bryant. Do I have to
remind you of a man's duty?"

I felt sullen. "I don't believe in duty."

"I beg your pardon?"

"It's like my mother says. Bugger duty! If you can't do a thing for love, you shouldn't do it at all."

"Yes . . . well . . . the Royal Navy has never found it possible to rely on love, exactly . . ." He suddenly straightened, coughed, and faced me. "Now listen to me. Do you know what I am?"

I looked up at all that gold braid again, started counting the rings for the umpteenth time.

"It's an Admiral of some kind, isn't it, sir?"

"I'm a Surgeon Rear-Admiral, Bryant. In other words, a doctor."

So that's what the crimson bit between the gold was. I had never really mastered the meanings of red, white, or purple between the gold bands. Or if I had, it had gone completely out of my mind these past unhappy weeks, since my return from civilian detention after the police had arrested me for importuning and soliciting one evening when on shore leave.

"Yes, sir."

"And do you know where you'd be this very minute if I hadn't been up there for Divisions this morning?"

"No, sir." But my unruly mind had already left his cabin for the makeshift passage up which one shooed the reluctant sheep before they had to plunge into the tank and, seconds later, scramble out, turned from woolly white into miserable, dripping creatures of violent rust-red.

"You'd be in cells, Bryant. You'd be in the bloody brig, that's where you'd be!"

But his words knocked only faintly at the edges of my consciousness.

"I should walk home, that's what I'd do. The minute no one was holding me I would just walk home. It's sheep-dipping time about now, I reckon."

"Desertion, according to K.R. & A.I., Bryant, in wartime, can bring the penalty of being shot. I presume you're aware of that?"

I made a huge effort to concentrate. "I don't know what K.R. & A.I. means, sir."

"Patently. King's Rules and Admiralty Instructions. The law of the Service, don't you know. The law you quite voluntarily put yourself under when you volunteered as an Ordinary Seaman for the Period of Hostilities—according to your papers here."

I sighed with tiredness. "I don't feel any hostilities any more. Anyway, we've had VE Day. It's all but over, really, isn't it?"

It was the Admiral's turn to sigh. "Sit down, Bryant. Over here. I want to talk to you."

As I crossed to him I thought I could detect some kind of perfume, and wondered whether it was one of those after-shave colognes I had seen advertised in glossy American magazines that sometimes circulated our messdeck when a U.S. ship was berthed next to us. It made him seem more of an Admiral than ever. It was not a smell I had ever come across in Cornwall . . .

I sat down where he had indicated but had to put my hands upon my knees to try and stop their shaking. But all it did was to make my arms shake violently too.

"What are you so scared of, son? No one's going to eat you."

There was an immaculate crease in his silvery hair, and the skin of his face looked softer, more clean-shaven, than that of most men. And his cheeks were slightly rosy. As I stared at these features from such a short distance I realized abruptly that he reminded me somewhat of my grandmother.

"I'm not going to hurt you—to the contrary."

"I—I know, sir. It's just my legs—they won't stop."

He swiveled on his chair and busied himself with the top drawer at the back of his huge desk. "Here, you'd better swallow this. It'll calm you down."

I always needed water to swallow pills, but I didn't like to ask him. I could feel the thing stuck in my throat, wanted to cough and return it to my mouth again. But I didn't dare do that either.

"Now, my lad, this is what I'm going to do with you. I'm going to put you into hospital for a little while. An Observation Ward it's called."

"But I'm not ill, sir. I'm very healthy, really I am."

"It's our psychiatric unit—and that's not half as alarming as it sounds."

But I was already on my feet. "But I'm not mad either. I'm—"

"Now stop interrupting and sit down." He spoke quietly but it was an order nevertheless. I slowly did as I was told, and then there was a pause between us. Letting it sink in who was boss, I thought. As if he need have worried with craven me!

"You'll be under the special care of a personal friend of mine, Dr. Alex McDougal. He'll run a series of tests on you and then he and I will consult."

I spoke out of a sense of overwhelming fatalism. "You're putting me into an asylum with a lot of loonies. You think I'm mad just because I want to go home. I shall be in there for years and years."

"Look at me."

As I did as I was bid his two hands came forward and took mine and held them between his—squeezing a little as he did so. When he spoke, his voice was softer than I thought ever came from admirals.

"Let me try and put it another way. You told me earlier you write poetry, right?"

"A lot lately."

"That's not the sort of thing one would expect from a sailor, wouldn't you agree?"

"I suppose so. I haven't thought about it much."

"Can you quote the last one you wrote?"

"No, not by heart. But I've got it here." My hand gladly disentangled from the embarrassment of his and reached inside my naval jumper.

"Like to read it to me then?"

I unfolded the somewhat soiled and creased piece of paper—a lined page torn from an exercise book. Then I licked dry lips and began to read:

A gray mist, leaden taut, is weighing on my mind tonight.
My head is throbbing with the overwhelming might
Of outside forces clamoring from near and far.
My soul is lonely: seared, a festering wound.
My grief has raised a latent barrier.
My ears are silent; now no sound to beard me in my den.
At last, at last escape from fellow men.

It was he who gently broke the silence after I had finished. "That sounds as if it were from the pen of a very depressed young man to me. I don't know too much about it but it also sounds a very nice poem. Do you have many others?"

I thought of my ditty box in my locker. "Hundreds of 'em. I write them in my hammock after 'lights out.'"

"And what about the others? Do you remember what they are about?"

"Well, like I said, not by heart, no. Oh, I don't know—about Cornwall some of them are. Lots about death. Suicide too. Then that's because I have a morbid turn of mind. Mr. Coles, my English master at school told me a long time ago." I thought quickly over what I'd just said. "But that doesn't mean I'm mad or need to be put in an asylum."

"I don't think so either, young fella. But I certainly think that Dr. McDougal can help you. After all, we don't want a repeat performance of this morning, do we?"

"All I want to do is to go back to our farm and write my poems. Why won't they let me go?"

"No one is saying they won't. But I'll tell you this. A few days in our Observation Unit is more likely to help than hinder. What about it, eh?"

I have always known when to bow to the inevitable—though knowing and doing don't come together so often for me.

"I've not really got any choice, have I, sir?"

He gave a little smile. "Not really."

That evening found me in a bed, not a hammock; moreover, there was no gentle rise and fall of a vessel at anchor or the rhythmic slap-slap of a running tide. I was lying there in H3 Ward, and one of the Sick Bay attendants was kindly explaining things to me as the ward grew dim and from various beds came the sound of snoring. "Half these sods are swinging the fucking lead—just so as to get demobbed early. The other half are so bloody crazy they should be properly locked up in the bleedin' bin."

I stared across at the rows of white beds opposite. Halfway down the ward a man sat up in the funny, old-fashioned nightshirts several of them were wearing in there. He was crying.

"What about him?" I asked.

"Dunno. He's been blubbering like that ever since he come

into H3. And that's over a week ago." He was speaking quietly but suddenly his voice dropped even lower. "But that's enough of the ole small talk, eh?"

The note in his voice made me turn toward him. He was pressed against the side of my bed as he leaned over me.

"Want to take care of this, then? It'll be worth your while, ops."

It wasn't difficult to catch his meaning. The bulge in his white trousers was very obvious, and he kept fondling it with forefinger and thumb—the way some men hold their cocks when peeing. I turned my head away.

"I—I don't go in for that kind of thing."

"What you mean you don't. You're a brownhatter, aren't you?"

I realized then that he had a slightly Cockney accent. Also that he was a lot older than I was. He wasn't very good-looking either—what with a harelip and something of a boozer's grog-blossom nose. I still refused to look toward him, wondering what to do.

"You needn't bother to deny it, ops, 'cos I seen yer papers. You was in the civvy clink, wasn't you, for importuning? I allus check up on my patients, see. Anyway, I can spot a 'hatter a mile orf. Knew what you was the minute you come in."

I wouldn't answer. The very memory of those months in Winchester Prison crushing me with misery and humiliation all over again.

"How about sucking on this, then? Make your time in here a bloody sight more pleasant, I don't mind tellin' yer."

I didn't have to incline my head to realize that he was taking it out. Even turned away I caught the faint scent of his genitals, and right after that could feel the head of his probing prick as he gently pressured my left shoulder with it.

"Fuck off," I said finally. But my words were without energy as I knew I had already stiffened between my legs in response.

"Come on!" he urged. "I knows you really want it. You don't have to pretend with ole Jack. 'Sides, it'll be better for you if we're real friends, like."

But it was not the implied threat of that to which I responded. I told myself I did not care for this man, this Sick Bay Petty

23

Officer who must be at least thirty and thus old. But I nevertheless felt excited by the subjection he was demanding of me.
That, even more than the insistent pressure of his knob, was
what made me finally turn round to face him and it . . .

"That's better, ops. Bet you ain't seen many that size, eh?
How's that for a piece of meat?" He lifted it from my bedclothes
and swung it, truncheon-like, before my eyes. Incapable of other
action, I put out my hand to take hold of it. I was surprised that
it was hotter than my palm, which had just come from my own
crotch.

"You're a nice-looking kid, do you know that, ops? Thought so
when you was being signed in. He's got a nice little bum, I says
to meself. And knows how to swing it, too. He's been on the
game, that one has, I tells meself. Oooh that's *nice* . . . Pull the
skin back hard . . . Ah, that's *good*, mate."

All the time he was speaking in that low voice of his I was
sliding my hand up and down his tool; and all the time the enormous mushroom end of it, with a bead of moisture protruding
from its little slit, came closer and closer to my face.

There were thoughts still bounding in me—not yet pushed
aside by my increasing lust. 'I am what he thinks . . . a whore
. . . a tart . . . I am just as the naval slang has it, a brownhatter
. . . a slut in a boy's body. And I love it. I love holding this ugly
man's big prick and I want him to come all over my face and
prove what an object of humiliation I am . . .'

I started to rub him even faster, but he withdrew a fraction
and put a restraining arm on mine.

"Not all at once, ops," he whispered. "There's no rush, kiddo,
no rush. Just play with it a bit, why dontcha?"

Free of my hand he thrust his cock forward and I could feel
the heat of its brownish smooth end against my closed eyelid. I
wanted to swoon. As he began to slowly brush the whole of my
face with it, I knew very well what he wanted me ultimately to
do. Something I had never done. Oh, there had been times when
I kissed men's cocks since donning the uniform of the King's
Navy to help win the war. And once, when lying opposite ways
with a boy my own age, in a dank, brick-smelling air-raid shelter
during basic training, I had taken advantage of the unembarrass-

ing dark to lick his prick. And he had done the same for me. But we had finished by my changing position so that our tongues and mouths were joined, while our hands served each other down below.

But this man, who by now was stretching so far over me that his balls entirely blocked my sight, was not looking for a sexual playmate; showed no interest in the fact that I had kicked some of the bedclothes away and was using my free hand to keep myself at erotic pitch. What he wanted was a service. The way I put it to myself, as I craned upward to kiss and smell the cooler skin of his scrotum was: 'He wants to fuck my face.'

He spoke again as he lifted his weight entirely onto the bed, the better to straddle me, and he now sounded almost maternal —or better, like a cow offering its udder to its calf. "You can play with them, ops. You can suck my knackers if you like."

At seventeen, going on eighteen, I didn't know that when a man offers you his balls his real gift is of vulnerability, but I suddenly lapsed back into infantilism and put up both hands as well as my nose and lips to his testes, playing there contentedly like a child with a comforter in its crib.

But as a warning bell in the swim of retreat to suckling babyhood as I hung on my man's balls was that growing sense that this was a mere stage on the path of his selfish fulfillment. And I suddenly wanted to finger myself again in order to achieve that blurring sense of passion which would finally free me of inhibition, would allow me to attain that degree of abandon where my mouth could be freely offered as proxy cunt for his cock. But I couldn't get either arm down to caress my own stiffness. I could only concentrate on my sight.

In the end, though, as he arched back and I found his stickiness pressed against my closed teeth for entry into the moist warmth of my mouth, it was not my own body's hunger that caused me to yield; to open wide to the point I was almost gagging as my eyes closed and my fingers held firm to the curls of his thick pubic bush. It was a sighing return to the land of self-degradation where, finally free of responsibility, as convicted pervert, as male prostitute, I could accept that brutal thrusting. It was his fine contempt I fed on as, with his climaxing spasms while he clutched my head tight, the urgent animal seed was pumped chokingly down my throat.

After that I can recall only the insolent wiping of his dripping dick on my lips before it made its softening way back to his pants; before the world of the ward returned searingly to confirm my shame.

"What about me, mate? Will you do me now?"

"If you loiked what he give you, boy-o, you'll fuckin' faint over this'm here!"

Fool! Bloody fool—to think they had all conveniently slept while my Sick Bay Attendant had insisted his great prick be paid tribute. Fool even more to think their silence had spelled respect for my privacy. Every owner of these hoarse voices now calling out their claims had only been waiting in line for the new whore to slavishly minister to themselves. No, not every voice—for amid the contemptuous requests, and fierce demands now came other commentaries. "Filthy little brownhatter! They should fucking well lock yer up!"

And from some dark corner a rising wail: "In the name of the Lord Jesus you will rot in hell for your sins!"

Had *none* of them been sleeping? Was it all a giant conspiracy?

"Crawl over here, homo. I want to fuck the bloody daylights out of you."

"Jesus and bloody Mary—get that pouf *out* of here!"

Sitting up in bed I thrust both hands to my ears, but their words still entered. I began to scream, shouted my frightened defiance at them.

"You're all mad! You're a bunch of loonies!"

"My God! Look who's talking!" The voice was one of those cultured, clipped, English accents that I had come to associate with naval officers—though there were certainly no officers in H3 Ward. It came from the next bed to mine where ever since my arrival that afternoon I had seen only a dormant form with even the head hidden under the sheets. I turned on him now, spitting with rage and fear.

"So what are *you* here for? All right, I'm a queer. What are you? A maniac or something?"

The Sick Bay Petty Officer touched my shoulder. "All right, ops. Knock it orf, mate. Here, I'll get you something to help you sleep. Something I don't pass out to these bastards." He gave me another nudge. "I told you it 'ud pay off to keep in with me."

But I didn't want any further association with him, for he must have known we were being observed; had probably inflicted himself on every newcomer to the ward.

"Go to hell!" I said to him, and leaned toward my neighbor in the next bed. "Go on, tell me, Mr. Superior. You like watching other people do it? Is that it—you just a bloody peeping tom?"

He was lying on his back now, quite motionless. When he spoke again he addressed the ceiling, still in those clipped well-modulated but almost expressionless tones. "I've tried twice to commit suicide. I'll manage next time. You should too. We're quite worthless, you realize that, I hope."

I didn't answer, his words shocking all vestige of anger from me and leaving me once more with that overwhelming sense of isolation from parents and family, schoolfriends, and that overall heterosexual world that I had been saying goodbye to for the past twelve months.

The clamor in the ward began to subside. And the return of the Petty Officer, and a few shouted orders from him for quiet, completed the return to the situation when the main lights had been turned off and he had come to my bedside.

"What you crying for? They ain't bothering you no more. Nor will they while I have something to do with it."

"I'm not crying."

"Snifflin' then."

"I hate it here. And I hate myself. When will they invalid me out?"

"Take this for a start. You'll soon feel too sleepy to worry about all that stuff."

He had even brought a glass of water—which was more than the Surgeon Rear-Admiral had offered. I did as I was told, realizing with a shudder as I did so that my throat was still full of his own deposit. I had never felt so unclean as when I sensed his semen sliding farther down me.

"I wish I could die."

27

"You don't have to get out of the Andrew to do that, ops. At least a couple of the bastards do it in here every week. Take that bloke next to you. Son of a Commander, R.N., that one is. Never has fitted into the Lower Deck. Well, he's twice jumped out the bleeding window. Spends his time picking out the stitches again after we patch him up. Silly bugger!"

"I—I thought you said this was an Observation Ward only?"

"Well, we're observin' the sod, ain't we? Anyway, the whole bloody place is overcrowded. It's odds and sods everywhere. Surprised we 'aven't got a pregnant WREN in here with the rest."

I turned over on my pillow, faintly enjoying a cool patch to my tear-hot cheek. But he went on steadily talking as if I were still facing him.

"Now I wants yer to be careful, kiddo. They're all quiet now, right? But I tell yer, anything can set this lot off. And you bein' a good-lookin' hatter and a Cornish janner an' all—well, there's them what sees Satan in every queer and them what thinks all Cornishmen is lying and thievin'. So you keeps yerself to yerself, d'you hear me?"

But it was only very faintly that I did. "Yes," I murmured as the pills he had given me took gradual effect. "Yes," I breathed again to his warm Cockney voice. Then drifted off into dreamless sleep.

I woke in the morning thinking at first I was in my white-painted iron bed over the farmhouse kitchen, and when I moved slowly into consciousness there was a moment when I thought I heard my mother shouting from down below that breakfast was ready. But only too soon I realized it was a man's voice I was hearing and that he was shouting the dismally familiar naval refrain: "Wakey! Wakey! Rise and shine! Hands off your cocks and show a leg!"

Through half-opened eyes I watched various nightgowned figures pass the foot of my bed on their way to the heads and bathrooms. I decided to wait as long as possible before emulating them. The final conversation with my Petty Officer came back to me. I looked at this patient and that, wondering which might hate homos and which Cornishmen. I also wondered which were real loonies and which were faking it.

But there was no real anxiety in these reflections. Although I was now fully awake I still felt caught up in some vast dream where all edges were blurred and there was no reality. I thought briefly that it was maybe a heritage from the sleeping pills but dismissed the notion as I lay there thinking of the succession of events which had brought me finally to H3 Ward and the company of madmen. It was such a long time, I told myself, since anything had been truly clear—except the aching wish to go home to the farm.

Even the encounter with the Surgeon Rear-Admiral had already taken on a fantasy quality and I found myself querying his existence—until I recalled his taking my hands in his, and my fleeting thought at the time that this surely wasn't the way admirals normally behaved with ordinary seamen.

Then the only events that did not seem wrapped in this great cocoon of haziness were those relating to my queerness. Incidents in certain Plymouth pubs where women were remarked only by their absence, a meeting with a Free Pole in the lavatory at North Road station, an encounter with a fellow sailor in the back of an American jeep speeding between Liskeard and Bodmin on a weekend leave pass—these things leaped quickly and sharply enough into focus. And, of course, there was freshest of all the sex of the previous night with my Petty Officer. As I finally permitted that to occupy the centrality of my daydreams I once more felt my body stiffen in response. If I had been alone, hid from all, I knew very well what I would have done next. But lying there, aware of those shuffling figures, I wondered instead if my constant masturbation was part of an insanity which linked me with the rest of them in the ward. For once my hand did not stray downward and instead I moved over onto my tummy and eyed the figure in the next bed.

He must have heard the movement as I rolled over for he suddenly turned his head and, for a while, stared at me in silence. Recalling his contempt of the night before, I kept my eyelids half-closed. I didn't want an argument with him, didn't really want him to to know I was even looking at him.

"Do you believe in God?"

To my surprise his tone was warm, conversational. He might

have been asking me if I liked fish and chips. Even so, I delayed answering.

"I don't mean like those stupid bloody chaplains at Morning Divisions. I mean, do you really believe there is some Almighty Whatnot who cares what you do or don't do?"

"Sounds like you don't," I prevaricated. "You seem to have a thing about it. Can't say I've thought too much about it," I lied, for I had a strong sense of God and knew that I was invariably punished for all my wrongdoing. I addressed long prayers to Him before sleeping each night and at home went regularly with my parents to the neighboring village church of St. Endellion where I was a server at Mass.

His tone changed then. "I shall know definitely if God exists long before you do," he said darkly. "Before any of these poor imbeciles in here."

I recalled his words the previous night about suicide, and what my Petty Officer had told me about him. "I—I think we know God differently at different times. When I am working upfield at home, say, I have one sense of Him which isn't at all like in church. It's much harder here in the Navy, though, I have to admit. Then maybe He's sort of local."

"What do you mean, 'local'?" His voice was edged with suspicion.

"Well, He's obviously easier to feel in church and churchyards because people are concentrating more in places like that." I thought a bit more, as he was silent and didn't answer. "You know, when I'm home I often go up on the moor. There's a special place. With an obelisk thing to a woman who was murdered there by her jealous lover. Now I always feel something special there. Maybe not God exactly, but certainly spirits. It's like—"

"That's not what I'm taking about," he interrupted. "I'm not taking about bloody *ghosts,* for God's sake! Pantheistic crap!"

There was the same sense of dismissal he'd vouchsafed me the night before. I bridled now as I had then.

"I'm afraid I'm not sure *what* you're talking about. Then you'd do better having this conversation with a priest or someone like that. I know what I know and I don't have to explain it to you.

In any case, I'm just a farmer's son. I haven't had your kind of education."

"Oh, don't come all that *faux naïf* nonsense with me. First the sweet little innocent who lets that Cockney lout of a male nurse have him the very first night he arrives here, and now the unspoiled rustic business. I know very well you're a cut above this bunch of illiterate dolts, even if you are a pansy. As if I can't see why that bloody trick-cyclist put you in the next bed! You're not playing the right game, you know. Instead of coming on as the village idiot, you're supposed to provide me with some intellectual stimulation. Cheer me up, don't you know, so that I'll cooperate in their stupid little games."

As he twanged on in that high-falutin' accent of his I tried to make out what he looked like. The night before, of course, there had been little light in the ward, but even now in daylight there wasn't too much of him to see. He had pale, wavy hair but all I could really make out of his face, which was partially concealed by the sheet he had drawn up high, was a pair of almost white eyebrows. I couldn't make out his length but for some reason suspected he was tall. I thought he was a year or two older than me—but then, I assumed everyone in the Navy was.

"I don't suppose you have too many friends." I didn't much like the sound of my own voice—too whiny, petulant—but he had somehow gotten under my skin with his remarks about my using my background as a kind of protection. It had happened before, you see. I mean, some months earlier, I had been standing in the bar of the Lockyer Hotel in Plymouth and a civilian had tried to pick me up. When I thought I'd made it quite clear that I wasn't interested—trying not to be rude—he had suddenly turned on me and very bitchily accused me of playing the innocent. I had just turned on my heels and left the pub. And now here was another attacking me in the same way. Well, whatever either of them said, I was younger than both—and just because I'd given up my Cornish accent except when I went home (in fact, I was experimenting with a broken French accent those days and was often called Frenchie by my shipmates who didn't know me too well) I didn't put on any snobby airs. I never sounded hoighty-toity like this Englishman in the next bed.

"I'm in the process of shedding people, not collecting them," he said in answer to my remark about his having no friends. "I've spent a week trying to explain to that little twit who thinks he understands the human mind that people only blur one's reality. Eventually there's only the flight from the alone to the alone."

I saw my chance. "Why start talking to me then?"

But he was skilled where I was only smart-alecky. I could sense his lip curling up as he answered me. "Beggars can't be choosers in a dump like this. And even your middle-class limitations are better than that proletarian oaf on the other side of me whose ideas of the comic don't rise above farting."

But I had had enough. I can't tell you just how much that laconic voice, so even with self-assurance, disturbed me. I had never met the likes of him before. I told myself fiercely I never wanted to encounter his type again. "I've got to get up and go to the heads. I can't waste time talking with you any more."

But even my attempt at rudeness he shot down effortlessly. "For Christ's sake, don't bother to *explain* what you want to do. That's so bloody bourgeois. Just get up and do it."

I did just that. I slid from the bed at the opposite side from him, took my toilet bag from my locker, and followed the few stragglers left toward the bathrooms. Most of them were nearly through when I got there. I took the farthest washbasin from the door as the two next to it were now vacated. I decided that I would put off using the heads as long as possible, preferably until I was all alone in the washroom.

I shaved the few hairs of an incipient mustache and beard carefully, wondering as I did so why they had left me my safety razor when they had taken my shoelaces away. I then tended my teeth (of which I was inordinately proud), brushing them up and down rhythmically as Mr. Penarrow, our dentist in Bodmin, had taught me. Before taking my toilet to the top of my head by moistening my hair from under the coldwater tap, I glanced about me and noted with satisfaction that my plan had worked: I was now alone in there, free of the thrall of being observed.

My hair I considered my crowning glory, and the kind of attention I paid it had only too often elicited the guffaws and crude comments of my fellow sailors. But now I could carefully part, comb, brush, and form water waves with my fingers without danger of ridicule.

I was well into the elaborate routine I had developed when, looking into the mirror to judge the effects, I saw that I was no longer alone in there. And even as I glimpsed the white soft-collared shirt of another patient, I heard him speak.

Speak? Speech? A grotesque euphemism for a quiet, ominous babbling, the memory of which causes me to shudder even now. As I turned to confront the idiot mutter I felt the hair rise on the nape of my neck—the only time in my life that has ever happened. What I saw coming toward me, arms swinging slowly from side to side, and an open cutthroat razor clutched tightly in one hand, was a face that summoned up everything as a child I had imagined as madness when passing the grim gray walls of the County Asylum in Bodmin, Cornwall.

I must have thought that if I strove for coherence it might have a comparable effect on this shambling shape, its loose-lipped mouth drooling, eyes staring without focus beneath a fringe of fine, crude-cropped hair. If so, my hope was vain.

"Can I help you? Is there anything you want?" My questions seem ridiculous now. They did not then . . .

But there was no time for reflection, for he kept on coming, the arm bearing that vicious-looking razor raised ever higher above his head. As I tried to take a step backward I felt the unrelenting edge of the washbasin pressure my spine. My mouth was so dry I knew no more words could come. Then I began to shake in all my limbs with quivering fear.

From what seemed an enormous distance—in that I heard the words about my ears but they would not enter—a man spoke.

"Don't move, lad. No quick movements, right? Jest keep looking at him. Smile if you can."

At the edge of my sight I made out the uniformed figure of a male nurse behind that creature who was still coming closer to me in that weird, dance-like shuffle.

"Get him!" I managed finally. "Get him away!"

With my left hand, which was slightly behind me, I fumbled and found my own Gillette safety razor—puny object that it was, compared with the lethal weapon in his hand. But at least it brought a small relief to me, a lowering of that clammy panic which had enveloped me on first glimpsing that patch of white over my bare shoulder. It was a consolation, too, for that terrible vulnerability issuing from the fact the whole upper part of my body was naked for the purpose of washing, and that I could almost feel that sharp steel in his hand coursing across my nude skin.

The male nurse spoke again. "Now, gently, without taking your eyes off him, move slowly down to that corner. He can't get to the side of yer that way. Get it?"

It was only then I recognized that the voice of my would-be savior was that of my bedside visitor of the night before. Controlling my breath lest even that seem too abrupt, I did as I was told, sliding along the edge of the washbasin and not taking my back away from it until I found myself in the far corner of the room from the door and escape.

The crazy eyes followed my every move—they were focused now all right! But the babble of sound from his mouth altered in neither pace nor inflection. And he still weaved in my direction.

"Stay there," I said, almost at breaking point. "Don't come any closer."

"He's not hearing you, son. You're wasting yer breath. Jest keep as still as you can. Here we go!"

Although the nurse's rubber-soled shoes made a soft noise on the tiled floor as he sprang forward, the man didn't turn round. I saw the burly arm flung about his neck, wrenching up his chin before he sank to the ground under his assailant's weight. The razor clattered across the floor, and there was my rescuer astride the prostrate figure, his knee in the small of his captive's back. It was all over so quickly that there were long moments before I could even sag in relief.

"Call outside, kid, will you? Tell 'em to bring a strait jacket wiv 'em."

But I just stared down at the moaning man beneath his knee. "How—how could he come in here like that? He could've killed me!"

"Well, the bastard's never given us no trouble before. Here for observation—jest like you, ops. You never can tell, see. He may be as sane as you and me—jest swingin' the lead to get out the Andrew, like I was tellin' yer last night. Then again he might jest have flipped. Like anyone could what comes into H3."

I stared at him, the fear reluctant to subside. "Meaning me too, I suppose. You mean I could end up like—" I indicated the pinioned man with my foot.

Looking up at me, my petty officer suddenly grinned, revealing two stark gaps in his teeth as he shook his head. "Aw, not you, ops. Not after last night. You're too interested in things outside yerself, still, to start frothin' at the mouth. It's blokes like this wot's too wrapped up in 'emselves that's got the problems. There's no sex for me with the likes of them—they're no good to themselves or anyone else."

He jabbed his captive slightly with his knee. "Now for Christ's sake go and fetch me some help, this bugger's strong."

But I continued to stare at him. The ease with which he could allude to the events of the night before, turning my fear back to shame . . .

"Hurry up now, Bryant! That's an order."

To the crispness now in his voice I finally responded, moving toward the door without even glancing again at my potential killer or the man I had sexually serviced upon my bed.

In the unreality of mental illness, Davey, you could find delay but no solution. But in the respectable role of the parson, did you think the wounds would heal? The scar tissue at least grow strong? Did you ache to yield to the heresy that there was salvation in the strength and protection of another? I let you learn, as I have not, that the pain of the past cannot be rolled away and a route back to the longed-for garden discovered through the invocation of childhood's nursery. But Davey, my shadowy self-love, your antics reveal that "white" possession can be as crippling as "black" possession: both of them strange entrances. You have taught me via your evasions and the allure of your teacher and mentor, Dr. Monk, the terrible dangers of handing over the self to the false authority of a fellow being.

Chapter Three

For me, at eighteen and three months, the London drawing room of the Reverend Symes Monk, F.R.C.P., L.R.C.S., was certainly the most beautiful room I had been invited into. And I was not simply being influenced by the depressing austerity of the ships and barracks I had experienced for eighteen months in the Royal Navy, or the farmhouses and cottages I had known all my life in Cornwall and which I had just left after my demob leave a few days earlier.

For one thing, in the late fall of 1945, the time I refer to, there was still no domestic use of electricity in the village I came from. And in such towns as Truro and Falmouth, where I had relatives, or in Plymouth which had been my base as a sailor, light bulbs tended to hang from cords in the center of ceilings and shades were rarely more than a plain white "coolie hat," with the occasional diversion of a heavy brass standard lamp with a cloth-covered shade which boasted hanging tassels.

But this splendid rectangular room (in retrospect all Cornish rooms seemed harshly square and excessively high ceilinged) had no light fixture in the ceiling but was softly illumined by several wooden standard lamps covered in which looked like fine linen, and as many table lamps which appeared to be converted from expensive and lavish-sized vases. These too had shades of an opulence to match their fellows.

If the warm glow of discreet lighting captivated me, the second feature to lay claim on my youthful attention almost took my breath away. I speak of books. In the front kitchen of Treworder, behind the latch door which scraped on the uneven slate

flagstones if pushed too far open, were a couple of shelves hous-
ing the few books we Bryants possessed—from the family Bible
and Pear's Encyclopaedia to the novels of Daphne du Maurier
and *Footprints of Former Men in Far Cornwall* by Parson
Hawker. But here in elegant Vincent Square, near Westminster
Abbey, Dr. Monk's books ranged every wall in long, creamy-
white bookshelves that rose only to the level of the window sills.
While on top of the shelves themselves, at discreet distances so
that there was no hint of clutter, were arranged such things as
small terra-cotta statues, expensive-looking crystal objects, and,
at various intervals, great bowls of flowers that bore no connec-
tion with the fact that it was November month outside. As the
trim, black-satin maid with crispy white apron and headgear
welcomed me across that enchanting threshold, I found my head
soon swimming with the unseasonal scents from vast clumps of
orchids and other strange blossoms.

In a huge blue cloisonné vase at one end of the long mantelpiece were several branches of yellow, furry buds which I would
later come to recognize as mimosa; while balancing that display
at the opposite end of the mantel was an artful arrangement of a
pure white flower with thick petals and even more fleshy leaves
of pale green. As I stood there, quite overwhelmed, I thought
suddenly of those travelogue movies I used to see as a schoolboy
in the cinema at St. Columb, with trips up the Amazon and the
Orinoco . . .

"Dr. Monk will be with you shortly. Just make yourself comfortable."

I thanked the parlormaid or whatever she was, and as she
quietly shut the paneled oak door behind me, I moved quickly
over the biscuit-cream carpet with its voluptuously thick nap to
admire more of what I had already decided was a veritable
Aladdin's Cave of good taste.

Looking back, I can only see myself that rainy, blustery night
as a piece of eighteen-year-old blotting paper. As I closely examined a cluster of dim icons on one wall and then moved to a
recessed shelf over which hung an exquisite holy water stoup, I
wondered if such things could ever be mine. Like a small puppy
for whom everything is both an invitation and a threat I wan-

dered about Dr. Monk's drawing room, appreciation and awe fighting for ascendancy in me.

A somewhat pale youth with two blots of high color about either cheekbone, I was not particularly strong in those days. "Neurasthenic" was the description applied by one doctor during the process of my being invalided out of the Navy, and my mental state was perhaps indicated by the fact that I had spent the last two months of my war service in the psychiatric wing of a naval mental hospital under scrutiny for "Depressive Reaction."

This, indeed, was a primary reason for my presence there at Dr. Monk's private residence. I had not been in the Navy very long when I had encountered a chaplain who had rather casually suggested one day when we were walking through the barracks that I might consider a postwar career as an Anglican priest. Subsequent to my arrest by the civilian authorities and my ultimate return by them to my base, the notion of ordination occurred progressively to me and by the time I left the Service I had talked to several more chaplains and had a substantial correspondence with various Church authorities.

However, because of my morals charge and time in Winchester Prison, the Ecclesiastical Board which handled prospective ordination candidates from the armed services had insisted I see this priest-psychiatrist before a final decision was taken as to whether or not my university studies in theology would be funded.

So, possibly from a combination of my awareness of how important Dr. Monk could be to the rest of my life with the novelty of appointments in his drawing room, after a few minutes more inspection of his possessions, I suddenly sank back exhausted on his large chintz sofa and stared dreamily into the flicker of flames from the log fire which burned so strongly in the grate.

I was staying for the few days of this, my first visit to London, at a Y.M.C.A. in Bloomsbury, and because I had left the Navy owning only the speckled brown demob suit, replete with vest, which I was now wearing, plus ten pounds in cash, I had elected to walk the distance from Great Russell Street to this part of Westminster, to save tube or bus fare. It was a long way and I was far from robust. Anyway, I must have succumbed to the room's warmth, for the next thing I knew was opening eyes and staring up at the becassocked figure who was leaning over me. I opened my mouth to apologize, but he was already addressing me.

"Hello. I hope I didn't frighten you. I did give a little cough when I came in but you were well away in the land of Nod! I'm Symes Monk, and you must be the intriguing young Cornishman, Davey Bryant."

Though still muzzy from sleep I was immediately aware of the musicality of his voice. To a Cornish ear, although one accustomed to a medley of accents in the Navy, he sounded very English, very educated. But there was nothing of that abrasive arrogance I had encountered with naval officers or the kind of ludicrous extravagance of vowel I was going to encounter amid my fellow theology students for the next four years.

"Oh, I *am* sorry." I started clambering to my feet. "I—I think it was the heat of the fire."

"But what an entirely sensible thing to do! Tell me, Davey, do you often have forty winks like that? It's a great gift. It was a great asset to Winston during the war. Now why don't you sit down again and I'll just squat over here."

As I sank back into the enveloping folds of the sofa's cushions, he crossed to a matching armchair and sat down, smoothing the skirts of his cassock as he stuck his legs out. I noticed as he crossed his feet that he was wearing expensive-looking, buckled shoes and that his socks were light gray.

"Now tell me something about yourself, dear boy. I know, of course, that you're a Cornishman, that you are a candidate for Holy Orders. Also that until recently you were a sailor boy and that the Navy made you—well, rather ill."

I stared at him in astonishment. "I didn't know you knew all that!" And because I suddenly thought that sounded rather rude: "I mean the Reverend Fairweather—I only got his letter two weeks ago about phoning your secretary. And I didn't think that he knew all *that*."

Dr. Monk chuckled. "Well, the Church isn't MI 5. It's simply that George Fairweather is an old friend of mine. As a matter of fact, he's mentioned you several times during the past year. Ever since your naval chaplain, Theodore McKay—another old friend of mine, by the way—got in touch with him about your possibly having a vocation to the priesthood. Mind you, all I know about are the things that have *happened* to you. And they don't tell one too much about the real person. That's why I invited you to drop by this evening. They can have all the forms, all the questionnaires they want, but there will never be a proper substitute for personal encounter, don't you agree?"

The smile he afforded me made me glow through and through. He was treating me totally as an equal. That had never happened to me before. It made me feel altogether humble. "Well, I think you know most of what there is to know about me. There really isn't much more to tell." I wouldn't have said that to anyone else, I'm not sure I even believed it, but there was something about this brown-eyed man with his round, boyish face and neatly parted hair which drew at me powerfully. The simplicity of his cassock with its worn leather belt, the warmly melodious voice that was so calming—it all made me want desperately to reveal all there was about myself. Yet at the same time I felt terribly callow and unformed and afraid to disappoint him. I need not have worried, though. If ever there was an expert at putting someone at ease it was Symes Monk. Within a space of minutes I was chattering away as if we were as close as my cousin Jan and me. There was nothing more reassuring than his ability to laugh at himself and when he wasn't telling me how silly he had been on this occasion and that, he was doing wildly funny impersonations of famous people such as the Archbishop of Canterbury, and Mr. Atlee, the Prime Minister, both of whom he seemed to know very well indeed. He told me about preaching his first sermon before the Royal Family, and being advised by an old Domestic Chaplain "to keep the standard at the level of the maids."

Then I started telling him things about myself, too. Told him things I would never have dreamed, before meeting him, of telling anyone. I spoke, for instance, of my passionate love of animals and those I had raised from infancy on the farm: of Rufus, my fox cub, of Castor and Pollux, my twin polecat ferrets who always followed obediently at heel around the fields of the farm, and of Grip, my young raven, who had been found with an injured wing at the bottom of my uncle's granite quarry on the edge of Bodmin Moor. I told him of all those boyhood things—fights with my cousin Jan, the Christmas we bathed nude in the ocean, the time my father had chased me through an alder hedge when Castor and Pollux had escaped from their hutch and wantonly killed a score or so of his prize Rhode Island Red pullets. All things, mind you, which I had carefully kept hidden from my fellow ratings in the Navy. And the mention of my dad, or mum too, come to that, were topics which had been strictly taboo with me in all my intercourse with the outside world beyond our farm.

When I embarked on all this stuff about me growing up at Treworder I may have been a bit hesitant, but he kept asking me further questions, wanting the exact names of all my animals, all my schoolfriends, and especially wanting to know all about my parents. At one point, I must admit, he embarrassed me. It was when he asked: "And what do your mummy and daddy think of your wish to be ordained, boy?"

Where I came from, "mummy" and "daddy" were terms only girls used, but I put it down to some English thing with him. Or perhaps an educated usage as yet unfamiliar to me as legitimate talk among adults. Oh, I was only too painfully aware of how uneducated, how uncouth I was, during that first session with Dr. Monk. But as I told him ardently at one point, I certainly did not intend to stay that way, especially if he would help me.

He seemed quite touched by my comment, for he leaned over and gave my arm a squeeze and murmuring: "We shall not let you down, boy. We shall not let you down." At that moment, from somewhere in the house, a telephone began to ring. But he went on quietly talking through the noise. It was then that he told me he believed I should be ordained. Indeed, that I should start at college that very term, even though it was more than halfway through.

"I'll tell you what I am going to do, Davey. I'm going to get you into King's here in London where I am myself on the staff. This first year won't count as such towards your degree, but it will give us a chance of getting to know one another much, much better and put you in the way of proper study again after all that upsetting time in the Navy. Besides, boy, there's no point in your moping about on the farm in Cornwall until next September. That, in fact, would be very *bad* for you."

Nothing could have pleased me more and I was about to say so, when the phone stopped.

"Well, if you're sure it's no trouble, sir. I mean I could go back and get a temporary job I s'pose."

At which point the uniformed maid who had initially let me in was announcing that the phone call was for Dr. Monk and could he come at once as it was something of an emergency. Characteristically, I felt, he was all apologies to *me* as he got up to go. And again I felt flattered, seeing who I was. Indeed, it ended up me urging *him* to go and that I would happily look at some of his books during his absence.

And that is what I did. I recall admiring his blue-bound set of the Wessex novels, and vowing to read Hardy myself at the first opportunity. I made a similiar vow over the collected works of Henry James. I came next to a fat volume of theology which, glancing through, I could make neither head nor tail of, and it was just as I was replacing that arcane tome between a book on the Council of Nicaea and one on the heresy of Arianism that I heard a faint noise which made me get up from my haunched position and stare toward the window.

Aware that it was both raining and blustery outside, I first thought it was merely a branch of one of the shrubs I'd noticed on climbing the steps to the front door, scratching against the glass. But then I heard the sound again and realized it did not sound so much like scratching as *tapping*.

Curious, I crossed the room. But before I had reached the heavy cream drapes the tapping had developed into an insistent if discreet knocking, only this time it seemed to be against wood rather than on glass. Very carefully I lifted the edge of the drape and peered out. At first all was black, save for the raindrops, glistening now from the room's illumination, on the small panes of the leaded windows. By this time the small sound was even more determined, and by craning my head to the left I could just make out some dark figure before the front door, huddled on the very porch where I had stood with such apprehension an hour and a half earlier.

I wondered why whoever it was knocking did not push the doorbell as I had done. More knocking. I stood there in a quandary, loath to usurp the maid's function, yet increasingly aware that the knocking was growing in frenzy. It was then I remembered Father Fairweather explaining to me that Dr. Monk was not only a priest but a psychiatrist which meant a medical doctor too. For all I knew this might be an ordinary patient, or perhaps the husband or father of one, for the figure's shape had the tall proportions of a man.

It was that which decided me. I opened the door of the room leading to the hallway, and made for the front door. But before my hand had reached the latch I was brutally aware of how cool it was out there in comparison with the cheery warmth of the fire-lit drawing room. I shivered just as I pulled the heavy door inward. But even as I did so, whoever it was who had been standing there pushed brusquely past me and almost rushed into the drawing room. I had the presence of mind to shut the front door again before moving rather crossly in the wake of the stranger.

As the man turned and faced me I had fleeting impressions of his pallor, of eyes wide with agitation, and the fact he was wearing a very dark, navy-blue raincoat. His few strands of sandy hair—for he was nearly bald on top—lay flat and glistening from the rain.

"Where's Doctor Monk?" he asked me hoarsely, even savagely. "Where is he? I've got to see him!"

But I hardly heard him, any more than I properly saw him, as he stood there his hands clenched before his chest in some kind of anguish, for there were other, more incredible things to lay sweeping claim upon my attention. For one thing the room's atmosphere now seemed utterly different. The warmth of it was gone and I saw my own frosty breath and his, meeting each other as the temperature dropped lower and lower. Instinctively I looked toward the burning logs in the grate and to my amazement saw the flames dying down before my eyes. Above, on the mantelpiece, those exotic flower displays began to droop, the thick, fleshy leaves to shrivel. From green they started to blacken, like dahlias licked by the first ice of winter. It was likewise on the low bookshelves where other bowls of flowers were kneeling over and drooping lifeless over the edges of their vases. I started to shiver violently, my bones to ache from the plummeting temperature.

I moved my legs, almost afraid that I would freeze solid there in my tracks. And as I did so there came the realization that the force of that awful cold was emanating from him. He, too, moved slightly in the direction of the window. Where I had pulled back the drapes to peer out I could now see the weird patterns of frost spreading over the glass panes . . .

"Please! For God's sake find Father Monk! I—I can't go on much longer. Can't you *see*—I'm dying!"

Maybe it was through an association of ideas at his words, or maybe from my horrified staring at that bloodless face and awful white hands, but to my nostrils came the cold, damp stench of the graveyard. The monstrous thought that flashed then in my head was: 'Not dying, but *dead!* It's a dead man standing here with me. A ghoul!'

With enormous effort I found live words with which to address him. As little more than a croak from my throat I managed: "I'll see. The telephone. He went to answer the telephone."

As I stumbled toward the door, as if in answer to some deep though inarticulate prayer, the slim youthful form of Symes Monk suddenly materialized there in the doorway. He smiled gently at me.

"I'm sorry, Davey, to keep you." Then he looked over my shoulder to the stranger, quickly surveyed the icy room. The gentle mouth was abruptly grim, and the boyish features dissolved as he seemed suddenly to stiffen in resolution, just as the tall stranger lurched toward him.

"Father, for God's sake, help me! I'm—" He had flung himself to his knees before the cassocked figure and his voice now dropped to a whisper I could hardly make out. What I *think* I heard him say was: "Help me, Father. I'm possessed."

But Dr. Monk was already speaking—intoning, rather—in a voice quite unlike anything I had heard from those lips before. I suppose I realized the language was Latin, but little more than that. I saw the priest withdraw a small crucifix from the recesses of his cassock which he held above the man's head in his right hand while his other fingers rested gently on the left-hand shoulder of the raincoat.

How long that bizarre scene was maintained I have no means of knowing, for I closed my eyes and tried to pray. Strange expressions that I had never, to the best of my knowledge, previously encountered, formed there easily in my head . . .

'O Lord Jesus Christ, Savior of the world, I beseech Thee to enter this man's soul. Cleanse it from its sins and imperfections, cast out its unholy dweller and fill it instead with Thy heavenly benediction and grace . . .' And all the time Father Monk continued his low-voiced invocation: *"De profundis clamavi ad te, Domine; Domine, exaudi vocem meam. Fiant aures tuae intendentes; in vocem deprecationis meae . . ."*

From the stranger there came low grunts and moans. Once, even, a strangled scream. I opened my eyes on hearing movement, in time to see the priest striding across the room to where I had noticed that holy water stoup hanging. He returned with it and, lifting the tiny lid, began to sprinkle the contents upon the figure now lying crumpled across the carpet. I saw the man twitch convulsively several times and heard a further hoarse cry followed by what seemed, incongruously, a burst of laughter. Then he fell still and silent.

There was a pause during which I could only hear my own deep breathing. From where I knelt—and, God knows, I never recall ever falling to my knees—I heard Father Monk exclaim a loud Amen and then observed him as he moved quickly about the room scattering the holy water from the miniature stoup in every direction. Even as he did so I grew aware of that awful cold being dispelled. In the fireplace the flames flickered into life once more, while the flowers above, and their leaves, gathered strength and stiffness before my eyes. Wobbly, but with the awareness that the ice had gone out of my soul, I got to my feet again. The stranger did not, though. He lay there very still, his body shaking gently, and I saw he was quietly crying.

For the first time since the man's entry I realized that with his presence the lights about the room must have dimmed, for now they seemed to grow in power until I had the distinct feeling that something like normality had returned to the drawing room. Dr. Monk, in spite of dark rings about his eyes and a generally haggard appearance, then addressed me and in doing so confirmed the impression of normalcy.

"Davey, be a good boy will you and ask Iris to phone the Westminster Hospital for an ambulance. This poor chap will need a bed there tonight. I'm going to have to sedate him, so will you first give me a hand to get him onto the sofa?"

Together we did just that and then I went for the maid. When I returned, Dr. Monk was in the process of using a hypodermic in the man's bared arm. He talked as he worked. "This will send him off into the land of dreams. The poor fellow will still feel exhausted, though, when he wakes up. Here, let's have a peek at that tongue. Thought he might have bitten it off during those convulsions. Ah, good! He'll still be able to blow a raspberry when he feels like it."

"Is—is he unconscious?" I asked, for I noticed that the man's eyes were shut and he seemed quite lifeless as he slumped there during the doctor's ministrations.

"I think he's drifting off now. In any case, he's utterly worn out. These things are very, very tiring."

I wanted to question the priest further, but at that moment the uniformed attendants from the hospital arrived and took the man away on a stretcher. After they had gone Dr. Monk suggested I settle myself on the sofa while he made a further phone call. When he returned he crossed straight over to me and tilted my chin is his direction.

"My goodness! I can see our late visitor wasn't the only one to be drained by all those strange goings-on. You look quite done in, child. I don't think you had better return to your Y.M.C.A. tonight."

I made a feeble attempt at a grin. "You look a bit pooped out yourself, sir! Then it isn't everyday that anyone goes through something like *that*. What exactly was wrong with him?"

"Well, let's just say that our friend is a very troubled man, Davey. Possession is a tricky business—the psychic and the psy-

47

chological lie so close to one another. Then in this case there were added complications. The man is probably an epileptic, too. There were at least indications of petit mal. He did throw a fit, you see. Then these cases are usually so much more complex than you think at first. There was a barrister who came to me not long after the Bishop had given me the faculty to exorcise in the diocese of Lincoln. Well, the exorcism worked all right but what we were left with was just a vegetable. The fellow's still in a mental home. And then I once had a woman patient whom I was sure was diabolically possessed. We dealt with that, but she still eventually committed suicide. They'll have to watch our friend of tonight very carefully indeed for the next few days. But at least the torment is gone from him."

I leaned forward on the sofa toward him. "Does—does this often happen to people, then?"

The priest gave a tiny shrug. "This is London, Davey. A large city. We tend to get more of everything here."

"Sounds exciting."

"It can be too exciting. Which is precisely why I think we should change the subject and that what you need is a nice hot cup of chocolate. And then off with you to the guest room. I shall now tell Iris to put a hot water bottle in your bed, while I put the milk on the stove. Back in a minute, all right?"

Alone in the room again I could only think of Father Monk; I tried initially to reconstruct the strange events connected with the stranger, but it all seemed vague, hazy. I tried to recall that intense cold, to remember the wilting flowers. But none of it would come. Not even the man's features could I now picture clearly. The only presence that loomed for me was that of the man who had just left the room, my priest-doctor host, the person of whom I could easily say at that very moment was the most wonderful I had ever met. I tried to put thoughts into the warm surge of love and gratitude which he evoked for me. I told myself that I must learn from his extraordinary humility and simple approachability, that here was someone on whom I could pattern my whole life. "I'll get you a nice hot cup of chocolate, boy," I said, striving to capture the rich sound of his voice. And I even got to my feet, tried on his kind of smile, and began to emulate that gliding walk of his. Fortunately I heard the sound of the door opening and was able to get back to the sofa before Father Monk appeared carrying two children's mugs with teddy bears and golliwogs patterned on them.

With an expression of rapt concentration—which I found altogether endearing—he placed the steaming hot chocolate on the coffee table, but instead of joining me on the sofa or taking the chair opposite he sat himself down on the carpet before me. This humble position elicited a fresh wave of candor from me. "I was thinking while you were out, Father Monk, that when that poor man came here asking for you, I hated him. Because I was frightened, I suppose. But I could see that you loved him right from the start. I think that's because you're a Christian and I'm really a hypocrite. I don't really have any right to be here, you know. I should never be a priest." He was smiling but it was a warm, encouraging smile and I longed to justify all this interest he was taking in me. "Sometimes I don't believe in God at all. Sometimes I think that Christianity is just a great big confidence game that everyone plays." I watched him carefully for his reaction to this rare show of inner feelings on my part.

"Well, start on your chocolate before it gets cold, child. And if I were you, I'd put that poor fellow out of my mind for the time being. I know it must have been very scary for you, Davey, but now you're tired and overwrought. We'll talk about it later, if you wish. As for your faith in God—well, I wouldn't let that keep you awake tonight either. You're what I call a *natural* Christian, boy. It's instinctual with you. Whether you think in terms of transcendental faith or not at a particular moment is neither here nor there. To tell the truth, I'm more concerned as a medical man over you at this juncture. That is why I would like to start seeing you at regular intervals. Going to King's College here in London is just the perfect solution. I'm glad we decided on that, child. Splendid idea!"

It was odd, but the more he reassured me, the more I craved further reassurance. "You mean, as a patient? You want to see me as a kind of mental patient regularly? I—I was rather hoping it could be—well, as my spiritual advisor or something."

But he only laughed and placed his cool hands fleetingly over my hot ones. "I'm not schizophrenic, child! When you come to my office in King's to see me, or here, you will be seeing Symes Monk. I shan't give you a Bible one day, a hypodermic the next, and dinner the next. Shall I tell you what the base truth is? I've always been fascinated by Cornwall, and now I've met my first lively and imaginative young Cornishman!"

I beamed back at him. "I—I shall tell you everything I possibly know about Cornwall. In fact, I shall study up on it so that I can tell you *more* than I know. And—and in return . . ." I faltered.

"Yes, boy?" His voice was so warmly encouraging I felt it as a caress.

"Well—" I gave a little wave of the arm not supporting me on the sofa where I half-sprawled. "All these books, for one thing. Oh, Dr. Monk, I haven't read *anything!*"

"Why don't you call me Father Symes. It's nicer than pompous old 'Dr. Monk.'"

But my self-pity would not be checked. "And the paintings you have . . . All these beautiful objects. Things I thought only lived in *museums* . . . This room . . . Well, I mean it's perfect!"

His voice, though still low, came a little harder. "It wasn't perfect earlier this evening, was it? Everything here is really transitory, Davey. And the objects, the possessions—all really nothing, you know. We only hire them, as it were. And really only for a very little space of time, if you think about it."

If I'd had a face like my cousin Jan I would have pouted at that juncture. As it was, the edges of my mouth turned down, just like my mother's. "You can afford to say that because it's all here. You've got things and you've learned to appreciate them. With me, it's different. They just show up my ignorance while they reveal your knowledge."

He gave me a soft look, though I was half-afraid I might make him cross. "My! What impatience! By the way, do you like music, boy-o?"

I believed that I did—only I was only too aware that I hadn't heard very much. Not of what *he'd* call music, anyway. But instinct told me that the more I stressed my ignorance the more I would lay claim on the teacher in him. Besides, there was something about Father Symes that urged me then and subsequently to play the innocent with him. Maybe it was because I found the innocence in him so lovable. "I—I don't know. I haven't really heard very much. But I'd certainly like to hear some of yours."

"Then you shall, you shall. But let me ask you something else first. Do you like gingerbread biscuits? They go awfully well with hot chocolate, I think."

I smiled—I hoped seraphically. It was funny. At eighteen, with everyone else, I wanted to appear at least twenty-five. But with him there was a sort of opposite effect. He made me want to flee back into little boyhood.

"Mummy always gave us a gingernut before going to bed," I lied, not unconscious of the fact that the lady in question had never been called "Mummy" by any of her offspring.

"Good," said Symes Monk, "then I shall play at being Mummy tonight, and bring you a ginger bickey for a bedtime treat." And with that he got gracefully to his feet and crossed the room to fetch a biscuit barrel of hammered pewter. "Now while you take out one for each of us, I'll see about some music."

As I replaced the lid after putting a gingerbread biscuit by each mug, I watched him take a gramophone record out of a cream-colored corner cupboard which I could now see was stacked with row upon row of them. He placed it on the revolving green felt turntable of a combination radio and record player, known in the England of that time as a radiogram. I had only ever seen one before and that was in the Armed Forces Centre in Plymouth when I had attended my one and only concert and failed to understand how people could sit silent and still on hard wooden chairs for so long while listening to gramophone records.

Before he had returned to his place on the carpet before me I was hearing the sounds of chamber music for the first time. "I like that," I told him, nibbling at my ginger biscuit while holding it squirrel-like with two hands and hoping he'd notice my cute pose. "What is it?"

"That's *Die Forelle. The Trout.* By Schubert. It was something I used to very often listen to when I was an undergraduate, with a close friend. I was about your age, I was hoping that you'd like it."

I tried to hum the tune but it was too fast so I gave up. Instead, I tried to imagine him at Oxford or Cambridge with one of those long scarves they wore. It wasn't difficult. After all, he still did look boyish and full of fun, in spite of the clerical collar and black soutane.

"What happened to the close friend?" I asked suddenly, wondering whether he'd been a bit like me.

"Simon? Oh, he committed suicide, poor chap." He said it so airily I was quite shocked. He might just have been offering me another biscuit! "I'm sorry," I muttered. "I wouldn't have—"

But he just put a finger to his lips until the music came to an end, which was shortly thereafter. "He was bound to have been killed during the war if he hadn't shot himself when he did. Simon was that kind of person. I knew he wasn't going to last." Then he smiled at me. "But you will last, my Cornish Davey. You're tough underneath. I can feel that. You look tired, but you still look tough!"

Somehow an image of appearing hale and hearty didn't appeal to me at that moment. It wasn't the Davey Bryant I wanted for Symes Monk to appreciate. "I was rather frail as a child," I informed him. "I was rather short for my age and was always seeing the doctor. And, of course, I wasn't too well during my time in the Navy, as you already know."

He got up again to change the record, and spoke in the direction of the radiogram. "We *all* walk on an emotional knife's edge, boy. It's simply that you have better balance than most."

I got up too. "Can I have a look at that, please, before you put it away?"

He handed me the shellac 78 disc with its red label and I concentrated hard to remember the title, the performers, and the record number. I was determined to purchase a copy as soon as I'd saved up enough money, even though I owned no machine to play it on.

After that I believe he played some Bach, but that did not hold my attention as closely as did the romantic Schubert. It is *Die Forelle* I still hear in my ears when I recall that long-ago evening when Dr. Symes Monk made his strange entrance into my life.

I am inclined to recall that blustery November night with reference to the stranger who came seeking freedom from whatever possessed him, via the ministrations of the priest-physician. But if I do, I am often tempted to smile. For if you had known Symes Monk, heard his voice, observed his mannerisms, and today knew me, nearly thirty years later, you would be inclined to say that it was I that night who experienced possession. For although I did not become a priest, or a physician, or a psychiatrist, and although I became a citizen of a country far from his and although the world we temporarily shared has changed out of all recognition, I still bear the marks of his pervasive influence and will continue to do so until I, too, am dead.

From the heady blandishments of Dr. Monk to the delights of sexual bullying and the solace of a sympathetic girl is a circle not a progress. A postwar world, the university promise and the sacerdotal defeat; the glow of being twenty-one and the chill of failure . . . the vise of memory will not let you go, Davey. Like an unhallowed bereavement, the distress of the earlier wound spreads like a damp stain on a distempered wall: over your feelings, over your relationships, over your destiny. Davey, can I chalk up the cost of the victims of my love to your account?

Chapter Four

"Shall I read another Shakespeare sonnet for you?" my new lover asked as we lay in shorts and sandaled feet in a quiet fold of Hampstead Heath on a warm June day.

"No," I said. "At least, not right now. Let's have sex again first."

"I can't, Davey. Really I can't. I'm worn out. Besides, I've got another exam this afternoon. I shouldn't be here anyway. I should be back in the library swotting up. So should you, shouldn't you. Or can theologs just pray for the right exam answers without studying?"

He was on his stomach the book lying open, his chin actually resting on the page. I reached over and began tugging at the tail of his blue shirt and exposed a portion of an already suntanned back. I ran my fingers over the smooth skin about his spine. "Bugger exams! You've got a beautiful body," I said softly. "It excites me, you know that."

"Let it excite you tonight then. After I'm through that damn history. If I fail it I won't get my grant next term. That'll be the end of King's College for me. *And* the end of my seeing you. I can't go running to Dr. Monk if I do badly, you know. There's no one to pull strings for me."

"You worry too much, Tim," I said, running my hand under the shirt toward his shoulder blades. It was nice and warm there.

"You've got too much energy. You wear me out," he said wearily.

"I don't believe anyone our age died of sex. Imagine this as a headline: 'Two Twenty-one-year-old Youths Found Dead from

Sexual Exhaustion on Hampstead Heath.' Only the *Daily Express* would run it. And only if they thought we were both Rhodes Scholars or something."

"You mean only the *News of the World* would run it," my companion commented, "and only if they knew you were studying to be a Church of England vicar!"

"How many times do I have to tell you that the last thing I want is to be stuck in some parish. I just want to scrape through those bloody exams and steal away. Right out of this godforsaken country, for one thing. And, do you know, I think old Monk suspects something of the sort. He's given me some odd looks the last times I've seen him. He doesn't ask me round for dinner much any more, either."

"Probably because he thinks you should be in the hostel studying and not keeping me up all hours like you did last night. And, don't forget, you promised that if I came out here with you this morning we could just be quiet and read to one another."

"Christ! I want to have you again *now*. Term's nearly over, do you realize? Then I'll be back on the farm in Cornwall, bored stiff, and you'll be up there in stupid, bloody Scotland!"

"I've already said I'll go to France with you in August. I'll have saved up enough from working with Dad by then."

I started to explore him netherward, my fingers like avid worms pushing up from the ground, trying to get at his flattened stomach from underneath. "Come on. It won't take long. I'm as horny as hell!"

But for the first time in the fortnight or so since I had first gone back with him to his digs in Kilburn and things had started, he resisted me. He turned right away from me, breaking some twigs of the fresh-leafed beech bush which screened us.

"If you keep on, I'm going back. Can't you understand when someone is just worn out?"

"No, I can't. I don't let myself be worn out any more. Nothing wears out Davey Bryant these days. If you loved me like you say you do, you'd just accept the fact you've got old super-sex lying here with you."

Tim spoke, looking away from me, and there was puzzlement in his voice: "You know, there's something the matter with you,

Davey. It's as if there's something inside eating at you all the time. You always want to spoil things."

Instead of pursuing his body across the small space we had crushed out for ourselves at the center of that sapling beech bush, I lay on my back, and stared up at the leaf-fractured sky. How explain to him how boring I was finding all that theology by that, my second, year of formal studies. How tell him that I had reached the point where I was no longer able to convince myself that I had a vocation to anything, except bodies like his. How ever admit to him that I was convinced I would never pass my final exams, as each year there to date had required "special handling" of my term marks by Symes Monk and his faculty associates, because I had done so poorly in all but a couple of subjects.

"Why you can't just relax and enjoy a beautiful day up here when we have it all to ourselves, beats me," Tim said. "And it was you who suggested bringing the sonnets. To think, Davey, just three years ago and the war was still on. We could easily, both of us, have been drowned at sea. And you're always going on about how much you hated the Navy. Well, here we are at peace and at the university, which is more than you can say for most boys our age, yet you never seem content for a moment. Well, except when you're doing you-know-what."

"Speech over? Or do you think you'd like to lead us in the General Thanksgiving?"

Silence from him. Hurt, of course. Christ! He was *always* feeling hurt! Frustration shaped into vindictiveness for me. "Who's that girl you keep flirting with in the library when you pretend to be studying?"

He starts another silence, but capitulates: "I told you yesterday who she was."

"I forget."

Tim sighs. "Her name is Sally Brown. And I don't flirt with her. We're just good friends."

"Odd that you never introduced us."

"Well, I haven't known you that long, have I? Besides, you never asked."

"So I'm asking you now."

57

"All right, then. This afternoon. She's taking the history exam with me. She'll be in the corridor just before two."

"I mean now. This morning. It's only just gone eleven."

"I don't know where she is. I expect she's home studying, like I should be."

"She always studies in the library. You told me that yourself. Come on. Let's go." I got to my feet, buttoning up my shirt as I did so and facing Tim, who still hadn't budged. "Come on, I want to meet Miss Sally Brown. She's got a boyish face. I think we're going to get on. And perhaps, just perhaps, she doesn't feel worn out."

He bit his lips and I thought for a moment that we were going to have tears, which was always rather nice. At least, the making-up bit afterward was. But when he spoke it wasn't like that at all.

"She's not 'Miss.' She's not 'Miss' anything."

"What do you mean, she's not 'Miss'? God! she can't be more than eighteen or nineteen. Twenty at the outside. You mean she's married already?"

"She's a Quaker. They don't use titles like 'Miss.'"

"So she's a Quaker. Good! I've never had a Quaker! Now are you coming or shall I leave you here to be raped by some wandering Free Pole who didn't get back to Poland?"

He got slowly up, and his shirt draped open like a coat, revealing the full length of that marvelous tan. His longish blond hair fell over his forehead and he brushed it back with a sort of petulant flip.

"You're only doing this to get at me, aren't you, Davey? You know, Sally's a nice girl. I wouldn't want her to get hurt just because of me."

"What a stupid idea," I said, stepping out into a sunwashed world of turfy slope above which skylarks hovered, singing. "It's simply I'm not in the mood for the old sylvan setting any more."

We didn't talk as we climbed the Heath toward the pond and the edge of bricks-and-mortar London. This was partly because I made it too difficult by keeping just ahead of him all the time. I had noticed that I tended to walk more quickly than Tim and that he soon became breathless from much exertion. It reminded me of my childhood with cousin Jan when he was always ahead of me, and the reversal of my status now gave me special pleasure. There was no way that Tim was ever going to know that once I'd been known as a bit of a weakling.

On the tube to the Strand I borrowed his Shakespeare and read some of the sonnets to myself. At least, I looked intently at the pattern of the print, the words themselves refusing to make much sense. In the courtyard of King's College I slowed down, so that we could ascend the broad steps together. Dick Winters might be hanging about. He was queer too, and knew I'd been after Tim the whole of that Summer Term. As he and I had once agreed that Tim McDougal was the best-looking of our year I certainly would not have minded bumping into Dick so that he would realize I'd got what I wanted.

Sometimes things just work out right. That late morning in June 1948 was the occasion of one of them. Just past the swing doors we did indeed encounter Dick Winters, who at once raised those extravagantly thick eyebrows of his. "My dear!" he said. "That was like a bridal entrance!" But I swept my Tim swiftly past him, calling back over my shoulder as I did so: "Remind me to tell you about Hampstead Heath. And how to keep warm up there at dawn."

Right after that, even before we reached the doors to the Arts Faculty Library, there was Sally Brown. I gave her an extra looking-over before Tim introduced us. She was wearing a simple white summer blouse, a red sweater thrown over her shoulders, a plain gray skirt from which two bare legs emerged to subsequently disappear into plain leather brogues. I also noticed she was wearing no jewelry (I was pretty quick on such things) and wondered whether that went with being a Quaker. There was nothing else about her, I reflected, which vaguely suggested such a thing.

"You two look as if you've been playing tennis or something. I can see that neither of you are worried about such mundane things as exams."

"Davey here doesn't have to be," said Tim. "He's a theolog and they can rely on divine inspiration instead of swotting."

"Are you panicky, then?" I asked her. "If so, you'd better hold hands with Tim. He's petrified."

"Petrified? Not particularly. What I don't know now I won't by this afternoon."

"So we can deposit Tim in the library and you can come for a coffee with me?"

Sally looks at Tim and she's suddenly soft rather than pert. "You all right, Tim?"

"I will be if I can get all those things that happened in 1848 right in my head. Oh, God!"

"What's up?" she asks.

"My history text. I left it at home."

My hand casts about the pocket in my shorts. "Here, get mine. You said you use that Cole's book, *1815 to the Present Day,* like we do? That's my locker key. It's in there somewhere. Underneath a big fat thing on psychology. I've never read it since I bought it, but our history prof said it was the best example of the secular humanist approach to history. I couldn't think of anything more boring."

"You sure you don't mind?" Tim looks at me, his eyes bright with uncertainty, though goodness knows why.

"Sure I'm sure. Then come back to the hostel after the examination and bring it with you, okay? You can have supper with us. I'll swing it with the subwarden."

Our glances met and held. "That would be nice, Davey. See you both later then." And he almost ran from us down the corridor and up the stairs in the direction of my locker in the Theological Faculty corridor.

"Now how about that coffee?" I said to Sally. "Come on. I know a nice quiet little place by the Law Courts that the students haven't ever discovered."

Students or not, the place was so crowded when we got there, with clerks and the like cashing their special luncheon vouchers, that we changed our plans. We went and bought sandwiches farther down Fleet Street, and then headed for the Embankment to eat them somewhere in the sun. Mine turned out to be of hard, stale cheese and soggy tomato. She had one of those composition meat things. They represented postwar British food at its most execrable, and the very sight of it, let alone the taste, depressed me.

The talk between bites and munches was pretty general at first.

"Where you from, Sally?"

"Cambridge."

"And you're here at King's? Coals to Newcastle a bit, isn't it?"

"My father teaches there. This is the only place I could get in. Even that was lucky for someone direct from school—I mean, with all the ex-servicemen and that. I understand there are still those demobbed after the war trying to get university places."

"That's what helped Tim and me. Both Navy types, you know."

"I knew that Tim was. Though I think it was all a bit tough for him. He isn't very strong, you know. Something about a kidney infection in the Navy?"

"I see you two have really talked."

"Yes, we have. Now tell me about yourself. Where are you from?"

"Cornwall." I knew my head must've dropped defensively. It always did when people started to ask me questions, especially about Cornwall, where so much raw love lay . . .

"Really? I was there last year with my father. What part? Perhaps I've been there."

"I doubt it. Our village is quite off the beaten track. No one ever seems to have heard of it. It's called Trequite, but it's really part of St. Kew. You're pretty thick with Tim, n'est-ce pas?"

Sally gave me a quick glance. I thought how English she looked. Well, maybe Anglo-Saxon is a better term. It was much to do with her being fair, but also with the way she wore her hair in a loose braid, pleated up at the back of her head. She might have been called Ethel or Wilfreda rather than Sally.

"Depends what you mean by thick, I suppose."

"Well, obviously not like those bloody sandwiches! Pals, chums, take your pick."

"Tim is a very dear person. Yes, we do get on very well. He's—he's different from most students in our faculty."

I smirked. "Yes, I think you can say that all right. Anyway, he's talked a lot about you. In fact, he's the one who thought we should get to know one another better."

"Well, that's what we're doing, isn't it?"

"I hope so. It's just like you said about Tim. The only people one can get to know at college," I told her, "all seem either old men who want to talk about their stupid war stories, or women who are just walking brains."

"Well, at least you don't have to worry about that with me! If I'm 'round people like Sheila Walters, I feel almost certifiable."

"You're intelligent, though. That's much more important than being clever. And you're pretty, too. God! our King's women are ugly. They have these huge heads that seem to grow right out of their bottoms and bypassing things like spines and necks. Then over half of them have got mustaches. And as for their clothes—"

"My goodness! I should hate to hear you talking about me behind my back. Do all the men feel that way about the women students? Or are you a bit more misogynistic than most?"

"The men are such a dull bunch too. I don't talk to them much either." I was beginning to feel restless again. I jumped to my feet. "Want to walk a bit?"

She also got up, only more slowly than I did, smoothing her skirt and brushing crumbs off her fingers. "If you like. How about the Embankment Gardens? There's a coffee stall, anyway, towards the Hungerford Foot Bridge."

So we sauntered along by the Thames, looking across the dark and sluggish water at the sun sparkling on the Shell-Mex House.

"You know, even now, towards the end of my second year, I'm still excited by just being here in London," Sally said.

It was my turn to glance sharply at her, for my thoughts were in an utterly opposed direction. "Not me! I hate it! Then, I hate the Labor Government, I hate England, I hate the whole damn thing!"

She stopped and put her elbows on the smooth balustrade of the Embankment wall. "That's a lot of hate, Davey. What has England done to make you feel like that, eh?"

I sighed with oppressive thoughts, picking at a dried splash of seagull lime on the flat stone. "Oh, it's all so ugly and dreary! Look at people's clothes. I'm sure Tim and I are the only two people in shorts today in the whole of this stuffy city. And think of those sawdust sandwiches we've just eaten. Then I only have to think of the filthy meal they'll serve us at the hostel tonight and I want to be sick!"

"Now come on," she coaxed gently. "Life's more than dull clothes and austerity food, surely? I mean, just look at the weather. Have you ever seen a more beautiful June day?"

I sighed. "That makes it worse. Just think of the same day in some place where the war is really over. Where people aren't wasting their lives worrying about furniture dockets, utility coupons, personal points, and all that."

"They'll all go, won't they? It's only a matter of time."

"Now you sound like my advisor, Dr. Symes Monk. But, Sally, it's *my* time. It's *my* life that's being wasted over fuel cuts and power shortages. This isn't what I grew up for!"

She gave a little laugh, but it wasn't hurtful. "Now you sound like a hundred!"

"I feel like a hundred."

"A hundred—or just someone who's a bit unhappy?"

"I don't suppose a girl like you, with a Cambridge professor as a father, has ever been unhappy. And I musn't forget you're a Quaker, too. That probably means you're not *allowed* to be unhappy."

"Don't be silly."

"Well, have you? Tell me when? Have you ever thought life just not worth living? Have you ever hated yourself?"

She made a little pause before answering and I wished I could be a little more like that instead of always blurting things.

"No. I've never hated myself. But I think that both Daddy and I thought life wasn't worth living when my mother died last year. For a little while, anyway."

"I'm sorry—I didn't know—"

"I didn't want to come back to London at first. Wanted to stay at home and help my father. But he wouldn't hear of it. Now I think that he was right. But not until this term. We had a good long talk again at Christmas, and he persuaded me to stay on."

"The only tragedy in my family is me. That was when Dr.

Monk said he could get me into King's and I jumped at it. Not somewhere closer to home, like Exeter."

"Isn't it a bit early for you to be talking about tragedy?" she asked. "I mean, you can't be that much older than me, and I'm nineteen next month."

"I'm twenty-one. And what I'm talking about happened ages ago—when I was eighteen, in fact, and in the Navy." My pulse quickened. Globules of memory, as harshly bright as the oil stains on the waters of the Thames at which I was staring, almost hurt my mind . . . that policeman's grasp on my wrist as I wandered through that Portsmouth park at dusk during my few hours of shore leave . . . the abrasive pee stench of the prison cell . . . my father's face white and anguished as the magistrates delivered their verdict . . . and the numbing shame when delivered several months later to the Navy as a technical "deserter" . . .

"Do you want to talk about it then?" Her voice, which was naturally contralto, now sounded even lower.

Amid the blotches on the Thames's surface I noticed a piece of wood bobbing. Black and shiny, it looked as if it had floated there for ages. "I've tried talking about it before. To lots of people. But it didn't really help."

"I don't want to pry, you understand?"

"I—I'd like to tell you—but I can't."

"Does Tim know?"

"Yes. Then he's not a girl."

The silence that grew frightened me. I was afraid it would get too immense to handle. It amazed me that I had let things get this far. I mean, talking to a *girl*—one I didn't even know . . .

"I—I had a nervous breakdown. When I was in the Navy. I wasn't really over it when I first came to King's. I'm not completely sure I'm over it now."

"They're not very nice things to have, I'm sure. But they're not the end of the world. That's what I first thought when Mummy went."

"Look, can we go somewhere else? I can't think standing here, let alone talk," I said.

"Where, then?"

"A pub, maybe? There's The Westminster Arms."

"I don't drink."

"Your place then?"

"There wouldn't be time. I mean, the exam is at—"

"It's only just gone twelve. We could take a taxi. *Please* . . ."

"Taxis are expensive."

"I don't care. I never care about things like that. Not when it's important."

"If you want, then."

We walked to the rank just beyond Cleopatra's Needle. My legs felt wobbly beneath me. I put the future right out of my mind, and all the way during the taxi ride to the address she gave in Bloomsbury, I talked frantically of Norman Douglas' *South Wind,* which I had just read.

The women's student residence where Sally lived was close to the soaring University Senate Building, and looked as new. As we climbed the stairs to the third floor and then went down the gleaming cream corridor, I imagined all kinds of strange female smells, and at one point I actually slowed down as I debated whether to call the whole thing off and run out of the place.

Each door had the owner's name typed on a card and neatly inserted in a metal frame. After an endless line of "Miss Rosemary This" and "Miss Mary That" we stopped, and I read "Sally Brown."

"Just like Tim said," I told her.

"Said what," she replied, inserting her latchkey.

"Just 'Sally Brown.' No 'Miss.' The Quaker way, n'est-ce pas?"

"The Friends way, we usually say. But 'Quaker' will do. Sit down and I'll put the kettle on. Will tea do?"

I nodded as I looked quickly around her tiny bedsitter. Searching for what? Female relics, I suspect. Stockings over a chairback, undies on the bed, a bra draped over a doorknob. But nothing. Neat as a pin. Neater than my room at the Theological Hostel had been since the day I'd moved in. On a small table a couple of photographs. I picked one up.

"Your parents?"

I heard the chink of cups and saucers behind me.

"My parents."

The other was a snapshot I had to hold closer to see properly. It was of Tim.

"I see you have your boyfriend?"

"A friend," she said firmly. "The first friend I've made at King's."

A small pain lanced from the picture of Tim standing with his bicycle toward me, and then, somehow, toward her. "I must get you one of me," I said.

"That would be very nice. Sugar and milk?"

"No sugar. An old Cornish custom." I sat on the bed, then, not feeling very comfortable there, crossed to the one armchair and sat on the front edge of that. It was made of wicker and it creaked loudly.

"I've never been in a girl's room before," I said to her back as she busied herself in the alcove.

"This makes you one up on me, then. I've never been in a boy's room in my life!"

"Here, you take the chair," I said, taking the cup from her and sliding down to the floor.

"There's the bed, if you want."

"I like the floor. I always sit there. Ask Tim."

She laughed. "I don't have to. I believe you." She spooned her cup and I did likewise. "Read any good books lately?" she said suddenly. "Other than Norman Douglas, that is."

I drank quickly at the tea, which was so hot it scalded my lips. But I kept on; I needed the hurt for courage. "When I was eighteen," I began, "I was arrested. It was while I was in the Navy. I was on shore leave just for one evening. But it was nearly three months before the Navy saw me again. I spent the intervening time in Winchester Prison. I was what they call remanded."

"What for?"

"A psychiatrist's report," I said quickly, deliberately misconstruing her question. "He said that I was perfectly normal. He couldn't have been more wrong!"

"You mean you were only imperfectly normal?" she said softly, as I felt her stroke the back of my hair.

I drew breath, turned and looked up at her, my lips almost forming the words I wanted so desperately to say—that I had been arrested on a charge of importuning and soliciting. But I couldn't! I couldn't! "Whatever I was, it was something they couldn't understand. The smug sods!" I noticed her contracting eyebrows, knew she was framing the unanswerable question.

"I'd—I'd rather not talk about it any more. Do you mind?"

"Of course not," she said softly. But I felt her ease back in her chair and her fingers gently disentangle themselves from the curls at the back of my head. "Would you like some more tea, Davey?"

"Would you mind if I kissed you?"

We got to our feet at the same time, confronting each other as I searched her dinky little face.

"Of course not."

I kissed her so hard I could feel her teeth against my closed lips. Then I hugged her hard, too, swinging her so that she almost lost her balance.

"Heh!" she said gasping, pushing away. "We're not bears!"

"I'm sorry. Let's do it again, though. I promise I'll be more gentle."

So once more I held her, kissed her lips, and then held my mouth to the hair of her head. Startlingly there came to me the scent of Tim's hair from lying on the Heath with him that morning. And the spell was broken.

"I suppose we ought to think about getting back," I said. "There's just that little matter of those exams."

Her mood seemed to change instantly. From acquiescent calm she suddenly became a flurry of movement. In seconds she was almost bustling me out of the door. "Let's walk down Gower Street, shall we, and look at some of those poor University College types. You can tell me then if you think their women are better than ours. Oh, and grab this book, will you? Turn to Chapter Eight. Now will you test me as we walk? There's a lot of questions at the end."

"Sally, we can meet again, can't we? I mean, I'd like that very much, if you would."

"Of course, of course! Now ask me about the Congess of Vienna, will you?"

The whole way back to the Strand and King's College was a

question-and-answer routine over such people as Castlereagh, Metternich, and Talleyrand. Neither of us ventured into the twentieth century . . .

That night in bed at the hostel with Tim, whom I had smuggled up and would have to smuggle out again before breakfast, he begged off sex again, saying his history exam had exhausted him but that he'd be all right in the morning, when he knew I liked it best.

"Know what happened today?" I address his shoulder blades.

"Go to sleep, Davey."

"I went back to Sally's room."

Silence.

"Guess what happened. Apart from my seeing that snap of you with your bike, that is."

There was an explosion of bedclothes as he turned over and faced me.

"What?"

I fought with myself, just for a second or so before yielding to my second big lie of the day. "I fucked her."

With another big heave on the single bed, he turned round once more and faced the wall. "I don't believe you."

"Well, I did. I did, I tell you. And it was super. The real thing, you know. There's nothing like it."

Tim made no reply, and I listened hard to hear if he was crying.

"Tim?"

No answer.

"Shall I describe it? The details?"

But the bastard was already drifting off. He could do that at the drop of a hat, I'd found. I hated him for it. So there in the darkness, a warm wind rustling the poplar trees out there in Vincent Square, I lay on my back and asked myself, yet again, why I did things for which I loathed myself afterward. But in the end, sleep took me too, that June night, without yielding any sort of answer.

Davey, I think you survive by laughter but are taught by tears. Already you are learning that nothing you do is ever clean-cut; nothing you think ever shines prettily in virtue or, for that matter, even stinks in unmitigated viciousness. Already you have discovered when it is vital to laugh at yourself. But I, your middle-aged nemesis, know better than your twenty-three-year-old self that there is no panacea in place. Having loved in London and been nibbled by professional ambition and social status, now try Paris, Davey, and see what an unpuritanical place offers. Learn to be a foreigner for the rest of your life.

Chapter Five .

I was walking the dusty, begonia-bordered paths of the Parc Monceau, endeavoring to fill the tired head of an eight-year-old Parisian with the rudiments of the English language.

"Now, Jeannot, what have you learned at school today?"

"La source de la Seine est le Saint Sacrement."

"Now come on. In English. You *must* speak in English. What was it you said?"

The flat, work-dulled voice of a rote victim of the French educational system started up again.

"Ze source of ze Seine is ze Holy Sacrament."

"That's nonsense."

"Zat ees what zey teach me, M. Bryant."

If it were possible on that stifling June afternoon, as my crew-cut charge and I maneuvered between nannies and baby carriages in that bourgeois oasis of the Eighth Arrondissement, my spirits sunk even lower. Given fewer anxieties about my own life, I might have smiled at Jeannot's conflation of his geography and religious instruction classes, but as it was, I looked anxiously about me for a bench on which to sit.

Suddenly a large woman in summery white, with hair blued to match the heavens above, got up and sailed majestically toward the exit on the Rue de Marceau. I gave my young pupil a sharp shove, propelling him toward the spot she'd vacated.

The day was so sultry, my face so sweaty that my sunglasses kept sliding down my nose. But before attending to such matters I first withdrew from my pocket a copy of *The Continental Daily*

Mail, spread it across Jeannot's bare knees, and told him to start reading aloud.

As he stumbled slowly over some boring account of a N.A.T.O. meeting, mispronouncing most of it without any correction from me, I looked around for some diversion.

I didn't have long to wait. Coming toward me was one of the most extraordinary creatures I had ever seen, and may I remind you that Paris was renowned, maybe still is, for its quota of odd, misshapen figures in bizarre attire, and with voices and gestures to match? This particular apparition was male, bearded, and afforded the general appearance of a corpulent dwarf in filthy clothes and of distinctly advancing years. This impression was further reinforced when he stood before me, raised that filthy hat, bowed, and, after listening to Jeannot, who still sat there reading aloud without looking up, addressed me in clear if accented English.

"Good afternoon, m'sieur. May I please join you and your young friend on zat bench?"

Two sharp brown eyes under bushy brows flitted their gaze toward the empty space.

"Of course. No one's sitting there."

Another formal little bow, and the strange bundle of rags was arranging itself next to me.

"Allow me to introduce myself to you two buggers. I am the Archimandrite Alexei."

"I—I beg your pardon?"

"Ze Trade Union leader said his members would not be bullied by threats of zat sort. In Geneva, Meester Dulles would be meeting with reprezentatives of ze Beeg Three. 'A penis is my answer to all problems,' says famous actress."

"'Happiness,' not 'a penis,' Jeannot. But read to yourself now."

But my eight-year-old now had the bit between his teeth, as it were: my request was blithely ignored. So turning to my other neighbor I had to raise my voice.

"I'm sorry. I didn't quite catch—"

"Here is my card, old cock."

From somewhere amid that voluminous bundle of cast-off

72

clothing a currently gray but once white visiting card was produced, and offered to me by a wool-gloved hand.

"The Very Reverend Archimandrite Alexei Levertov," I read. There was no address, nothing else whatever, on the dog-eared piece of cardboard.

"It is good for the young man to read the newspaper aloud thus. That help-ed me in my learning of Greek, of Arabic and Russian."

"Russian isn't your native language, then. Your name . . . I thought perhaps . . ."

"I have Russianized it. I am a Grenoblois by birth and a British subject."

I could only stare.

"Sex-change describ-ed by Danish doctor. American soldier to become a lady," persisted my pupil.

"Your English is very good, sir. I wish Jeannot here would take a lesson from you."

The Archimandrite Alexei obviously took me literally. "I would be delighted to assist you. He is a nice little bugger, yes?"

So my ears hadn't deceived me just now. He *had* used a cussword. Now normally such language meant nothing to me. I swore all the time. But from this ancient Archimandrite, well, to say the least, it was very unusual . . .

"The leetle fellow is a good learner? It is a gift, you know. For some, like me, languages is no difficulty. For others it is all bloody hard work."

It was then it dawned on me that he was quite unaware of any incongruity. "Where?" I asked, not without guile, "where did you learn to speak English so fluently, Archimandrite Alexei?"

He was obviously pleased with the implicit praise. "In the Great War, 1917, I was attach-ed as liaison officer between the French army and the Welsh Guards. It was those Welsh bastards who taught me the English vernaculaire. I was very lucky. The same when I was in Russia. I learn-ed there from the sailors in Murmansk."

I wondered if he had similar problems in Russian. Greek and Arabic too, for that matter . . .

"That is very important, you know. To speak the bloody languages like the natives. Then you understand the soul of a nation. You are at one with the peoples."

"True, very true," I murmured; only too aware that I spent vast tracts of time in disassociating myself from "the peoples," not least the Parisian herd with which I did battle day by day.

"Army of rats threaten royal residence."

I turned my back even more firmly on Jeannot.

"I have many good friends in the Church of England, young man. Perhaps we have the mutual acquaintances?"

I thought quickly back over the past ten years of my life, back to when as a schoolboy of thirteen I had been confirmed by the Bishop in Truro Cathedral, and doubted it. I shot another glance at the Archimandrite and thought it also highly unlikely that we would have joint friends in any other context either.

"I took English at university. I can't think of any clergyman offhand that would—"

"At Oxford I know well the Anglican, the Lord David Cecil. English is his field, the dear old sod. He was perhaps your tutor?"

"Afraid not. I was at King's College, London. We were rather short of lords there."

"Ah, a scholar at London University. Then you would have doubtless work-ed much at the British Museum. That is where I spend most of my fucking time. In the Reading Room. Perhaps we have been there at the same time. Come to think of it, your face is very much familiar, Bach. You don't have a bloody fag on you by any chance?"

As I handed him a Gauloise protruding from its blue package, I noticed a large wasp alight on the shoulder of his overcoat. "Wait a minute, there's a wasp on you—I'll get my handkerchief out."

But with the cigarette between mittened fingers he waved disapproval. "Do not harm heem! I have a great reverence for all life. I kill nothings. I am at one with the great Saint Francis in these matters. Let the little bugger rest on me if he so wishes."

He took a long and meditative draw at the cigarette and I watched with fascination as eventually clouds of smoke escaped both nostrils and mouth, and lingered for what seemed ages about the tatters of his beard, amid his bushy eyebrows, and even under the edge of his broad-brimmed hat. He appeared, in fact, to be simply *enveloped* in smoke, and from just that one long draw.

"You find my appearance fascinating, no doubt."

I started in my realization that he had caught me out staring at him. "I—I'm sorry. It was just the smoke—"

"A form of fumigation. I seem to be a bloody magnet for most insects. This way does not hurt them but they tend to move on faster if they catch the scent of tobacco on my person."

"What a good idea! I should think these Gauloises especially good for the purpose."

"Excellent. Otherwise they are bloody horrible cigarette, do you not think?"

"England sends ze West Indies packing. Visitors 'ave gloomy day at Leeds."

I turned once more to Jeannot and took the newspaper firmly from him. "That'll do for today. Now say hello to the Archiman-drite Alexei here."

"Hello. What you got all them cloth-es on for?"

I had rarely heard Jeannot speak English more fluently, but could have wished for a less personal question from my charge.

"You have not done the sciences at school yet, young man. That I see. It is fucking hot day, no? So with my cloth-es the body sweats and that is nature's cooling system. I remain at the 98.6 in the Fahrenheit."

"What is fucking mean?" asked my evil eight-year-old.

"Forget it!" I said sharply.

But the Archimandrite leaned toward me, waving his cigarette reprovingly. "Do not deny the right of a child to acquire wisdom, my son. That is his sacred right. 'Fucking' is the English dialect for 'very.' It is constantly in use with the Welsh Guards."

"C'est comme *merde* en français," I told Jeannot, quietly but quickly. "Ce n'est pas poli."

"Fucking hot day," repeated Jeannot, then lapsed into silence, but nodding his head in some kind of arcane agreement.

I looked at my watch, then got up to go. "It is time I took

Jeannot home. It has been a pleasure meeting you, M'sieur Archimandrite."

"You are walking?"

I fingered the few francs in my trouser pocket. "His mother likes him to have the exercise."

"Then perhaps I may accompany you? I too believe in the bloody long walks."

"Bloody," says Jeannot, before taking a chewing gum strip from his pocket and beginning to masticate rhythmically. "It is bloody fucking hot!"

Instinct told me to ignore him. "Well, if you like, m'sieur. Though I'm afraid it's all the way down the Avenue d'Iena."

"That is perfectly in my direction," the old man said, also getting to his feet. "Now let us proceed in the name of the Lord, amen."

As we climbed the steady slope toward the Arc de Triomphe, the Archimandrite rambled on freely. I learned he had for several years been on the staff of the Ecumenical Patriach in Istanbul (which he only ever referred to as Constantinople) and for equally substantial portions of time he had been prison chaplain to a White Russian contingent in Vladivostok (where he had witnessed an execution by the ax); had served on some interfaith committee of a Pacifist nature, with headquarters in New Delhi; worked at the Missions to Seamen in the Port of London (where doubtless his command of the English vernacular acquired from the Welsh Guards stood him in good stead); and had been in recent years frequenting the British Museum researching for a biography of a somewhat disreputable Irish Bishop of the nineteenth century who had eventually fled to Scotland, become secularized, and ended up editing the *Edinburgh Review*.

Dodging the rush-hour traffic around the Étoile, I both noted how nimble he was and at the same time reflected that if even half of his stories were true, sheer pressures of time would demand that he be now into his eighties. Jeannot, still walking between us and obviously listening to every word, was apparently thinking upon similar lines.

"You must be highly old, m'sieur."

I winced, but those quick brown eyes of the old man didn't

harden. Indeed, his lips parted to reveal a hideous array of stumped teeth as he cackled warmly. "Very old, young man. As old as the bloody hills. When I was your age the Champs Élysées, where my uncle, the General, lived, was only the private residences. And the Avenue de Bois over there"—he pointed to the Avenue Foch—"was the most beautiful in Europe—well, outside of St. Petersburg, that is. The world then was full of beautiful horses—not these fucking cars!"

"My father 'as a Rolls-Royce and a Alfa Romeo. And—and my grandfather 'as a Mercedes-Benz. He is also as old as ze bloody hills, but he 'as not got that barbe."

"Beard, Jeannot."

"Beard. He don't smell the same as you, as well."

"That's the building where Jeannot lives," I said crisply, still anxious over the unduly personal trends to the boy's conversation. "I must get him in before he's late for supper."

"I will attend you here, then? You have only to deliver the little bugger and then come away? I will then walk further with you—unless, that is, you have the other plans."

"Not at all," I said, though suddenly suspicious of his motives in wanting my company, and thinking (Cornishman that I was) that this was all leading up to an opportunity to touch me for some of my precious francs. "See you in a minute, then." And I was soon propelling Jeannot into a rickety glass-doored elevator which took us, swaying and jerking, up the five floors to the Martus' apartment.

As the tall double doors of varnished oak were opened, his mother stood there as usual to greet us. Her orange-dyed hair looked as lifeless as ever, her makeup as excessive in rouge and lipstick, culminating in vulgarity with those curiously plucked eyebrows and their false, painted successors. I did not like her.

There was plenty of evidence that Madame Martus did not like me. She never lost an opportunity of complaining that I cost too much and did too little. However, her way of bemoaning these facts as I stood there on the threshold was to question Jeannot about me as if I were not there. This particular encounter began as had its predecessors. I offer it in English, but she

77

spoke a shrill, staccato French that I personally considered in perfect harmony with her appearance.

"Darling, you look so pale! What has he done with you? Did he make you walk all the way in this heat? Why did he not take a taxi? Did you learn some English for once? Speak to Maman in English, my treasure."

For once in my presence Jeannot bothered to look up at her and answer, in part at least, her endless stream of stupid questions.

"It is bloody fucking hot day," he said with a grin. "Bloody fucking hot!"

Now Madame Martus was not fluent in my native tongue, but she was not wholly ignorant of it either. As those painted eyebrows knitted and the blood-red cupid of her mouth contracted into a vicious slit, I knew with sickening spirits that she had grasped every word.

"So, he fills you with the language of the gutter! The degenerate hypocrite! Now go to your room at once, darling, and let Marie help you wash up for supper. Now go! I will deal with this—this corrupter of youth."

Eight-year-old shoulders shrugged Gallically. "Goodbye, M'sieur Davey. I—I am sorry."

" 'Bye, Jeannot."

"Jeannot!"

"Oui, Maman." He slouched past her and didn't look back as he walked slowly down the long parquet-floored corridor toward his own room. As I watched him go I felt something close to affection for the kid. I certainly pitied the poor little bastard having her as a mother.

"So, m'sieur. That is that. Our business is obviously terminated. I should report you to the Embassy, but I shall tell only my friends who were persuaded into recommending you. I shall see you do not corrupt any other child, if I can help it."

I continued to stand there. I wanted to put my hand out for what she owed me, but my pride wouldn't allow that.

"So, m'sieur? Why do you not go?"

"Well, there's just the little matter of what you owe me." My voice was low, mainly a mumble. But she responded instantly.

"You expect me to pay you for putting those horrible words into a little boy's mouth?"

"He did not learn them from me, madame. And I have had him in my care for two hours. You owe me two hundred francs. That was our agreement."

"Absolutely not! We owe you nothing. You owe M. Martus and myself our little boy's innocence. Now go or I shall call the concierge to have you removed."

With my realization that she was not going to hand over a single franc, my temper exploded. I spoke both loudly and in English, and for her pendant-drooping ears, with great distinction.

"You are a mean old bitch. A tight-wadded old cow. And I am sorry for that poor little sod having such a vulgar slut—"

But before I had really begun to warm to my task, those twin tall doors had been slammed in my face. It was only as I started to descend the white stone stairway (I didn't feel like waiting outside her doors for the elevator) that it dawned fully on me that a major portion of my very slim livelihood had just been taken away. In fact, I didn't have enough cash to pay for supper that evening, and I refused to think about such things as the rent and the next day's shopping.

I almost bumped into the Archimandrite, for I was walking with my head down, feeling immensely depressed, and quite oblivious of his existence. My glum mood must have been very manifest. "What is the matter, my young friend? Something unpleasant has befallen you, I can see."

I have always been reluctant to share my miseries, and in those days, during my early twenties, far too proud to allude easily to my perpetual poverty.

"That little kid's revolting mother has just cheated me out of two hundred francs. I was rather banking on it." I couldn't help a hefty sigh surfacing in me. "Life is a little difficult at present, Archimandrite Alexei."

We started to walk farther down the Avenue d'Iena, though I hadn't the vaguest notion of destination. After a few moments of silence, the old man gave me one of those quick, bird-like glances of his.

79

"May I ask the occasion of that woman's dishonesty? She is of a criminal disposition, perhaps?"

"Just plain stingy. French, that is." Then I remembered. "Oh, I beg your pardon. Perhaps it is a *Parisian* trait."

"It is a *French* trait," the Archimandrite said firmly. "Forty million misers. It play-ed a large part in my decision to take out the British papers."

"So you joined another forty-odd million hypocrites. It doesn't seem much of an advance."

"You must not yield to cynicism, young man. That is bloody self-defeating. However, let us sit down to talk of these things. We shall go across to that café over there." The mittened hand emerged from the deep recesses of his long coat and pointed.

I rapidly estimated the price of a vermouth, or even a beer. "I am not feeling particularly thirsty," I lied. "Maybe a bench somewhere?"

"A small gesture of gratitude for accepting my company. You will please be my guest. No fucking argument, old chap."

Until that moment I had thought it unlikely that the muffled bundle of rags was concealing as much as a sou. I recalled all his traveling. Maybe the Archimandrite was one of those eccentric millionaires who choose to appear otherwise. I stopped thinking about my own plight and speculated on the old man instead.

Consequent with such reflection, when we sat down I ordered a Pernod—something I would not have dreamed of doing if spending my own money. He ordered an apéritif called "banyuls," sipped it and then leaned toward me, close enough so that I could detect the whiff of what I took to be gentian about his whiskers.

"You are hard up, my young friend? Bloody broke, yes?"

I could see no more point in concealing the fact. Besides, the kindness of his voice was further spur to confession. "Pretty much so. By the way, Archimandrite, my name is Davey Bryant. Please call me Davey."

There was a slight pause in which I took out my crumpled package of Gauloises Bleues, offered him one, lit up and watched him go through the previous process of fumigation of his upper person. When most of the smoke had disappeared he finally spoke, though not looking at me but across the street to a row of plane trees, their broad leaves lifeless in the heavy air.

"I think I have a good idea, young Davey. It could be a bloody good solution for you and of some special benefit to me. You are a good listener, that I know. Now you must tell me how you are with the women."

It was the last question in the world I was expecting and my lower jaw drooped. For a wild moment I was prepared to believe that beneath all that hair and clothes there lurked some kind of magician. For apart from the endless nag of wondering where I could earn enough money to stay in Paris, the other overriding obsession of mine at twenty-two was the sexual attractions the City of Light offered. Twice already I had journeyed out to the American Hospital at Neuilly, falsely suspecting I had contracted the clap. In the space of one week I had seduced Barbara, who worked for W. H. Smith on the rue de Rivoli, *and* her visiting brother from Wolverhampton. Graduating from more or less orthodox bordellos, I had sampled the various "exhibitions" of Pigalle with their subsequent corporate corollaries when sometimes as many as a dozen or so of us had been gathered together, as it were . . .

Qualitatively, I was still experimenting with my sexual identity, but if quantity could yield the answer to where my final preferences lay, then I was fast on the way to getting there.

"Naturally, I have many women friends," I said guardedly, "but I fail to see—"

"You find them *sympathique?* That is very important."

"Oh yes," I said, feeling at once on safer ground, "I find many ladies *sympathique.*" (That was no lie. If it had not been the case then things would have been considerably less complicated than they were. I mean, the business of Barbara and then her brother Frank had proved most embarrassing when each had found out.)

"Then I think I have the bloody answer for you, young friend. There is this woman I know here in Paris. She has what you call the damn frail nerves. She is not strong, you understand?"

"Uh uh." I didn't but I nodded my head.

"She is an American. A lady of the high social position from the South. Halabama, I think."

My mind turned vaguely to *Gone with the Wind,* which I had seen for the first time a few weeks earlier, and quickened at the image of Vivien Leigh as Miss Scarlett.

"Well, this lady inhabits a clinique and is very lonely. She is also fucking rich. Now, she has the habit of telephoning deep in her. At night she makes the phone calls to me—here in Paris, or London, in Beirut, Constantinople—wherever I am being. And always she is asking for the news. Archimandrite Alexei, she asks, what is happening out there?"

"How old is this—this lady?" I asked.

But on that point he seemed somewhat vague.

"Yes, I would say younger rather than older. But she does not talk of such things. No, she wishes to know what is going on in the world. Now you will understand, old boy, that I have bugger-all knowledge of these matters. I am pursuing the life of the unfortunate bishop who had to flee to Edinburgh for his indiscretions, and this means little to her. And the Inter-Confessional Institute for Peace—she has no interest in that either. Now I should tell you she is not so bloody ignorant, this woman. But her interests are not those of the Archimandrite Alexei, understand?"

"What makes you think her interests might be mine? I presume that's what you're thinking."

"It is *life,* what is going *on,* that consumes her. It is, as the great English writers say, her devouring passion. And you, young man, are so full of life. I tell it at once when I sit down in the Parc Monceau. You smell, I tell myself, of all that pulsates. It is the spring season that verily runs in you, you old bugger."

"Thank you," I murmured, thinking it might have been the traces of the previous night's lust he had scented, and wishing once more that I had the facilities for taking a proper bath in my one-room slum. "And what exactly is it you felt I might do for her?"

"To zat I was coming. Now I have told you she is rich. In fact, she is loaded with the fucking dough, as ze Americans say. Always I am receiving the checks and on those few times when I am able to call upon her, there is money for my work and some expensive gift which is quite bloody useless for me."

"I see. Did you have some kind of—er—*erotic* role in mind for me, then?"

"Ah, here I must make the warning. She is very sensitive, this lady. And once I made an unfortunate mistake with her. I sent her a young man of good family, well educated, all those things, and he leap-ed upon her with the animal savagery. That poor woman had a relapse; her already tortured nerves snapp-ed and she spoke with no one in the clinique, or even on the telephone, for almost one year. She is now, let us say, a little suspicious if I make mention of sending someone in my place. I think she feels I am making the excuses for not being there. She is bloody right, of course. She wears me out. I am not as young as I was and she is without the understanding of the position of a clergyman. You follow me, I hope?"

I thought I did.

"Well, I certainly wouldn't rape her," I said forcefully. "That is not my nature at all. But how can you be sure she would even want to see me? I mean a complete stranger—"

"For me that poor creature has the implicit faith, my old pal. She is afraid of meeting the strangers, but she has nowhere else to turn. If I say I cannot go but will send a young friend instead she will, with all bloody reluctance, come to agree. I have not seen her on this visit, for frankly I have been putting it off. It is not just the journey to the Clinique de St. Eustache, but the hour."

"Hour?"

"Always so fucking late. The woman suffers also from the damn insomnia, you understand? She has turn-ed night into day, and day into bloody night."

That didn't bother me. I was a night owl myself. Besides, with no Jeannot to instruct, my daytime obligations were now at an end.

"I am interested, Archimandrite Alexei. Very interested. Now what precisely do you propose?"

"You are busy tonight?"

"I needn't be."

"Good, then we will have some bloody grub together and then I will telephone to her and say you will visit. I shall explain that you are a poor young man—"

"Well, there's no need to—"

"Leave all that side to me. I assure you there will be no problem. Your financial troubles are over. You will find her of much interest, too."

It was only later, when recalling that last comment of the Archimandrite, that I realized he was even capable of understatement . . .

Rattling along on the oil-smelling Métro that evening, after leaving the old man at the Gare St. Lazare entrance, where we exchanged addresses, it slowly dawned on me what an incredible thing I was doing. Here I was, tearing across subterranean Paris, headed for a rendezvous with a complete stranger, simply on the assurance of someone whom I had known only for a few hours that she would welcome me.

My sense of apprehension received a decided spurt when I presented myself at the main gate. The clinique oozed that grim, gray quality which makes any French institution exude a prison atmosphere.

The very same attendant who made use of an intercom system to announce my arrival to Madame Elfrida as the Archimandrite had informed me she was called, accompanied me down the maze of harshly lit corridors. A taciturn, blue-jowled fellow of quite villainous appearance, he merely shook my sleeve when we arrived at Room 318, banged violently upon the door, beckoned me to stay put, and then shuffled away without even a word escaping his tightly compressed lips.

It was something of a welcome antidote to all that grim silence to hear a woman's voice call out gaily: "Come on in, honey. The door's unlocked."

At first I could not locate the owner of that lilting Southern accent. Then I saw the huge four-poster bed at the far end of the long, rectangular room and thought I saw movement amid piled pillows—and realized that the mound of lacy material sprawled across it contained the person I had come to see.

"Over here, sir. Come right on over here!" It wasn't so much a command as a sultry invitation. I felt my mouth suddenly dry with nervousness.

"Don't be shy, Davey Bryant. Just take that chair over there and we can start getting to know each other."

Now I could make out which end of her was which, as within yard upon yard of the creamy pink material which composed her gown and which she seemed to inhabit like a cocoon, I could finally detect a face. I sat down where I presumed she indicated, my knees tight against each other, my hands clasped on my lap.

"So you're Davey Bryant of the Cornish Bryants, and I am sure the Archimandrite told you my name was Elfrida and that I am a daughter of the State of Alabama." Coyness invaded her voice. "What *else* did that saintly man tell you about me?"

"That you were old, old friends."

I thought her length stiffened amid all that foamy, filmy cloud of material and I became aware of silence.

"That's to say, you are very *good* friends."

"The Archimandrite Alexei Levertov possesses one of the most brilliant minds in all Europe. Unfortunately, it is not of the kind that can possibly understand a woman like me."

I said nothing. What was there to say?

"Did he by any chance mention my problems?"

Now here I felt on firmer grounds, for not only had the old man told me of her fear of the world beyond her room, you remember, but I had taken pains to formulate a reply if the subject were raised.

"He did explain that you were reluctant to do very much in public."

"I have not been beyond these quarters for ten years."

"I did gather that you have been somewhat unwell."

"It is not illness that plagues me. It is my emotional fragility. I was raised in an atmosphere of extreme gentleness and now I pay a terrible price for my sensitivity. Would you say I was a beautiful woman, Davey Bryant?"

I was thinking it was hard in that light, and through that sartorial sea, for me to discern whether the head had a body and whether the body was connected to limbs, but as she spoke she moved. Lace wafted, floated, and suddenly she was lying, her head toward me at the foot of the bed and resting on clenched fists supported in turn by her elbows. For the first time I saw Madame Elfrida's countenance. The ghostly white of it was perforated by huge lemur-like eyes and a mouth dark red with lipstick. Dense black hair now cascaded prettily on each side. It was a striking face which in less dim light might easily have been revealed as beautiful, in a singular way, that is.

I cleared my throat. "Yes," I said firmly. "Yes indeed, Madame Elfrida. You are very beautiful."

"Good," she murmured. "That is a bridge crossed. I could not have continued with this visit had I thought you felt otherwise. Now will you stand up and come closer?"

Fear washed at me afresh. Were things to be so precipitate? I almost panicked at the thought that I might well be 'no good to her'—as our village women in Cornwall were wont to say of their menfolk who couldn't get it up.

Somehow I got to my feet, though I believe I was swaying as I stood there, wondering what on earth to do. I could almost feel the hot intensity of those huge eyes staring at me.

"You are not very tall, Davey."

"Not very, I'm afraid."

At that she slowly let out an enormous sigh. "What a cruelty it is that what is a blessing for a man is a tragedy for a woman."

Her words caught me by surprise. "I beg your pardon?"

"Height for a man is a dignity. To be stunted, an object of mirth. For us, the opposite."

Rather blindly I sought to cheer her up on the point. "Oh, I don't know. I think short men rather attractive. As a matter of fact, I wanted to be a jockey when I was still at school. When I grew too tall I remember being quite disappointed."

"What do you mean, you find short men attractive? Are you? Do you? Well, do you have that *thing* some men get about each other?"

I got her drift. "Not particularly," I babbled on. "I see life as a great experiment. I am still learning, still finding out about myself."

From the abrupt change in her tone it was obvious that something I'd said had offended her.

"Really? Come, you're not *that* young. I should've thought you have had ample time for the more *basic* discoveries."

I backtracked rapidly. "Oh yes, of course! All the more basic stuff has been taken care of. I was thinking more of—well, the refinements, if you like. That's why I came to Paris. I've discovered that I like stinky cheese for one thing. And I never thought I would when I was back in Cornwall. Then there was the matter of teaching. I thought I might see if I had a vocation in that direction. But I find I nurse homicidal tendencies toward the very young. Do—do you find children attractive, Madame Elfrida?"

"Please stop using that ridiculous 'Madame' business with me, Davey. No. Children are quite repulsive to my temperament. The very sound of them could put me to bed for a month. On one of the few occasions the Archimandrite really addressed himself to my problems, he told me that such beauty as mine was at variance with the maternal instinct. Unfortunately I suspect he was rather drunk on the bottle of Beaujolais we had been sharing."

The thought of the Beaujolais seemed to move her to greater restlessness, for with a sharp flurry of garments, she slid from the bed and, for the first time, revealed an extraordinary aspect of herself. Elfrida Proudfoot of Alabama was a giantess. The long, long nightie thing she was wearing made her look even taller, of course. But as I reared back in alarm—for she was undulating violently—I thought mistakenly that she must have topped seven feet. However, when she finally came to a halt I had to admit she was less than that by several inches. It still made me feel little more than a dwarf, though.

She was standing now at the far end of the room from where I stood by the foot of her vacated bed. She had her back to me as she spoke, not bothering to turn around but raising her voice instead.

"I who have suffered at the hands of men, Davey, have been rendered incapable of bringing forth their offspring."

I felt a fool answering only that long black mane of hers. "I suppose the world would be a dull place if we were all mothers,"

I said lamely, and, when that neither turned her around nor elicited a verbal response: "What beautiful hair you have."

All that evoked was a somewhat equestrian toss of the locks so that even from that distance I could see glints of light in its waves. I decided therefore to try another tack and appropriate one of her own more dramatic idioms. "It—it looks as if it has never known the wound of scissors."

Like an enormous moth, the billowing shape moved swiftly along the room's edge, turned and faced me, the long arms with material flowing from them, spread-eagled on the wall behind her. I was reminded of a scene from *Lucia di Lammermoor*—which was probably what she had in mind, as I recalled the Archimandrite telling me she had been an ardent operagoer in some distant past and nowadays consoled herself many a night through with operatic recordings.

"An early suitor, now a most prominent figure in Washington, D.C., attempted to strangle himself with these strands." She shook painful recollection away with a gigantic convulsion. "But you are right, young man, this hair has never, never known the knife. You are very observant. Yes, indeed. No wonder the Archimandrite spoke so highly of your wits."

I wondered, in fact, what old Alexei *had* told her about me, considering most of it, under the brief circumstances of our acquaintance, would have had to be fiction. I tried to coax her on the subject.

"The Archimandrite is too kind. I hope he gave you no false impression. I am a very simple person, really." I made an attempt at an endearing smile.

"The Archimandrite does not understand women—that is to say, this particular woman. But then, no man has for so very long." She sighed extravagantly. "It makes my present desolation all the more unbearable."

"Oh don't say that, Madame—I mean, Elfrida. You make me feel my visit less than worth while." I eased my position, feeling pleasantly smug. If she wouldn't talk about me, I could register protest too. "If I am an intrusion . . . Well, I'd hate to be a burden."

Rarely, I suspect, has complacency been so short-lived. With an animal cry of protest Elfrida flung her sinuous length in the direction of me and the bed. I struggled briefly against the soft but enveloping drapes of her, but as oxygen became progressively difficult to procure, I subsided. Besides, she was shouting something up there above me, and I had no wish for the commotion to attract that grim-lipped attendant in white who might so easily misunderstand my smothered position beneath Madame's fluttering folds.

"Ah, my dear young man! My dear Davey! Honey, don't doubt your worth in my womanly eyes. The Archimandrite could not have sent me a sweeter gift. That saintly man has intuition. He must have known the depths of my despair this evening, until his phone call."

From the inky darkness of her imprisoning clothes I vaguely realized she was stroking my hair.

"You cannot believe the agony of waiting for your arrival. I must have crossed this prison a thousand times in my impatience. And you are more virile than I had ever dared hope. Oh, my handsome Davey, with that cute British accent—there is going to be such a marvelous friendship between us!"

"Madame," I managed to splutter, "I cannot breathe."

"There, there, honey child. Don't cry. Elfrida will take care of you. The days of your lonely wandering—searching for a mature relationship—are mercifully over."

Was it my imagination, or were those long fingers moving down from my head to less public parts of my anatomy? No, I realized, as a nipple was traversed on a downward path, no I was *not* mistaken! "Madame Elfrida, you are suffocating me!" And with that I made a further heave, aiming my bunched hands at what I hoped was the pit of her stomach.

Then her exploratory movements suddenly ceased—though not as a result of any winding from me, I sensed, as she called out in a quite different tone of voice: "That's all right, Jerome. Just leave it there. That will be all."

From the restriction of her garments I had heard no door open to permit the entry of a third party, but such was my sudden embarrassment that I ceased to struggle. However, she had hardly finished speaking when she rolled off me by her own volition and

89

slide from the crumpled crêpe de Chine bedspread and onto the thick carpet once more.

"Come and look what we've got here, honey. No—wait until I've lighted the candles."

I complied readily. Leaving the bed the opposite side from Elfrida, I hastily rearranged clothes and carefully recombed my thick mass of curls. By now there was only one thought dominant beneath that hair—escape!

"If you could move those two chairs closer, kind sir."

I threw up my wrist dramatically before my face (dramatic gestures were catching in that boudoir). "My God! I had no idea it was so late!"

"There is no *time* in this room." It wasn't a casual comment but a bared-teeth challenge to the world at large. My arm dropped at once and my watch slid under the cover of my cuff once more. I went straight to one of the upright chairs she had indicated and took it to the table where the candles now burned prettily.

And then, looking down at the polished tabletop, my feelings underwent a violent change of mood. For what I was beholding was a feast. Amid snowy-white napery, with silverware glowing dully in the warm candlelight, I quickly noted caviar, a pâté en croûte, a huge platter of crustacea, and several lidded dishes whose contents, of course, remained a mystery. An ice bucket contained what I felt sure was champagne, and more wine bottles—it was too dim from where I stood to read their labels— also stood there on the table.

Immediately hunger obliterated any notion of freedom, as it did the other fear of further physical entanglement with my impulsive hostess. I say hunger, but there was more to it than that.

Whether the pig or peasant in me was at work, I neither knew nor cared. At that precise moment I lay wholly under the thrall of that enticing spread, so remote from stolid pasties and filling yeast buns in Cornish kitchens. Indeed, I recall now the rationalizing reflection that for such gastronomic adventuring I had come to France.

"I sent to Fauchon's for most of these things. But if there is anything you like especially, let me know, Davey, and I will see we have it next time."

Five minutes earlier I would have shuddered at the threat of "next time." Now I merely conjured up images of those pricey little birds on skewers in the window of Fauchon's, of exotic-looking Indonesian crabs and weird-looking fruits that I had never seen before, let alone tasted . . .

We sat at opposite ends of the oblong table, which she informed me was Sheraton, and during the repast the conversation set mainly (and satisfactorily) upon me. By the time it was over Elfrida had been drawn a highly detailed portrait of a young Celtic nobleman whose family, of course, had known better days. But even before we had consumed a second bottle of wine after the champagne, she had also been made aware of my brilliant academic career at Oxford (under the tutelage of Lord David Cecil) and of the novel that was about to appear which, in galley proof, had already excited the admiration of T. S. Eliot, Grahame Greene, E. M. Forster, and D. H. Lawrence. A slight worry that it might occur to her that Lawrence had been dead for twenty years and that the Archimandrite might one day tell her I had flatly denied any knowledge of Lord David Cecil (or the University of Oxford, for that matter) had been entirely dissipated by the time we embarked upon a third bottle of wine—a claret which I guzzled as if it were 7-Up . . .

By the time I had staggered around to move her chair back from the table—a request she had to shout three times before I cottoned to that charming American usage—I had the muzzy feeling that our heights had been entirely reversed. It was I the giant who now gallantly, if unsteadily, escorted the little lady toward the bed on which she had somewhat crossly indicated she would like to enjoy a brief rest.

Brief rest appealed greatly to me too—that is, if I were not to be desperately sick as alternative. But in spite of earthquakes in the head and unpleasant promptings below, sleep finally took me. Took me, in fact, till 5 A.M., when I woke abruptly, looked at my watch, saw her gently heaving shape on the other side of the bed and felt immense relief at the fate I was convinced I had managed to escape. Taking infinite care not to wake her, I stole from her bed and finally from the clinique to greet a gray Paris dawn.

Somewhat later that day (I repaired quickly from hangovers when I was twenty-three) I sat once more with the Archimandrite Alexei to proffer my report on Elfrida and our meeting.

"She is a bloody beautiful woman, no?"

"I—I *think* so. It's funny, I'm not altogether sure."

The Archimandrite's eyes twinkled under his enormous brows. "Ah, she give you some of her American cocktails, I see. Those buggers are very strong!"

"No. Though there was quite a bit of wine, I remember. No, it was more to do with the light. It was so dim you couldn't see too much. Mind you, she gave me supper and the food was smashing!"

"She gave you something elses too, I understand."

I looked at the old man with astonishment. His vocabulary might not be suitable for my mother's ears, and his attitude toward sex and things was obviously poles apart from that of the Bishop of Truro, but his hint seemed crude, even by Continental standards.

"I'm—I'm not sure what you mean. Nothing *happened* between us, if that's what you're suggesting."

"You have your wallet with you?"

My hand fled to my inside jacket pocket. "Yes. But why . . ."

"Take it out, Davey, and look inside the bugger."

He watched me closely as I did as he said, leaning forward slightly as I eventually withdrew three crisp thousand-franc notes.

"So the Madame Elfrida gives you more than the supper, my old shit!"

"What? I mean—I don't understand—"

"When I talk-ed to her on the telephone she wish-ed to apologize. Something of a poor wine which might have upset your stomach?"

I shook my head. "A possible interpretation. But look at this." I fingered the notes with almost awe, never having seen such high denominations before. "There was no need. I mean, she needn't have . . ."

"It is the fucking old rent and the food, is it not? It is easier than the pedagogy, no?"

"Yes," I admitted. "But now I feel—well, a gigolo or something."

"So? You cannot make the omelettes without breaking the shell-eggs, as the Welsh Guards say."

"Eggshells," I corrected automatically. "You know, if—er—I were to find part of my income that way—just for the present, that is—I should start at a slightly less exotic level."

He was eyeing me intently, but I couldn't really make out his expression. I colored suddenly. "You've got to admit that your Madame Elfrida is *very* peculiar."

"Her money is not. And I myself, my young friend, have often been so describ-ed."

His persistence was slightly embarrassing me. "Ah, but, Archimandrite, there's no comparison. It is true—"

"It is true that I am in no position to offer you zat!" A mittened finger emerged to tap the three crisp notes on the table between us.

For one nervous moment I thought the Archimandrite Alexei was going to scoop them up.

"I should very much like to talk to her again," I said quickly.

The old man suddenly leaned back on his chair, a smile now playing about his lips. "So you will accept my old friend's gift?"

"Why yes . . . of course." Even as I spoke I picked up the three thousand-franc notes, folded them, and replaced them neatly in my wallet. "As a matter of fact, I'd like to see her again. Perhaps you could arrange—"

The Archimandrite's chair tilted forward again abruptly and his whiskers were only inches from my face. "Ah, that I do *not* think necessary, Davey, my dear young sod." He was smiling even more broadly, though I had already decided it was hard to say whether it was humor or mischief in those beady eyes of his. "No, Elfrida and I have talk-ed on this matter. We have decided that no further meeting will be necessary."

93

My mind raced back to the events in the clinique. "Of course I did get slightly muzzy on the wine. Maybe I got carried away. I mean, Lord David Cecil—"

But the Archimandrite waved my words away. "It was nothing of such details. Simply that Madame does not feel you are quite the type of visitor she is looking for." My discomfort was growing acute, the thought of no more of those nice, clean thousand-franc notes alarming. "If I misbehaved in any way . . . I mean, if I upset her. Perhaps if I called her to apologize?"

"Do not upset yourself, my dear old shit. It is nothing you could help."

The Archimandrite was already collecting garments prior to getting to his feet. "Let us say you are just too young for a woman of her experience and suffering. It is just the bloody life, eh? I think you will have to search out the very young again for the English lessons." He was already standing. "And now I must go. But I go with gladness in my heart that you have something to live on until you find another young bugger for the teaching. Got another fag I can smoke later, Dai Bach?"

Wordless, I handed him one.

"See you in the British Museum, I hope?"

And he was shuffling away in the direction of les Grands Boulevards.

I don't remember now exactly how long it was I sat there, wondering what had happened, but I am sure it was over an hour . . .

How does a young man of twenty-six end up being kept? There are surely as many ways as there are older lovers seeking the consolations of youth. But for you, my wound-dazed Davey, there was no decision, no dramatic gesture of escape from self-reliance, because the weight of the past was just too heavy.

Instead, there were a million and one tiny steps, a subconscious knitting of circumstance, until too many places in Europe had been visited, too many handsome shirts bought, too many delicious dinners consumed, for there not to be recognition of the fact that it took another's income to provide these things.

But unlike your progenitor, you will not give up, will you? So there is still the longing for the Cornish garden and the hope that religious liturgy might lead back to safety. But not to be . . . not to be . . . my own beloved wound of the imagination and final defense.

Chapter Six

If you were about Europe in the early fifties, you might have glimpsed us. Or if it had been your wont to stay in middle-priced hotels in some of the less obvious places, you would at least have stood a good chance of *hearing* us—through a bedroom wall as we quarreled our way loudly through the night.

You would not have had much difficulty in recognizing us. A balding man in his late thirties, clad in rumpled tweeds whatever the weather, with clipped British accent to match—that was Alfred Barnes, a librarian with U.N.E.S.C.O. in Paris. While I was a curly-headed youth whose slim figure was invariably clad in as "Frenchy" clothes as I could persuade Alfred to buy me. And over colorful shirts was a soft-complexioned face and a mouth that was a mite too pretty, even when it was pouting—which was much of the time.

Staying in Vianden, Luxembourg, lolling on the beach at Thonon-les-Bains in the Haute-Savoie, or amid the marram grass and dunes near Banyuls—all these places often proved to be something of an embarrassing mirror for both of us. For we kept meeting our doubles, or at least our equivalents.

"Look, Alfred. Over there. There we go again."

Alfred looks over rather than through his spectacles. "You mean that old aunty with his pouf? Speak for yourself, Davey Bryant! But if you just mean there is someone else who is *kept,* I'd have to agree."

"I was thinking more of the other one. He's just as jealous as you are. Look at him hovering over that poor boy!"

"Doesn't look poor to me. That's good flannel covering that

twitchy little bum. I bet it costs a fortune in clothes to keep that one happy. And by the way he's looking at you I should think he's about as faithful as a randy tomcat when he gets a chance!"

"Which I would think, Alfred, is about once every leap year. Isn't that a ball and chain he's wearing? Oh, it *is*, you know! I can see from here it's the same model you got for me."

That would be more than enough to start Alfred off. "I know you can't help having the instincts of a whore but you could at least try and lift your sense of humor out of the gutter. It's so very boring for me, you know."

"I've told you before, dear, if you don't like my Cornish peasant background, you know *exactly* what you can do. You may have rescued me from some hack English teaching but you didn't buy me lock, stock, and barrel. And you certainly didn't buy my sense of humor. Anyway, what do you know about my humor? You never listen to a word I say. It's only my body you're interested in, though you're too hypocritical to admit it."

"That's exactly what I mean by the gutter! Just because you're obsessed with the sight of your own body doesn't mean everybody else is. You're not *that* good-looking, you know."

"Aren't I? Funny, last night in bed you said I was. In fact, you said it over and over again."

Then Alfred hisses, his eyes ferocious behind the rather thick lenses. "Don't be so fucking vicious! Do you hear me?"

His voice would raise over the sea of metal tables on the freshly washed sidewalk and I would look about me apprehensively. In over a year of Alfred's company I could still so easily be embarrassed by him.

"I tell you, Davey, I can't stand it. I don't mind what I spend on you, where we go and that. But I can't take your cruelty. It's destroying me, understand?"

Then I'd jump to my sandaled feet, especially if I could see anyone else in hearing. "I'll see if I can get you a copy of *The Times*, my dear Alfred," I'd say. "You'll feel better when you've done the jolly old crossword."

That conversation was one I have virtually resurrected in its entirety from the last time we stayed in Villefranche. I mean, the whole bitter exchange and then my leaving him to search for

The Times. I left him there, drumming long fingers angrily on the flaking tabletop, and ambled along the quay, smelling the early morning Mediterranean smells, toward the tabac where the foreign newspapers were sold.

Madame, with her terribly swollen ankles, sat on her kitchen chair by the revolving postcard rack. She knew me, for Alfred had brought me down several times before on the P.L.M. from a cold and wet Paris to the clemency of the Riviera.

"Madame."

"M'sieur."

Flicking the cards around: "Je prendrai trois cartes postales, et vous avez le *London Times?*"

"Non, m'sieur. Seulement le *New York Herald Tribune*. J'attends les autres de Nice."

"Ça va. Donnez-moi le *Tribune*, s'il vous plaît."

She looked me up and down as I searched for the exact change, to save her the effort of getting her bulk out of that rickety chair. "Et le m'sieur? Ça va bien pour lui?"

She always referred to Alfred as le m'sieur. And once, when inside the tabac with Alfred, she had referred to me as 'Madame' and then profusely apologized, but I knew what was going on in her head all right . . .

"Oui," I said, "il va très bien. Un peu fatigué peut-être, après un hiver à Paris. Mais c'est comme ça pour moi aussi, vous comprenez?"

She stuffed the filthy franc notes into the large leather satchel on her lap, and then the tiny gray curls that covered her head bobbed up and down as she exploded in laughter. "Vous, m'sieur! Mais vous êtes un jeune homme. L'hiver—qu'est-ce que c'est pour vous?"

A futher rumble of mirth from her was even more dismissive, contemptuous.

I thought her darty black eyes were doing a swift accountancy of my new spring suit and my pigskin gloves with string backs that Alfred had bought me in Madelios. "Well, fuck you!" I said aloud in English as I gave her a tepid smile in response. "I bet you've been an evil old cow in your time." But before turning away I addressed her in French again: "Savez-vous les horaires de la Banque—Le Crédit Lyonnais—madame? Parce que j'attends le chèque mensuel de mon père."

"Non, m'sieur. Je ne sais pas."

'I bet you don't know what time the bloody banks open,' I thought as I sauntered back in the direction of the sidewalk café and Alfred. 'I bet all your ill-gotten gains are stuffed under your smelly old mattress!'

Alfred was still sitting there. As well as his coffee cup, I noticed a part-emptied glass of milky white Pernod before him. I looked at my watch. It was just gone 9 A.M. I wondered gloomily what kind of state he'd be in by midday . . .

"What's this?"

"*Herald Tribune. The Times* isn't in yet."

"Who wants to read this bloody American muck?"

"Me, if you don't want to. You know I find American things so much more interesting than all that dull English stuff."

"You would! Like you they thrive on predigested pap."

"And what's that supposed to mean? That neither they nor I are interested in your silly old snob games about who went to which school, and all that old malarkey?"

"I was thinking more of the fact that they have no history and you're too ignorant and idle to learn yours."

"I've only heard you going on about dates when you're boasting about your old Felstedians or whatever and that dreary Founder's Day. And, incidentally, that seems to get a hundred years earlier every time you mention it."

He gave me that irritated look over his glasses again. "That bothers you, doesn't it? Then I suppose it is rather difficult to find genuine pride over Bodmin High School, or whatever it was called."

Then before I zeroed in on his failed B.A. (he once foolishly admitted to me that he was sent down, as they call it, from Oxford) he turned to the newspaper I had handed to him. For a moment I watched him, or rather watched the paper as he held it out in front of himself, searching for another bloody crossword puzzle. When he found it he did as he always did—folded the sheet lengthwise, then bent it over from top to bottom. This way, when he was finished, only a small square of newspaper showed, with the crossword at its center.

"Did you happen to notice whether World War Three's broken out?" I asked. But he didn't even look up.

"Cannot be taken away. Eleven letters across, beginning with 'I'. 'Inalienable,' of course. God Almighty! This must be composed for the kindergarten!"

Out came his slim propelling pencil. His neat lettering filled in the blanks. I got up. "I'm going to get my book. See you later, I expect."

That made him look up. "You might see about a taxi into Nice. There's a rather pleasant little restaurant in the old port I've never taken you to." His voice was softer now. I knew I mustn't yield though, or there'd be one of those interminable discussions about "US" and about our "RELATIONSHIP." And he'd get progressively maudlin as he steadily downed those Pernods.

I made for the hotel entrance, but, when out of Alfred's sight, felt I wanted to stay in the fresh air—to walk, to think things out. So I took the narrow alley away from the quay, where in contrast to the bustle before the row of seafood restaurants overlooking the water, all was silent and rather gloomy, cut off from the morning sun.

The tiny bars and bistros that catered deep into the night to the crews of the luxury yachts riding out in Villefranche Bay were now tightly shuttered. I detected a faint scent of urine in the shadowed air, and, once or twice, as I climbed the steep, winding streets, noticed the dried-out course from a wall or doorway where some drunk had emptied his bladder a few hours earlier.

But all of that was very exterior to me as I toiled toward the higher levels of the old quartier. I was thinking of Alfred—or, rather, trying *not* to think of Alfred. There had been so many occasions when I could have cheerfully kicked him, indeed there had been the time in Rapallo when he had found me with that young fisherman when I had done just that. My Italian friend had fled down the seawall, pulling up his pants as he went. Alfred and I had started to struggle (he was jerking like a spastic with jealous rage) and from aiming at his shins I had actually pushed him over the side of the jetty and, apart from the soaking, he'd permanently lost his glasses.

I sighed heavily and shook my head: the scenes, the rows, the fights, the embarrassments—there had been so *many* of them . . . Then I forced myself to admit there were other sides to Alfred. Kind sides. Like the time when I was suffering from a dreadful bout of diarrhea in Seo de Urgel and he had nursed me and looked after me when I had really thought I was going to die. Or in Paris, when I was really down on my luck and finding it more and more difficult to find French brats who wished to learn English. I hadn't known Alfred very long and when I had so imprudently lingered outside the pissoir at the Rond Point des Champs Élysées and panicked when a policeman approached, it had been Alfred who'd come straight from bed down to the station where they'd taken me. It was he who had taken me back to his place and calmed me when I was babbling with fear over repetition of that earlier incident in my life. And he who had finally paid off this lawyer and that so I was left free and in peace.

It was shortly after that I had moved in with him and my life had undergone such an abrupt change. After mere subsistence for long bleak months, my twenty-fifth birthday blossomed with me as Alfred's guest, downing a fantastic dinner at Ramponneau's. I had gotten so drunk that afterward I had insisted he carry me pick-a-back all the way up the Champs Élysées. Oddly enough for such a precise and fastidious creature, he had really entered into the fun of that. Nothing stuffy or pompous about him then. But nor in those early days, of course, had I begun to fret and rebel against those invisible but still chafing bonds of being kept . . .

I reached the steps that led up to the little square where the parish church was. I climbed them and stopped at the top to catch my breath. Below me was a sea of red-tiled Mediterranean roofs, broken here and there by patches of gardened courtyards from many of which peeped either the milky mauve tresses of wisteria or the bright yellow pom-poms of mimosa. Of human sights or sounds there were none, and I suppose it was that which encouraged me to speak out loud—that and the fact that when someone is standing above a whole section of a town he's tempted to do the Pope's balcony thing and address the multitudes below.

"Why do you have to be so bloody possessive, Alfred? If you'd only trust me it would be so much easier. And why do you have to treat me as some kind of halfwit just because I grew up in Cornwall and failed to get that stupid theology degree? You didn't do any better, after all!"

I thought I could hear pigeons or doves cooing, but I couldn't make out from where.

"You address ze roofs of Villefranche, huh? Do zey reply?"

I turned quickly. "I—I beg your pardon?"

Facing me was a young French priest—replete with long black soutane, big, farmer-type boots, and, at the other end of his stocky length, a black beret that didn't quite manage to conceal a clump of blond hair.

"They—they say it's a sign of madness, don't they?" I said weakly.

"Madness?" His eyebrows raised.

M. l'Abbé, or whatever he was, certainly spoke English all right, but maybe he had a bit of difficulty understanding it when someone else did. Like me with my French.

"When you talk out loud, they say you are a bit—" I tapped the side of my head with my forefinger. He understood that. Laughed.

"I do not think you are mad, m'sieur. You have intelligent face, non?"

I'd already decided *he* had a very nice one. Not really handsome, but open and honest. Nothing of that blue-jowled scowl which so many of the French clerics I'd noticed seemed to wear.

"You are enjoying your stay in our leetle town? It is warmer than England at this time of year, non?"

"I live in Paris, as a matter of fact. And I can tell you there's not much sign of spring there yet."

"No. I remember what it was like where I come from. Now zere would be—how you say?—les jonquilles?"

"Daffodils."

"Daffodils. But not yet ze blossoms."

"Where was that then? In the north, I suppose?"

"A small place. You would not know eet. But not far from Rennes."

"I've been to Rennes. That's Brittany, isn't it?"

"Where I am from is just in Brittany. From Normandie just a few kilometers."

"That's very interesting. You see, I'm from Cornwall. Cornouailles? And the Bretons and the Cornish—"

"Ze same peoples, non? We are both ze Celts, is that not so?"

"*Exactly!* Tristan and Isolde and all that."

"You are a student, per'aps?"

"Yes," I told him. It seemed the easiest thing to say.

His gray eyes searched my face and I wondered uneasily what he was trying to read there. "I'm studying library methods at the Bibliothèque Nationale at present," I lied. "When I've finished I've been more or less promised a job with U.N.E.S.C.O. Ça veut dire O.N.E.S.C.O., vous comprenez?"

He nodded. "My father has much to do with zat. He is—how you say?—curator of ze museum in Orleans."

"But you didn't decide to follow his footsteps?"

For the first time he looked down at the ground instead of directly at me when answering. "No. When my mother died I went to the 'ouse of my father's brother, here in Nice. Then I go to the big seminary in this diocese."

"Which is why you're here in Villefranche? A nice place to work in, I imagine."

"Ze peoples. They are not so young. They are very conservateur, you understand?"

It was my turn to nod. "That your church, then, behind us?"

"I am the vicaire."

"That's the curate in English. For some reason we put it the wrong way 'round. A vicar is M. le Curé and the vicaire is the curate. Bit confusing that!"

"You are a Catholic, perhaps?"

"Sort of. Anglo-Catholic. Not Roman Catholic."

"Ah! Ze High Church! I know of ze Lord Halifax and all zat. It was my special studies you know. You haf everythings except the Pope."

I laughed. "You've put it very well."

Even as I spoke, memories of my being an altar boy, a server in the broad spacious sanctuary of St. Endellion Church, began to surface in me. I was also conscious, I think, that here was something over which I had no need to exaggerate, to lie, to borrow Alfred's experiences and pretend they were my own. "I was an altar boy, and sang in the choir, too. That was all back in Cornwall, of course . . ." I tailed off, thinking of how much I had left behind in the Cornwall of my childhood. Like feeling clean and innocent for one thing. Like the way this young priest seemed to me now.

"You are remembering, yes? Nice things?"

I turned quickly away from his smiling face and looked out again over the rooftops of Villefranche. I spoke to them as if he were not there by my side. "Things happen to you, without asking. They just steal up. And one day you wake up and realize you're cut off from everything you once thought would be there forever."

"Zat is very true. For me too."

He was standing very close and I sensed his sympathy strongly. Then I thought of Alfred still sitting there at the sidewalk table, playing with his crossword and getting quietly stewed. I also recalled the so many strange beds I had woken in . . . "It—it must be in a different way, for you," I said. "It can't be the same."

"You would not think me impolite if I asked how old you are?"

"Twenty-two," I lied, suddenly deciding to shed four years. "And you?"

"I am twenty-seven. The difference is important, I am feeling."

"How so?" I said, startled that there was only a year between us.

His shrug could only be French. "For me—how shall I say?— there is less of ze *promise* already. For you there are still all ze choices. But for me it is all decided. It was when I was twenty-six, come to that."

I nodded in the direction of his black-clad body. "Meaning you're a priest?"

"Of course."

"And you regret it?"

"Ah, zat I did *not* say, m'sieur." True, he smiled when he spoke. All the same, he didn't look very happy. "But my work, my life, it is all now so settled. When I was twenty-two like you, it was not quite so clear. You understand?"

I didn't feel like reflecting on the implications of my being twenty-six rather than twenty-two, so I concentrated on him instead. I wondered if he was trying to tell me something about himself.

"You miss something in life maybe? Perhaps you are not quite as free now as you were then?" As if in objective confirmation of my suggestion, the single bell in the roof of the church behind us suddenly began to clank away. The priest's hands which had been tucked into the pockets of his cassock flopped to his sides. "That is for the Mass—" He broke off and searched my face for a second or third time. (It seemed to be almost a habit with him.)

"I am thinking—would you care to serve at ze Mass, m'sieur?" And before I could answer one way or the other: "There will only be one or two of ze old ladies. You tell how you did serve ze Anglican Mass. We could make it a votive Mass for the reunion. Zat would be wonderful, I think! Pour l'Église de France et pour l'Église d'Angleterre."

"Well, I've forgotten—"

"It would make ze history in Villefranche—though only you and I would know."

That rather appealed to me. "All right," I said. "Only, you'll have to show me."

"It is very simple. Like your Holy Communion, n'est-ce pas?"

"I can serve a Low Mass in English all right," I told him firmly.

He nodded at that as we started to walk together toward the tall, pitchpine doors, one of which was now slightly ajar.

"Thees one will be in the Latin unfortunately. We are not allowed to say Mass in French yet in thees diocese."

He smiled. With a jolt of embarrassment I felt his arm alight about my shoulder.

"We are—we are—how do you say?"

"Backward," I supplied. And hurried ahead of him into the darkness of the building.

He indicated where the lavabo things were and where I could kneel by the altar until he emerged from the sacristy. As I walked over toward the rail an old witch dressed entirely in black, with lace over her head, fled from the place he'd pointed to. It was obvious that I was about to do her out of a job. Even so, she inclined her head politely as she passed me on her way to a pew farther back. I noticed a rosary was tightly knotted about her gnarled hands. I wondered if she would have nodded her head like that to me if she had known what I had been up to the previous night . . .

Picking up the missal, I busied myself with an exploration of its pages, until I suddenly noticed the priest already standing there in his crimson chasuble at the foot of the altar steps. As he began praying quietly but still audibly, it all came flooding back to me. That bent red back with the gold cross emblazoned upon it . . . the low words . . . It could so easily have been Father Trewin there in the granite cool of our Norman church above the Cornish cliffs. As I struggled with the Latin Responses I remembered the English ones:

'I will go unto the altar of God.'

'Even unto the God of my joy and gladness.'

'Our help standeth in the name of the Lord.'

'Who hath made heaven and earth . . .'

'I confess to God Almighty, to Blessed Mary ever Virgin . . .'

And then the Kyries in the Greek that both Rome and Canterbury shared: 'Kyrie Eleison, Christe Eleison, Kyrie Eleison . . .'

But soon my mind refused to stay with the words I was offering in response. As the young French priest proceeded through Epistle and Gospel, I heard not him but the incessant wind as it moaned through the telephone wires on the road through Pendoggett and St. Endellion; I saw the cluster of mossed roofs of the adjoining fishing villages of Port Isaac and Port Gaverne. To my nostrils came neither the dust and damp of where I now knelt in Villefranche, nor the blend of furniture polish and incense that spelled Endellion Church on a Sunday morning. But the manurey blends from cowsheds and stables, the acrid smell of rain-dampened straw in the ricks of the farmyard beyond my childhood bedroom window.

I rang the sanctuary bell as first the host and then the chalice were elevated during canon of the Mass. But I was watching another Davey Bryant, sitting happily on the broad back of Duke, the carthorse, a sack for a saddle, slithering down the fern-fronded lane to St. Tudy—to white-haired Mr. Tregidgo and his blacksmith's forge.

With sudden fierceness I felt love for that twelve-year-old self on that coal black horse, riding the Cornish morning in Wellington boots and corduroy pants about my bouncing little bum.

"Seculae Seculorum," said the priest.

"Amen," I answered as the long, silent prayer came to an end.

But was it love for that vanished Cornish me (so vivid there in the mind's eye as the young equestrian anticipated the sharp stench of burning horse hoof as the white-hot steel was pressed to it and the blue smoke rose in the blacksmith's shop), or was it hate for the whorish me who knelt there now, hypocritically responding to another man's faith, which made me squirm?

"Agnus Dei qui tollis peccata mundi . . ."

"Dona nobis pacem . . ."

But there was no peace as I shifted my weight from leg to leg: only this anguish over mental snapshots of a happy boy under a long-gone sun and last night's image of lusting lips at work. Then suddenly my thoughts rushed back to the place I was in. Only vaguely had I noticed the priest go to the tabernacle, take out the Communion hosts, and stand there looking at me as he held up the ciborium. Then I realized. He wanted to give *me* Communion! I panicked. I shook my head violently. But he still walked slowly down the altar steps toward me.

"Non. Merci, non."

He was smiling, whispered softly: "À cause de l'irénicisme. Pour l'unité de l'Église."

I pulled myself to my feet, stepped back to the side aisle where the church was in deepest shadow. For what seemed an eternity he just stood there. And then I realized there were tears streaming down his cheeks.

I couldn't bear it any longer and groped for the wall. I refused to focus my eyes on the two or three hunched women scattered about the church as I made for the door and daylight, for freedom from all that suffocating innocence.

Once outside in the little square I don't know why I didn't just hurry away down those steps. Partly, I guess, because I immediately felt calmer out there. After all, I was back in *my* world as opposed to his—I mean, squares, streets, alleys, that kind of thing. And also, I suppose, because I felt I owed him an apology. After all, I had agreed to serve his Mass, however reluctantly.

So I wandered back to the balustrade where he and I had first talked. I felt rather than saw him emerge from the church. In fact, I heard those heavy boots of his on the cobbles of the square. Frantically I tried to arrange what I would say to him. I felt I could not, certainly wouldn't, tell him that I had left things like Holy Communion behind me at King's College, London, when I had also left behind an incomplete degree in theology and an abortive vocation to the priesthood in the Church of England. And under pain of torture I would never have told him that as recently as yesterday I had done things with my mouth which made his invitation in the church—well, out of the question.

My skin started to prickle again, as it had inside, and instead of just standing there, awaiting his inevitable questions, I started toward the steps. He intercepted me and fell in beside me just as I was descending the first one. The fall of our feet sounded in unison as we went down several more. Neither of us spoke or even looked at each other.

Then he finally addressed me. "I—I am sorry. I have to make ze apology. You were right, of course. It was very stupid of me. I am too sentimental. My superiors, they 'ave told me that."

"Right?" I couldn't hide my surprise.

"It would have solv-ed nothings. There is, after all, the schism of the Church. You were willing to give témoignage—how you say?—to *witness* to zat. But I was trying to forget it was zere."

"Schism of the—"

"It was so hard for me to think of you not being able to share ze Body of Christ with me. Nous sommes Chrétiens, tous les deux, n'est-ce pas?"

I licked dry lips. "I didn't mean to let you down. It—it was more complicated than perhaps you think."

"Eet would 'af been nice, though, if we had at least made ze Pax."

"The Pax?"

"It is usually for ze High Mass only. We do this."

We were halfway down the winding slope of the narrow Rue des Pêcheurs, and were in the deep shadow of one of the covered, tunnel-like lanes that led ultimately out onto the quay. I felt his hands on both my shoulders as he brushed my face with his lips, on either side.

Whether it was the uprush of sadness I suddenly knew—for him, for me, for what had taken place in the church—or whether the fact of being held thus by him sparked a more earthly response, I still am unsure, but my reaction was certainly immediate. My own arms reached out to his shoulders and my lips found not his cheeks but the fullness of his mouth. There was nothing of Gallic or liturgical ceremonial about *my* gesture. And by the way his lips pressed back against mine in response I felt sure he was aware of it.

I remember the pale fragrance of wine about his mouth, and then the slight turn of his head as he attempted to speak. I wasn't absolutely certain whether he was addressing me in French or English, so low were his words. As it turned out, I never was to know. For at that point his voice was wholly drowned out by another. A loud, rasping voice, sickeningly familiar:

"Jesus Christ! You little slut! You fucking little slut!"

I didn't even say goodbye. Just violently pushed the young priest from me and turned to face the threat of Alfred. There he was, at the far end of the covered passageway, peering short-sightedly at us through the sunless gloom.

"Coming, Alfred," I called. "Now let's not have a scene. You've got it all wrong, of course."

"Scene? I catch you whoring with a priest in the fucking daylight, and you talk about a *scene!*"

I looked back quickly. The curate of Villefranche still stood there, his black silhouette quite motionless. I almost ran on down toward Alfred, talking all the time. "He—he asked me to serve his Mass. Then he wanted me to make my Communion. I couldn't and that upset him. He was showing me what they call the Pax."

"Don't tell me what he was *showing* you. The whole bloody town could've seen that!"

"Alfred, I don't care *what* it looked like. You've got it all wrong as usual." I kept on walking, wanting him and the savage hate of our relationship removed as far as possible from someone who could still weep over the division of Christendom. "You must've heard the bell for Mass. You aren't that pissed. We'd just walked down from the church. We'd just reached that place when you called out. Surely you—" Then I stopped trying to explain. There were no more explanations possible between us.

Am I my creature's keeper? Maybe. More often than not I refuse the reflection, relying, rather, on you, Davey, to take the brunt of my obligations and free me of moral complication. But in so doing you learned before you were thirty what I have only learned later, that sometimes we belong to our sisters. In saving up money to join your male lover in North America you are also saving up memories of what you might have been. You whose sexuality refuses my personal confines, how could you know of a possible chance missed, or perhaps of a further one taken? And I who created you can only record and not explain. You are too close to me, Davey my quintuple senses, for me to have omniscience. All I can say is that you are also saying goodbye to the physical location of a garden as you prepare to put a continent and an ocean between yourself and a Cornish childhood.

Chapter Seven

Some of the details are a little hazy. It was in the late-fifties, for example, but I am unsure of the precise date. Which means I cannot pinpoint my age either, but let's say I was pushing thirty.

Where things become crisply focused is over the kind of day it was that September morn I walked the quiet streets of an ugly military town called Aldershot, in southern England, on my way to a new experience. On that bright though chill morning, as a few sycamore leaves rolled lazily in the strength of a mild breeze, along the gutters, and as I walked past the privet-hedged gardens of tall, red-bricked Edwardian houses, to the occasional tune of dogs barking, I thought with a nice sense of buoyancy, of the novel prospects before me.

For once in my life, it seemed, I was no longer to be wholly at the mercy of another's whims for my livelihood as it had been with Alfred in France. Nor, I was convinced, would this specific and even respectable employment which I was jovially approaching contain any unhappy echoes of the fiscal risks and intellectual frustrations attendant upon my brief career as a freelance tutor of the half-witted young of the Parisian rich.

Crossing from one tree-lined street to another, all of them apparently named by an early twentieth-century developer with a passion for poets, I hummed happily to myself as I headed my sports-coated self toward St. Benedict's Preparatory School where Davey Bryant, internationally traveled gay lecher, was already known as Mr. Bryant, the new teacher of French and master in sports and athletics.

I spoke the description aloud to the sycamore tree I was

approaching, and had to grin at the last bit. The only sport I had ever pursued in high school was the one we boys referred to as "pocket billards," while my athleticism was rarely displayed beyond the confines of a bed.

The French, on the other hand, made more sense. I had been able to turn mere schoolboy French into something more useful, if not all that more profitable, during my three years based in France after leaving London and ideas of priesthood behind me. And, after all, had I not fallen finally in love with someone in Paris who was directly responsible for my walking that morning toward my first really bona-fide employment? If Ken, now back in California finishing his Ph.D., had stayed in France, I would not that moment have been implementing my plan to save as much money as possible in as little time as possible, in order to join him in America.

Of course, I had not explained *that* to Father Grimble, my prospective headmaster-employer, who thought, poor dear, that I had finally found my vocation in life and would be patiently teaching his little charges for long into the future. Then I had not told him very much about my personal life, its gay aspects or otherwise. It was his money, not his intimacy, I needed, and I was not in Aldershot for its social whirl or potential in friendships. I was quite determined to remain as aloof as possible from Father Grimble, Miss Crocker his sidekick, and the rest of the staff whom I had met on my previous visit, when he had interviewed me and I had landed the job.

Two more streets to go . . . I noticed just ahead of me a horse-drawn milk dray with the name of a local dairy emblazoned upon it. The milkman, metal crate of bottles in his hand, was chatting with a postman in his navy blue uniform. Both of them wore peaked caps. A small sigh moved against my general sense of euphoria. In a little while, a few months at most, all that Englishry would be left behind. Even the tinpot prep school which was unwittingly to provide me with my passage was also part of that peculiar British mosaic which I was soon to turn my back on—for all I knew, forever.

Perhaps not surprisingly, my thoughts turned next from that immediate scene to the rugged farmland on the edge of the moor where I had grown up and which could always and so easily tug painfully at me. I thought of that hurting Cornish terrain where Mother and Father still lived and from where they continued to worry over their feckless son who still, at nearly thirty, had failed to provide them with a daughter-in-law, let alone the grandchildren their letters suggested they ached for.

But that way led to ever grimmer reflections and I was damned if I was going to depress myself on this meaningful Monday on which so much of an exciting future was hinged. I quickly made a decision to spend at least a couple of weeks on the farm in Cornwall before sailing on the *Liberté* from Southampton. The remaining minutes on the way to the gates of St. Benedict's were spent estimating precisely how long I would have to play at schoolmastering before sending off the magic letter to Ken, informing him that I was on my way . . .

Shortly thereafter, though, all such pleasant anticipation was blotted out as I stood before my first French class. That particular group—they seemed to be about ten or eleven years old—knew not a word of French. But as it soon became apparent that their English grammar was itself vestigial, we turned to, for them, more congenial topics, and, for me, less arduous ones. I discovered that most of them were sons and daughters of servicemen, and that although they had never heard of a past tense, they were quite familiar with the Suez Canal, the inclement heat of Aden, and the swimming prospects on Cyprus. By the end of that initial session I had them standing up in turn and telling the rest of us their favorite overseas adventure. When the bell rang we had only reached the end of the front row so I knew I had enough ammunition to keep that particular class engaged for some weeks to come.

Next came the Common Room encounter—my first real meeting, in fact, with my colleagues. There was Mrs. Howells, for example, whom I at once recalled, from my previous visit, had a wonky eye that disconcerted by only looking outward and upward. Before, we had only exchanged vague niceties; this time she was more direct.

"Welcome to St. Benedict's, Mr. Bryant. I gather we're the

only two graduates on the staff. I'm a Girton woman myself. Are you a Cambridge man, too?"

Her one good eye stared at me with such intensity I thought it was doing double time for the irregular one.

"King's," I said blandly (neglecting to add that it was at London rather than Cambridge and omitting entirely the detail that I had in fact failed my degree). "And please call me Davey. Everyone else does."

"French, of course? You read French?"

By that period in my life my policy to combine dissimulation with intermittent candor had become second nature. "As a matter of fact, no. I took theology."

Her good eye glistened. "Theology?" (She made it sound like "sewage.") "But I thought—"

"My *second* degree was French, of course. The Sorbonne," I added, "or to be quite precise, the Institut Catholique," thinking that I would be happily wandering arm in arm with my lover on the edge of the Pacific Ocean before she could check the accuracy of that.

"My goodness!" she exclaimed, crossing her plump, nyloned leg and smoothing her Harris tweed skirt, "we *are* becoming academic at St. Benedict's. Although I would have thought—well, we're such a potty little prep school . . . And with your qualifications . . ."

"I just fell in love with Aldershot," I murmured. "Such a quaint little town."

She stared at me, wondering, I'm sure, whether I was pulling her leg. "Mr. Bryant, if I'd known Major Howells was going to spend most of his army career in this *dump* I would never have married him. It is only the teaching here at the school that has kept me sane."

Looking at her and remarking her iron-gray hair for the first time (it looked as if it had not seen a comb in weeks) I wondered what Major Howells' opinion might be as to her sanity. But I recalled my decision to remain socially unentangled during this stint of teaching, and steered the conversation away from her matrimonial affairs.

"Well," I said brightly, "I'm looking forward to teaching here too. From what I've seen of the kids already, they seem a bright-enough bunch."

She took the bait, relaxed back in the only armchair the common room boasted, so that I could see the end of her stocking where it clung to the top of her fat white thigh. "I have never met children with more accumulated experience than those we have here at St. Benedict's. Unfortunately the experience seems quite unrelated to knowledge, Mr. Bryant. They have seen everything and learnt nothing—except perhaps cynicism."

"You've taught here a long time, Mrs. Howells? English, isn't it?"

"Since the blessed day dear Father Grimble founded the school. Isn't that so, Miss Crocker?"

Mrs. Howells' good eye was fixed on somewhere behind my shoulder. I turned to greet the headmistress of St. Benedict's, with whom I had already talked fleetingly before taking my first class. Physically speaking, I suppose you could've called Miss Crocker almost the opposite of Mrs. Howells. Whereas our English teacher was ample in bulk, matronly in her tweed suit and unpolished no-nonsense shoes, Miss Crocker was a mere slip of a thing with her raven hair tied in a bun and her thin little body hunched into a position just this side of deformity.

"I suppose so, Mrs. Howells. I suppose so." Her voice was so low as to be almost a whisper. Its inflection, which was entirely dismissive, was backed up by a quick flick of a bony wrist.

No love lost between these two, I thought to myself.

"Has anyone prepared Father's soup? It's Monday—it'll be the onion of course."

I raised eyebrows and looked inquiringly at Mrs. Howells, unsure what Miss Crocker was talking about. But I encountered only the wonky eye and looked quickly away again. "Soup?" I queried.

But Miss Crocker, apparently answering her own question negatively, had whisked her tiny self in the direction of the small kitchen where I had previously made myself a cup of Nescafé at the invitation of Mrs. Howells. Miss Crocker addressed a steaming kettle, but her words were obviously meant for me behind her back.

"Father Grimble *always* has soup at break. Only he likes to vary the flavor each day. The poor man has been on his feet since the early hours, remember. And we mustn't forget that he carries the weight of the parish as well as the school on his back."

On the subject of Father Grimble I immediately noticed her voice had switched gear. There was a tremolo now in its huskiness, even an incipient hysteria, and I realized for the first time that my priestly boss owned a slave. A slave who no doubt had lived for years in the hope she might one day be elevated to the status of lover, with the ultimate satisfaction of achieving the title of "Mrs. Grimble." My suspicion was that I had more chance of ending up Father Grimble's lover than did poor Miss Crocker, if that cleric had anything to do with it. But I continued to pursue my role of neutrality with vigor. I addressed her back: "Anything I can do to make Father Grimble's cross lighter to bear I should count an honor."

From behind me I thought I heard a little snigger from Mrs. Howells. So apparently did Miss Crocker. "Mrs. Howells, I do hope you feel rested from your one hour's labor, as someone must go at once and supervise the Juniors' milk. And by the way, Miss Ellis-Wynn is sick again so I must ask you to take her Arithmetic, History, Nature Study, and Junior Art Class today."

"Maybe I should cook lunch, too."

"I do not think sarcasm helpful, Mrs. Howells. I would take some classes myself if I were not assisting Father Grimble in Senior Liturgics."

I was wondering what in hell Senior Liturgics were as Mrs. Howells scrambled to her large feet, snorted, and waddled out of the room without casting a glance in the direction of either of us. Miss Crocker, her mouth the grimmest slit, watched her go. Small, wizened, she might be, but there was no doubt who Father Grimble's henchman was and on whose side I should try and keep on. She confirmed it seconds later.

"I'm afraid I had to change things generally, Mr. Bryant. This afternoon, for instance, you had better take the Juniors for sports as Miss Ellis-Wynn won't be able to take them for her subjects."

My heart sank. Those bloody sports! I had hoped, indeed had

every reason to believe, from the posted schedule downstairs, that I would have my first day devoted exclusively to ordinary teaching before encountering the kids on the playing field. Apart from my general awareness that I myself was wholly out of trim for running around blowing a whistle, I had no idea what to blow a whistle *for*. Father Grimble had said something vague about my taking whichever sport I wished, but I had neglected to tell him that it would make no difference: I was as ignorant of one game as another, and, what is more, detested them all with equal fervor.

"Yes, Miss Crocker. I see your point entirely. I shall be delighted to take the youngsters out on the field."

By the time the afternoon arrived I had come up with a rough strategy. Walking amid a stream of boys making their jabbering way in the direction I'd been told the playing fields lay, I quickly remarked the tallest and fell in beside him. He turned out to be a rather porky boy, too. From a few steps behind I noted that his navy blue shorts were stretched so tight that I would not have been surprised if the bulging cheeks of his bottom hadn't split them up and down the seam. Walking with him, while studiously avoiding the sight of glistening mucous trailing from a podgy nose, I listened a while to his shrill-voiced boasts of his prowess at rugger.

Then I moved in, as it were. "Rugby's your game then, is it, boy?"

"Yes, sir. Rather, sir. I scored three tries in the final match last Lent term, didn't I, Rodgers? You should know 'cos you were fullback for Epistle."

"Epistle?" I had a disturbing vision of them kicking a football around the altar in church.

"The other team, sir. We always break into two. Gospel and Epistle."

"Extraordinary," I murmured.

"It's the Grim's idea, sir. Sorry, I mean Father Grimble. Then the girls' hockey teams are Incubi and Succubi."

"Jesus Christ!" I burst out.

"We thought of that too, for the two teams, sir," contributed Rodgers, the fullback, who walked on my other side. "But Father

Grimble was quite chokker. Said he wouldn't have any blasphemy. But there's a Jesus College at Oxford and Cambridge, isn't there, sir?"

"There's a Queen's too," I began, but tailed off in the face of their obvious puzzlement. "Look," I told them, "Epistle and Gospel, Ancient and Modern, Wafers and Wine—I don't care *what* you call yourselves. But you, boy, are going to be referee and everyone else will play on one side or the other."

"But we've got enough chaps out today for four teams, sir."

"I don't care if you're forty a side. Just two teams, get it?"

Ahead of us I saw the main road and a green doubledecker bus passing down it. That gave me an idea. "And by the way, you'll play an hour and a half each way." I looked at my watch. "That's the field over there, isn't it?" This time my question elicited a mighty chorus of yesses. "Right, then. By the time you've changed and on the field it'll be 2 P.M. I expect you to blow the final whistle at 5 P.M. Get it?"

They looked at me as if I were slightly dotty, but they obviously got it. Indeed, one grinning youth with more gaps than teeth had the effrontery to interrogate me thus:

"You going into Aldershot, then? There's that war picture about the Eighth Army at the Odeon."

I had, in fact, been contemplating a visit to the shopping center and a pharmacist, as I had run out of my favorite shampoo, but his question made me freshly aware of how chill the breeze had grown and the fact that it was now spitting with rain. "As a matter of fact," I said, returning a smile of my own to his toothy grin, "I had something else in mind. But in this bloody weather maybe a film about the desert would be the best."

I waited there until the last boy had crossed to the open field across the road, then turned to look for the bus stop. It was as well I did so, for otherwise I might not have seen the cassock-flapping figure of old Grimble bearing down on me. Fortunately, the tall white-haired priest seemed a man quite unaccustomed to haste, and by the time he reached me my words were formed.

"Hello, Father. Just making sure there were no more boys to come. I hate these main roads for children to cross. There should be a proper marked crossing."

"How thoughtful of you, dear boy. Well, I've been thoughtful too. I decided I'd come and give you moral support as you make your debut on the playing fields of St. Benedict's. You see, I know how difficult it is for some brilliant, imaginative young man like yourself to play with that nasty rough ball." He put his arm lightly around my shoulder. "When dear Father Monk replied to my letter about you he stressed just how sensitive a person I was getting. But all of us teachers have had to shoulder the burden of sports at some time, when we would rather be attending a concert. All of us, dear boy, at one time or another."

I scowled, though he couldn't see. I had no difficulty in imagining some of the things he had gone through in his time and conjured up several obscene cameos involving the lanky cleric. I also had no difficulty in understanding the true motive for his presence with me at that moment was to see personally that I didn't wriggle out of my obligations as sportsmaster. I sighed heavily as the cars swished wetly by. Ah well, if getting chilled to the marrow was the price I had to pay to be reunited with my Ken, it was surely worth it.

Father Grimble then gave me another irritating little squeeze. "There, my dear, don't sigh! Things could be far worse. And you'll soon discover our little St. Benedict family is full of love and understanding."

More to escape his clutches than to get on with the job of supervising juvenile sports, I dodged the traffic and hurried ahead of him across the road. During the next hour or so—for the first thing I did when taking over control from my surprised young appointee was to cut the playing time by half—I had numerous occasions to curse that solitary black figure haunting the touchlines.

But my frustrations were by no means confined to the presence of that inhibiting old clergyman, for as I got colder and wetter, muddier and more out of breath, my excited charges got progressively out of hand. War-whooping like irate Iroquois, they hurled themselves upon one another as much as upon the ball, and on those frequent occasions when I slipped and fell they would smother me too.

Whatever it was possible to sprain I felt I had sprained before that black afternoon was over. Ankles, wrists, back ached madly, while my lovely new clothes bought with such fastidious care at Simpson's, Liberty's, and Austin Reed's, for the delectation of this brutish place had soon been rendered by my neglecting to bring alternative wear, into a condition that would have suited a George Orwell in his most masochistic longing for identification with the ragged and unkempt. Even the hot shower I took with my little bastards afterward was not so much a pleasure as the kind of relief one gets from jerking a hand away from a deceptively hot iron. And as my eardrums winced to the screams and yells of excited youths reliving their athletic prowess I made a vow (to this day unbroken) to never voluntarily take part in any organized game involving physical effort.

Incidentally, that ghastly experience on my first day of teaching: the ubiquity of those nose-running, sweat-smelling little fiends on their elected battlefield and again in the showerstalls, confirmed my belief that I had no taste whatever for classical pederasty. However, the following day there began an ongoing experience which took me in a matter of weeks from feeling merely disconcerted to a state of violent alarm. At 10 A.M., after a lengthy discordant Sung Mass which old Grimble had arbitrarily attached to some remote saint I couldn't even find in my Knott's missal, I met for the first time with the boys and girls of the Upper Fourth. Within seconds I was aware that the atmosphere here was radically different from the one I had found among those who had begun to tell me of their adventures as sons and daughters of serving officers or NCOs in the Armed Forces.

Not so much the boys. These fourteen- or fifteen-year-old youths were merely untidier, more malodorous and larger versions of their twelve-year-old counterparts of the day before. But the girls were a different matter. There sat row upon row of neat little women with brushed hair shining and frequently enlivened with colored ribbon. But the difference did not stop there. For I soon discovered that my girls of the Upper Fourth were actually interested in learning French, indeed, already had a firm grasp of the basics of the language and were eager to acquire more.

Only another teacher, I suspect knows what that can do for a flagging pedagogical spirit . . .

There is not a boy whom I can now specifically recall from the classroom context of my St. Benedict days, but will I ever forget fair-haired Pamela Noyes, breathless with knowledge in the front row? Or dark little Harriet Shapiro, her arch-rival, who sat in the back row and swiveled those bright brown eyes where I paced, flopped, or simply camped in front of the blackboard?

A question was scarcely formed upon my lips before the arms of my two star girls shot forward and upward in a manner that would have graced a Nürnberg rally.

"Please, sir. Oh, Mr. Bryant, sir. It's avoir—j'ai, tu as, il a . . ." Or from the even more coquettish Harriet: "M. Bryant, je le sais, je le sais. Vous voulez savoir si nous sommes prêts . . . Alors, je suis prête, M'sieur Bryant . . . Je suis prête." She was half-standing in her desk with excitement, with the sheer vigor of youthful enthusiasm to reveal acquired knowledge.

After those dull clunks of boys who just sat there, patient as spaniels and with comparable intelligence, these two shone as beacons of encouragement. They more than anyone else sparked memories in me of my own schooldays. It darted wickedly into my head that I had been more like Harriet and Pamela than like the rest of them in this class. I too, you see, had been an outrageous flirt with my teachers.

I was sitting on my desk, bouncing a piece of chalk from one hand to the other. "Miss Shapiro, am I to understand from your standing position that you wish to leave the room?"

Her little bum flopped back onto the seat as the class started to giggle.

"Oh no, sir. I was just answering your question. That's what you wanted, wasn't it, sir?" Her face was one wide grin. "P'raps I was speaking too quickly in French, sir?"

"Not at all, young lady. But I gather in this ancient and learned institution of St. Benedict that it is customary to respond when one's name is called. Neither your Hitler salute nor your standing up is sufficient claim on *my* attention."

With a pang of conscience I realized that even now, some

halfway through this my first lesson with the Upper Fourth, I had learned only the names of Harriet Shapiro and Pamela Noyes. Harriet, wicked sprite, must have been aware of it too.

"But you don't ask any of *them*, Mr. Bryant. You just asked all the class and *I* got the right answer." The pout to her lips was enormous and she had the gall to actually bat her eyelids at me.

I took a deep breath. "The top of page twenty-one," I announced." Look at the photo of the Parc Monceau and then study the questions underneath. I'll be back in a minute."

Slipping into the masters' washroom I lit a cigarette and crossed to the mirror. I was distressed to see that my tie knot had fallen away from my shirtcollar and, even more, that my clowning antics in the classroom had caused several strands of hair to fall into disarray. A quick plunge of my comb under the running water from the cold tap and transferral straight to my head and my coiffure was restored.

With a speed and precision evolved from years of practice I ducked my head almost to the ground to see if the solitary sit-down toilet was occupied. Satisfied that I was quite alone I undid my trousers, letting them drop to my ankles. Then I deftly pulled my penis and testicles through the slit of my underpants, dressed the full battery of my genitalia to the left, and pulled up my pants again. A quick glance downward satisfied me that my manhood now bulged prominently through the gray flannel of my slacks. I then returned my attention to my face and with a freshly licked forefinger moistened my eyebrows before pinching cheeks to excite color and stretching lips in a dazzling smile which also provided me with the reassurance of nice white teeth in the mirror.

But as I stood there in narcissistic trance, the smile suddenly vanished and my eyebrows arched abruptly. For it hit me with force that the routine I had just undergone, a routine I had accomplished hundreds of times in the past, when about to sortie for an evening's cruising, for example, had no such familiar goals now. For what I had just done was for the exclusive benefit of Harriet and Pamela—girls both, and child-girls at that!

Now apart from a handful of rather self-conscious female pursuits with copulation as goal in mind, when I had been living in

Paris, this was the first time I had felt the allure of the opposite sex of such tender years since I myself was of that age. I touched the softness of my cheek fearfully, wondering as I did so whether this was some kind of prelude to a nervous disorder. But even apprehension did not deter me. Feeling perhaps a little queasy about my nether regions, I hurried back to the source and inspiration of my distinctly unorthodox behavior.

The return to the class, though, at least on that first occasion, proved somewhat anticlimactic. There was a loud hum of conversation which died instantly as I entered the room. And with the reassurance of that my poise grew, and from then until the bell sounded I coolly quizzed each child in row after row over the pedestrian questions some textbook hack had invented to accompany the photograph they had been asked to study. But the responses were so monotonous and the accents in which they were delivered so atrocious that I soon forgot my efforts at self-titillation and spared not a thought for the strategic replacing of my privates.

It was not, in fact, until a few days later, by which time I had already had the Upper Fourth through my hands several times, that my equilibrium was again to be disturbed by thoughts about myself and thoughts about my two girls which could in no way be construed as normally part of a teacher-pupil relationship.

It was an afternoon session and both the class and I seemed dulled by the day's labors. I decided that the most congenial way for me to get through the period was to give them a dictée.

My first impulse, after slowly enunciating several sentences from an idiotic speech by General de Gaulle, was to collect their exercise books for correction. But a hasty glance at my watch suggested that if I were not very careful I would be hauling all their stuff back to the bedsitter I'd rented, to correct that night—a pedagogic practice against which I had been warned by a trick met at the Piccadilly Underground station who had been at the business of prep school teaching for some years.

"Now just exchange your book with your neighbor for marking and I'll write the correct passage on the blackboard."

But in an impossibly short space of time my arm ached from

chalking up the correct words; moreover, my writing deteriorated to such a point that as my sentences wandered up and down the blackboard it became so illegible that voices kept calling out in complaint that they had no idea what I had written and whether I was using acute or grave accents.

With relief I let the chalk fall back in the groove below the blackboard.

"The rest I will do with each of you personally. Now as I come 'round, the others can start learning the vocabulary on page twenty-three. What you don't do now will be your homework tonight."

In seconds the room was filled with the low drone of French words repetitiously muttered as the class strove to memorize them. I started at the front row, standing behind a thick-necked boy whose ruler proclaimed in large ink strokes that he was not only a denizen of Aldershot and inhabitant of England, but that he was also a European, and that he lived on the planet Earth and was part of the Universe. I also noticed that this boy's indulgence in ink extended to his shirt collar, his fingers, and the sheet on which his dictée was written. In fact, blots, smudges, and doodling made his efforts wholly unintelligible. I murmured something encouraging and passed quickly on.

There were, I think, two more boys, and then, suddenly, I was standing by the side of a squirming Pamela Noyes. Hers was the first dictée I examined which was completed and it was as neat and decipherable as those of the three boys had been messy. Giving her a slight nudge, I slipped onto the bench of her desk alongside her. Her body trembled against mine as she whispered: "I—I wasn't sure of the last word, sir."

"It's perfectly okay," I told her, "except it needs a cedilla."

But my words, though warm, were mechanical. It wasn't her work that excited and held my attention. I breathed in the warm, clean smell of her hair which fell so prettily about the white blouse and navy blue tunic of her school uniform. Slightly turning my head, I could just see the tiny pink of her earlobe, and I could feel the cool of her bare leg against the worsted flannel of mine.

She fluttered even more. "We've—we've never done a dictée

before." The heat of her small body was so palpable . . . did little girls have a higher blood heat than 98.6?

"You've done excellently, Pamela. Oh, that's *la* gloire. It's feminine, so it takes an 'e' on the end." I scanned her carefully written work once more, realizing that there were no more mistakes and suddenly feeling forlorn about it. I didn't wish to leave her side.

"When do you put in your accents, my dear? As you write each word, or at the end of a sentence," I pushed a little closer against her. She didn't budge.

"I put them in afterwards. That's what Miss Belmont told us to do last year."

"Well, I suggest you put them in with each word. That's what the average French person would do when writing a letter. That's what we do with English, isn't it? I mean, with dotting I's and crossing t's. We don't do them after, do we?"

It was no good though. I could spin it out with her no longer. A rather ferocious-looking, somehow overgrown girl across the aisle from us was staring angrily in our direction. Besides, the vocabulary exercise was turning into a mighty roar of repeated words. Reluctantly I got to my feet, silenced my youthful hordes, and quickly continued along the rows. But I was careful not to sit down next to anyone else that day.

In the weeks that followed, my caution abated somewhat and I found myself longing for those moments of certain St. Benedict days when, however rarely and however fleetingly, I was able to sit as neighbor to both Pamela and Harriet. Mind you, cunning and residual discretion dictated that I did not single out my two nymphs exclusively for this attention. I sat next to all the girls eventually—though a concept of boys as "jail bait" from a cautionary reading of the *News of the World* and its accounts of unfortunate vicars and choirboys, plus an innate distaste for that effluvium from so many of my lads, determined that I only *stood* alongside the boys and just occasionally placing an encouraging hand upon a male shoulder when the work was good.

Harriet, possibly because of her position in the back row where she was less observable, dithered less than her rival up front. She would suddenly turn and look me straight in the face as I praised or gently corrected her French. And after the second or third treat of sitting next to her, meeting her glances while those about us remained seemingly indifferent, I was emboldened to address the whole class without moving from her desk.

She never even bothered to move over voluntarily as I sat down, but allowed me to slide her along. It was then I could feel the electricity from the hardness of her thigh, along our adjacent shins and down to our shoes, which, more often than not, were touching each other.

By the second dictée I was resting my arm along the back of her desk, even timorously touching the fringe of the back of her hair. By the third time around not only had I already made an extra visit to that masters' washroom for a spruce-up (on joyfully deciding it was to be a "Harriet session") but I had the distinct feeling that via E.S.P. or whatever, she was expecting me to sit with her and had dabbed a little eau de cologne on her neck and given those sable tresses of hers an extra brushing.

I may say that by this time my earlier worries over the pull of my two young ladies upon me had been thoroughly rationalized into the framework of boring classwork where, relatively at least, they stood out as both mental and physical oases. But this sense of pleasant dalliance, which had begun to so ease the burden of my teaching days, was to come, under dear Harriet's auspices, to an abrupt end.

It was, I recall, the last class of the last day in the week in late November when, if I had not been sitting there next to Miss Shapiro, I would have already seen to it that the lights of the classroom were switched on. We were doing "unseens"—that is, beginning with Pamela's row, each student had to read aloud from *Cinq Mars*—that dreary romantic novel by Alfred de Vigny —and then translate aloud the same selection before I called out "next" and the following child took up where the other had left off.

Very occasionally, when a French accent achieved grotesque proportions, or translation verged on the idiotic or obscene, I would make my presence felt by leaping to my feet and shouting for the culprit to shut up. But already the weaker brethren had been passed and I realized with quiet satisfaction that the only interruption of my sitting there enjoying Harriet in the gloaming was the occasional need for me to punctuate the air with the necessary "next!"

By this time, although it was totally unspoken, Harriet and I had worked out something of a choreography to accompany our propinquity. There was the usual fact of my arm going out behind her desk (along the back wall of the classroom in fact) and then would follow the series of pressures between our knees and feet followed by her giving the arm of my jacket a sharp tug from the concealed area under the lid of her desk. This afternoon, however, possibly by virtue of being darker than usual and thus limiting the risk of our being observed, such actions took on even firmer definition than in times past. Indeed, the pushings and brushings distinctly quickened tempo, and after some ten minutes I was suddenly and devastatingly aware that I had been sexually aroused by Miss Shapiro.

For a moment I sat there immobile in the horror of the thought that she would accidently discover my tumescence and shriek the terror of her virginal fear to the class at large. Why then did I not rise instantly and there in the aisle attempt to conceal my stiffness before striding down to the front of the class? That way may have lain embarrassment but surely safety! Yet even before the mind focused enough to ponder, fourteen-year-old fingers had already firmly encircled the length of my swollen object, and I was temporarily lost in the swoon of lust.

All this, though, proved to be but the delirious beginning, for with the speed of a seasoned angler flipping his fish ashore Harriet had opened three fly buttons (these were pre-zip days in Britain) and had landed my pulsating member across the palm of her upturned hand. I wanted to lay my head back against the wall and close my eyes, but at that moment with her free hand, she suddenly reached over, nudged me sharply and sotto voce but fiercely whispered: "Next!"

Only in the vaguest sense was I aware that the room was all but silent, save for sudden accesion of heavy breathing from me. But my response to her command was well-nigh instant.

"Next!" I croaked. "Next!"

As a boy's husky alto broke the spell once more, I felt as limp above my waist as I felt tense in those regions now subject to the nimble discovery of Harriet's four fingers and thumb . . .

Protected by the drone of the boy's French, I strove for poise. "Put it away!" I muttered. "Do you hear me, Harriet? Put it *away!*" Suiting action to words I tried to ease back on the seat to aid that particular suggestion. I do not boast when I aver that it was too big, too stiff for any such automatic remedy on my part. Nor was she of any assistance when her fingertips, light as butterfly wings, described the length of the glans penis and finally fluttered on the exposed end—that arena of so much erotic male joy.

To be free of the thrall of pleasure, desperate to produce its size to more gainful proportions for manipulation back into the safe harbor of my pants, I made myself think of strident newspaper headlines: MOTHERS OF ALDERSOT LOCK UP YOUR DAUGHTERS! . . . FRENCH IS NOT WHAT IT SEEMS AT ST. BENEDICT'S . . . EX-HOMO REVEALS TASTE FOR NYMPHETS . . . COLONEL DEMANDS RETURN OF THE STOCKS IN ALDERSHOT HIGH STREET AS VENGEANCE FOR DAUGHTER'S SEDUCER . . .

But it was quite obvious that my fears were not shared by my young companion. "Relax, Mr. Bryant. Gosh, it's a whopper, isn't it! Bigger than Jim's over there. He has his out all the time, but even with us helping him it never gets like this."

The flush of passion across my forehead turned to cold sweat. Was this some kind of conspiracy? Did the whole back row know that their teacher sprawled like some "flash Harry" with his expanded penis wedged between the base of the desktop and the increasing activity of a schoolgirl's hand?

Then finally, from God knows where, the certainty came to me that it was now or never. Even seconds more of that exposure and her skillful caressing and my last veils of caution would be in threads as I tossed and tumbled toward an inevitably messy climax. Although she pushed back and tried to pin my encircling right arm to the back of the seat, I managed to roughly pull it free. With a fierce stab of pain I grabbed my exposed part (just as she was questing my balls, presumably to give them an airing too) and almost bent it in half as I thrust it back behind the safety of my fly.

What began as an involuntary scream from me turned into another "Next!" as from somewhere in the darkened room the translation from *Cinq Mars* came to a halt. I staggered to my feet, buttoning as I did so. I *thought* I heard a ripple of titters along the back row as Harriet quite distinctly told me to sit down again. But that way lay madness—as well as such minor factors as my being kicked out of St. Benedict's and hauled off to prison. With knees almost collapsing, I hurled myself down the aisle to the front of the class, switched on the lights, and faced them all.

"Questions on page thirty-three of *La Belle France*. You can start writing now and finish it off at home tonight."

With an awful sensation that thirty youthful faces were riveting their attention on the front of my pants and the stain I dreaded might be growing there, I rushed from the classroom, fleeing once more to that sanctum, the masters' lavatory at the top of the stairs. There I undid my trousers and rearranged my private parts and the garments which housed them in such a way it would have taken a small forest of hands to bring my jewels once more to light.

As I stood before that now familiar mirror, recombing my hair, I made a promise to the ghost of Polonius that, forsaking the Pamelas and Harriets of this world forever more, I would to mine own self be true.

Head high, jaw jutting in proud resolution, I returned to the Upper Fourth and smiled upon Harriet and Pamela—but only as I smiled upon them all. I never did dally with either of my feminine favorites again; indeed, can honestly say I have never sat at a school desk with a pubescent girl from that day to this.

Davey, you who surface from the murk of my misunderstanding and fear in order to make things clear, you suffer more than I do. I think you learn more, too. (We gods, we almighty creators, lack the laughter and tears of our subjects and cannot know the riches of moral dilemma.) But when you discovered that a long and loving relationship carries its own price tag, you may well tremble for yourself and your own loves. But this again is your lesson, not mine. I will see and smell and taste your fear of the frost of death, but refuse personal implication. David Watmough cannot as yet accept price tags for his joy . . .

Chapter Eight

I awake on a hard bed. My feet are freezing. The room is damned cold. But through a dirty windowpane I see a blue sky awash in sunlight. I listen carefully. No surfy sibilance from the tide at Kitsilano beach. I sniff quickly. I cannot smell the sea. Tenderly I lift my head, apprehensive of the hangover thumps I expect to be pounding there. Now I can see a motley of red-brick chimney stacks through the lower half of the window: chimneys, the broken-down back of a deserted house, and clumps of ragwort and other wild weeds clinging precariously to outcrops of crumbled masonry. There are no high-rise apartments propping up a lead-gray sky. I am not, definitely not, at home in Vancouver.

Then comes the clash of bells, Sabbathy loud and soaked in Englishry—certainly not St. Mark's, Kitsilano in Vancouver, with its half-hearted tape tucked high in a carillon nervously nudging the Sunday stillness for a very short time and that only when the morning is reasonably established. But this wild noise, triumphant, incessant, is an early affair. I imagine men hanging on ropes in the ecstasy of it, and the peals seem to brim the confidence of centuries on their breath.

I am in London and if they are not Bow bells they might just as well be. City bells they surely are, for this cramped little room with its low ceiling, its peeling paint and worn grime, can only be part of the huddle of London Town.

Then it's all cleared up: persons usurp places—even that dislocated sense of place which is all tied up with too fast jets, anonymous airports, and pushing five new pence into a telephone box instead of a dime.

"Davey? Have those bloody bells woken you up?"

In comes Charlie. Charlie Goldman, white quiff of hair that earlier used to be black, still lopping off one side of his forehead and stopping just before the arch of a seemingly perpetually raised eyebrow.

"I've brought you a cuppa. The boozer doesn't open till twelve and we drank all the beer in the place last night."

I closed my eyes. Blood bells bang there in my head, in unholy communion with those outside the window.

"Oh God! It—it wasn't intended that way." I screw up my eyes in unpleasant recollection. Charlie, benign behind spectacles, short rotund body including protruding beer belly, all wrapped in a shiny, rust-red dressing gown (very old-fashioned) puts the tea somewhere near my pillow. "Well, it never is, dear, is it? I mean, no one says, 'I intend to have a hangover in the morning.'"

"That's not what I meant," I expostulate wanly. "I meant to do with meeting you after all this time. The extraordinary coincidence . . . and then everything happening so *quickly*." I give out, the effort of shaping things just too much. But Charlie was on to it. I remembered how during those few hectic months after teaching at St. Benedict's, when he and I had been working together for the same publisher in London, he would gently josh my serious torrents and threaten to write to Ken in San Francisco and tell him what a solemn little fart he would soon have on his hands.

"I don't call all that time you've been prowling 'round the United States and Canada a sign of undue haste. Hardly a matter of *quickly* anything!"

With difficulty I find the tea, rattle the cup and saucer, and drink gratefully.

"What I mean is . . ." I began.

Charlie let the top part of his robe fall to his girdled waist, put on a rumpled blue shirt he'd picked up from the floor, and then sat down on the end of the bed. He looked at me fondly. "What do you mean, sweetheart?"

"That I hate it when things are rushed. Like meeting you after all this time. I wanted to, well, *savor* it. Like slowly."

"All right, then. Let's do that. Let's go back to that ghastly hotel in New York when I held your hot little forehead over the loo and you vomited everything up. What's happened to you since? I presume you left the hotel and have kept a few meals down?" He took out a cigarette, offered me one which I declined, and stuck his in the side of his mouth. I recalled from eight years before, or whatever it was, that the cigarette would stay there until it was just a mottled stub almost burning his lip.

"Well, I'm a Canadian citizen," I said eventually.

"That's nice."

"And I suppose I know a bit more about me."

"That's even nicer."

"I'm still living with Ken—"

"Now that's quite splendid. When I met him in New York I told myself that if I couldn't have you I'd rather him have you than anyone else. As a matter of fact, he's far too good for you."

"And we have two dogs and a cat."

"Next you'll be telling me about the weather."

"I *love* my dogs and cat," I said defensively.

"Of course you do. Nature boy always doted on his furry friends. Do you think I'll ever forget you and your badger Giulietta?"

"Remember the whores along the Bayswater Road wanting to buy her off me, as a come-on for trade?"

"We remembered that last night, dear. Just before they slung us out of The Coach and Horses."

"Did we? What else did we remember, Charlie? I should hate to repeat myself."

"We remembered there were lots of bottles of beer here—which is why you missed the last tube and never got to your aunt's where you were supposed to be staying."

I covered my face with the crumpled sheet. "Oh Christ! Oh Jesus Christ! You mean she doesn't know? She's still waiting?"

"You telephoned. Explained the plane was late and all that."

In the intervening silence I enjoyed the reprieve the phone call would provide from domestic strife. It was then I realized that the bells had stopped. "Thank God," I said quietly. "Thank God I called her."

Charlie beamed.

"Why are you grinning? On my aunt's behalf?"

"Because you're here, idiot. I'm enjoying seeing you again."

That did my morale good. I even think my headache receded somewhat. In any event, I felt like getting up. The pervasive cold of that unheated English room probed deeper than any familiar alcoholic memento of success. As I began to dress, Charlie flitted hither and thither, finding a towel and face cloth here, a luxury bar of soap unwrapped from Christmas gift paper there.

I realized as I pulled on pants, stood shivering in the tiny, makeshift kitchen where the only water for my face was cold from a verdigrised tap—only one faucet—that *Carolus domesticus* was really an unknown phenomenon for me. The few months he had been my immediate boss in that murky publisher's office in Bloomsbury when I had been both recovering from the debilitating rigors of St. Benedict's School and saving more money more quickly for my transatlantic progress, our friendship, our laughing companionship (to put a finer shade to it) had swiveled between ecclesiastical chitchat and gay gossip about the London literary establishment in either that stuffy, gasfire-popping room or in a handful of surrounding pubs.

But the image of Charlie in every dredging of the past as I put my clothes on was of him in a stiff white collar over a striped shirt, a navy blue suit, a red carnation in a buttonhole, and, when outdoors, of a coat with a velvet collar and a bowler hat tilted raffishly on the angle of his left-falling lock of hair.

Now in his weekend clothes, crumpled and lived-in, though his memory-stirring banter filled the air, there was an unfamiliar ingredient which had nothing to do with the passage of time. Once, when stepping barefoot over the tacky floorboards into the bedroom to find my socks, I noticed a battered wardrobe, the door slightly ajar. I peeked in. I thought I recognized a suit or two hanging there, and a few fifties-thin neckties. But what certainly did loom as familiar was that bowler hat on the upper shelf. I could hear him pissing in the john, so took the hat down and looked at it. It was gray with dust and I realized it had not been brushed or worn for a long time.

After replacing it, I left the bedroom, closing the door softly behind me. While waiting for him to finish in the tiny closet of a john and busy himself in the kitchen-cum-bathroom, I stood there in the strangely shaped triangular living room with its floor-to-ceiling shelves of books, and stared out at the sun-washed square in the littered aftermath of its Saturday night debauch.

'Hello, London,' I thought to myself. 'Well, I'm back . . . But like a swallow, not a sparrow. I'm a visitor now, you know. And that means I like you more than I did. Now that I don't have to wrest a living from your stones, now that I can let you be more than just a painful memory of unhappy studenthood, of failing that degree and letting down poor old Dr. Monk, who put such faith in me . . .'

"What on earth are you up to, *Il Papa* addressing the multitudes of Clerkenwell? Why don't you open that window more if you want to give 'em a Papal blessing?"

"Because it's too fucking cold in here as it is," I growled, pulling up my metaphorical pants as best I could. "Anyway, why the Papal bit? You become a Roman Catholic?"

"You might as well ask if I've taken out Italian citizenship! My dear boy, have you really forgotten what a dutiful son of the Church of England I am?"

He stood there stiffly, almost at attention, the cigarette dangling in character, his eyes blinking behind the glasses in their accustomed way. I smiled suddenly. Charlie hadn't changed one little bit. That accent, the way he stood . . . he was so *incredibly* English.

"No, Charlie, you're right. That was a silly question. I can't imagine you as other than a son of Canterbury—a very High Church son at that!" But Charlie, as I now had occasion to recall, had always enjoyed the role of my gentle admonisher.

"To think you could forget! Why, we've attended St. Bartholomew's, Brighton together. We've both listened to dear Father Hutchinson—now, alas, no longer with us."

"Oh, is he dead?" I asked. But it was really mechanical, as I was busy letting all the jigsaw pieces fall into place. The T. S. Eliot plays we had crossed half of London to see in the most fourth-rate amateur production . . . the endless conversations about Charles Williams, Evelyn Underhill, and "mystical" Maisie Spens. The best Anglo-Catholic churches to be found across the realm, the idiosyncrasies of Father X, the sexual goings-on at St. Blank's, the peculiar pieties of Bishop Blinks. Inexhaustible, largely profitless, as arcane to an outsider as Indonesian freemasonry . . . yet there was our tremendously shared enjoyment, hour after hour, day after day in that scruffy little publisher's office when we were supposed to be coming up with the titles of trashy paperback possibilities for the back-street trade.

"You'll be telling me next, Davey Bryant, you don't remember taking me to St. Mary the Virgin in New York—and sitting me next to that filthy old woman who stank to high heaven."

As he spoke, I did remember it—and something else at the same time. That must've been about the last time I had darkened the door of *any* church—Roman Catholic, Anglican, or bloody Baptist. But even as the thought took form I knew a growing reluctance to pass the information on to Charlie Goodman.

"As a matter of fact, old boy, talking of St. Mary's—I was going to give you a choice. We can bugger off all the way to St. Mary's, Bourne Street, if you like. In which case we'd have to leave right away. Or we can nip round the corner to Holy Redeemer, Clerkenwell. Or we can do a typical Anglican compromise and embrace Holy Mass at St. Alban's, Holborn."

"I think I'd prefer St. Alban's," I said slowly, remembering sitting adoringly beneath the pulpit, aged about twenty, when Father Monk had been the guest preacher.

"Good! Personally I love St. Alban's—always have. It's Whitsunday, of course, and they'll pull out every stop. Tremendous old carry-on in the sanctuary and enough incense to sink the *Queen Mary!* Well, better change me clothes. Holy Church's birthday, after all."

"Something white?" I suggested, gently malicious, to his retreating figure. And wondered as I said so, why he had bothered to put on his other clothes in the first place.

I personally couldn't have cared less what I was wearing. Then, of course, I wasn't Charlie. I doubted whether Charlie had been other than dapper since he quit his perambulator. In any case, I had other worries than my clothes and not the least of them was my supine agreement to attend St. Alban's, Holborn with the devout Charlie.

As I gloomily scanned his bookshelves while waiting, I noticed the considerable number of theological tomes there, and recalled that he had in fact worked for a religious publishing house before joining Ace Books, where I had subsequently met him. One or two of the books I recognized from my King's College days . . . I passed quickly on to where his fiction was housed, and at once felt better. Even so, I was not at all sorry when we descended the rickety stairs and emerged into sunlight.

Upstairs the early morning Sabbath tranquillity had been appealing: out in it, knowing that it would soon be exchanged for the gloom of an Anglo-Catholic church, outdoor London took on the qualities of paradise. Sooty pigeons cooing and starlings and sparrows prattling became the voice of the turtledove and the cheerful chatter of feathered cockneys. I grew immediately alive to the unshouted charms of Victorian cottages, screened from the hurly-burly of London life by Sunday-deserted giant warehouses and gaunt distilleries which fed upon the special qualities of the subterranean River Fleet. I enjoyed the spasmodic yellow-brick outbursts of Georgian terraces, and the unbidden gardens of London wildflowers which still in places covered the wounds of wartime.

"I didn't know all this still existed," I murmured. "It's so much nicer than the West End."

"Never go there if I can help it," said Charlie, who was born, I suddenly remembered, in St. Bartholomew's Hospital, just a few blocks from where we were walking. "It's just a gigantic emporium for Americans and Europeans. Davey, would you mind crossing the road here? That's my newsagent's on the corner and I haven't paid his bill since Christmas."

I hadn't thought much about Charlie's financial state. But now that I fleetingly did it occurred to me that his tiny flat and spartan appurtenances hardly added up to a flush existence. Not that I was rich, exactly, but somehow I seemed to dodge the sense of having to forever cut corners. For instance, here I was wandering through London on a sunny Sunday morning with a buttoned-down roll of traveler's checks in my pocket and the certain knowledge that there was more where that came from, back in Vancouver. I took a quick glance at my companion. I had a sense that if all his assets were realized he could still hardly have made Scotland . . .

On the other hand we *were* on our way to Charlie's bank in the heavenly places—and I didn't have one of those any more . . . I thought of despair on a rainy night, trudging the ugliness of Vancouver's Granville Street for God-knows-what; of wild flights on last-minute ferries to Galiano Island in the vain hope of catching content. I quickened my pace along those calm back streets in an instinctive attempt to escape the hobgoblins of the past. I was glad when he interrupted my bleak reverie.

"The one thing about earlier Masses is they're over in time."

"Time for what?"

"The boozer, sweetheart. It's twelve on Sunday. Don't you remember? My God, you *have* become a Yank! There's only two hours before they close again. Then there's that awful wait till the evening—seven o'clock."

As a matter of fact, I had forgotten that item of English life. But the very notion of sitting through that impending Mass made my throat feel ready for a gin and tonic.

"Let's hope they keep up a steady clip, then," I said. "I couldn't bear to waste any of those niggardly drinking hours."

Then suddenly we are there. Charlie's world, not mine. But one I have led him into thinking I still embrace. The little children in the street . . . a couple of black-clad "fathers" flitting in and out of the open church doors, a handsome youth in his late teens flirting with two church-spruced girls with newish-looking handbags . . . an organ warming up as we enter and several tall gray-haired men lurking at the back, presumably waiting the machinery of the service to creak up before they can function . . .

Charlie walks in confident, a quick passing of a hand over a holy water stoup, his wet fingers then brushing mine. A bob to the Reserved Sacrament and then we are halfway down the central aisle, taking the first two seats in.

As I fold my raincoat and place it on the adjacent chair (after taking it off and wishing now that I hadn't, as the church was

frigid to my Canadian-acclimated blood) I watch Charlie surreptitiously. He flops forward on the hassock, brushes his forehead and chest with a casual sign of the cross, and closes his
eyes tightly. I think, 'Well, I haven't forgotten any of the rig-
marole. Or if I have, I'll just follow him a fraction of a second
later.' That was the way, I remembered Ken telling me, he had
picked up the mysterious up-and-downing of Anglo-Catholicism
when we had started to attend the Anglican church in Paris together.

Not much time for idle thoughts, though. The six great candles
on the high altar are lit, the organ swells, the incense swirls, and
I am spiritually undone. On this holy feast of Pentecost, as I
stand and sing, prostrate and pray, the saintly bric-a-brac flows
over me in tumultuous waves. Incense stuffing memories through
the nostrils . . . a myriad lights dancing childhood visions before
my eyes . . . the sonorous liturgical words and rousing Anglo-
Catholic hymns, reshaping a reality on my lips that had held me
firm in its spell for the first twenty-odd years of my life . . . I am
reconverted with every chink of the thurible chain, proclaim my
childhood in Mother Church at every closing of my eyes. A soul
I'd forgotten I possessed lifts on choirboy voices, and every
white-robed acolyte holds me tight in the vicarious spell of his
endearingly familiar activity.

I am lost, stunned with vision, numb to the world . . . Someone is nudging me. With a gut sigh I turn my head. It's Charlie,
fussing with his outdoor clothes while I am still kneeling, draped
over the chair in front of me. Up in the sanctuary a golden-
haired server extinguishes the last of the great six candles.
Slowly it dawns on me that my knees ache like hell. They are not
used to hard floors through thin kneelers.

"Come on, sweetheart," Charlie stage whispers. "They overran.
The boozers are already open."

Outside, I feel worse than coming out of a gripping movie at a
matinee performance into the banality of a rain-washed afternoon.

Charlie says: "Wasn't that magnificent? Didn't I tell you?"

Guilt oozes from my pores. I want, oh how I want, to be that
dutiful little boy again who turns up on a Saturday evening at
St. Endellion Church and sweats outside the confessional box at

the prospect of telling Father Trewin how many times he has masturbated since the previous month. High Mass isn't grand opera, I keep telling myself as we walk. There are strings attached: moral strings, ethical strings. And I have severed them all—years ago.

"I shouldn't have gone, Charlie," I say eventually. "It was a mistake."

Charlie darts me that odd look of his, like an old cockatoo, huddled, head-cocked, to one side of its perch. "Should? Shouldn't? What do they mean? I mean, what else *is* there? It's all there is, isn't it?"

I was silent. What to say?

Charlie seemed content with my silence. In fact, he seemed somehow to put me aside as we journeyed through the narrow maze of alleys and side streets to the pub of his election. We stopped at a delicatessen—Greek—and Charlie bought feta, a long loaf, and some resinous wine. There was much banter with the bulky Cypriot owner and his shy daughter with pulled-back, black-braided hair. Then, at the next corner, an old woman hailed him from her doorstep. "'Ello, Charlie-boy. I knows where *you're* 'eadin', mate. Save a seat for me?"

"If you're good, duckie, I'll buy you a stout. All right, Mabel?"

"Come into the spondulics, eh?"

"Never out of it, my dear. It just looks that way sometimes."

Such interchanges, brief, familiar, grew in number at every little outcrop of domestic life amid the sea of commercial and industrial premises. Charlie was cock of the boardwalk, I reflected as he strutted through his bailiwick.

"Mornin', mate. How's things, then?"

"Good morning to you! My friend and I have just been to a *marvelous* Mass at St. Alban's, Fred. You should've been there."

"Me? I'm a fuckin' pagan. Leave it to you buggers to pray for me."

"Hello, Maggie. Have a good night, dear? At least it wasn't raining."

"Might jest as well have been, Charlie. Only four bleeders, and the last sod never paid up, at that."

"Never mind, sweetheart. The tourists are coming. Can't you hear the rustle of those green dollar bills?"

"That's the West End. I leave that to them foreign bitches and all the Irish poufs in Hyde Park. Wouldn't be seen dead alongside any of 'em. Give me our own boys, that's what I say."

I didn't hear Charlie's reply as I was a few steps behind, and he turned sharply down a further alley as I caught up.

"You're like a rat," I told him.

He did his horsy duchess thing. "A *rat*, dear?"

"You've got your own little runs and never seem to leave them. You know what you've done? You've turned the threshold of St. Paul's into a rat warren. A Charlie warren, that is."

He seemed rather pleased by that. He beamed. "Thank you! I rarely get compliments these days. But it's nice to be told you belong. One doesn't always feel so."

. . . Now we're at the pub. It isn't the same as the one we were in last night, and I say so. Charlie uses his churchy whisper, which can be heard for miles. "Certainly not! On the Sabbath I always change. *All* the publicans have to live, you know."

Even so, he seems as well known here as everywhere else en route. He introduces me around as "my Canadian friend who used to work with me," tells everyone we've been to Mass (God! *Why* does that embarrass me so much?), and shares banter with some fifteen fellow patrons. Mainly, I see, they are workingmen. Charlie, I notice, scorns the saloon, and prefers the proletarian vigor of the public bar.

He orders a light ale and I have a bloody mary after explaining to the publican that I want Worcestershire sauce in it too. This is not the West End and my request has to be fully spelled out. Afterward, Charlie leans over to me and upbraids me: "You might try using a few pleases and thank-yous, sweetheart. You sound so rude."

I shrug. Something else I had forgotten. In England, before the abolition of capital punishment, I'm sure the hangman and his victim exchanged a score of polite pleases and thank-yous . . .

By the fifth or sixth drink Charlie is telling me that A Very Exalted Personage (try as I might I can't get him to divulge the name) is addicted to the bottle. A few drinks more and he seems to be getting maudlin and I decide I've had enough and suggest we go. I think he's about to remonstrate when the landlord calls time. Charlie clutches his two bottles of Greek wine (I thought he'd only bought one—or maybe he'd bought the other here in the pub when I was away taking a piss) and lurches toward the door. I am right behind him.

"You're drunk, my friend," I tell his back. Two backs maybe. I'm having a little difficulty myself!

There are fewer people about now than on our way from the church to the pub. Or is it simply that we aren't noticing everyone? In any case, Charlie is this time addressing more of his remarks to me. I have to make an effort to focus. In The Unicorn he had gotten back on the subject of St. Alban's and by now that's become something like an undigested dinner: makes me feel somewhat bilious.

One thing that I do notice, though, is the change in the weather. We are no more than a block away from The Unicorn when I realize that the erstwhile sunny day has degenerated into an altogether more sullen affair. Dark clouds pile fretfully above our heads and a sharp wind has materialized which stirs the new leaves of plane trees, rustles paper in gutters, and brings grit stinging to the eyes.

I am about to comment on all this to Charlie, look at him as I open my mouth to speak, but hear him instead:

"You know something, sweetheart? I *hate* Sunday afternoons."

I don't like the look on his face. It isn't just that the booze has loosened his facial muscles, making him look older. But somehow the glint to his eyes that has been there, drunk or sober, since we met, is gone. An old exasperation sweeps over me. Drunks . . . Christ knows, I drink! But when that awful scrim descends on someone with whom one's trying to communicate, I find affection flying out the window and a muting frustration taking over.

But this is Charlie. I haven't seen him in ages and God knows when I'll see him again after I've gone home to Vancouver.

"They've even made movies about English Sundays, haven't they, Charlie? It's the national misery hour—or hours."

"Mine's personal, old boy."

Charlie doesn't call me "old boy" . . . I guess I look quizzically at him.

"This is something you'd call personal."

"I see." (Though of course I didn't.)

Charlie-boy sighed, and that too was out of character as far as I was concerned. "No, I don't like Sunday afternoons, Davey. Especially cloudy ones."

So he'd noticed the weather. I decided he couldn't be *that* high, then.

"Do—do-do you mind if we don't go straight back to the flat?"

I had noticed earlier that Charlie had just the slightest tendency to stutter after a few beers, but usually when he was trying to argue something.

"Not a bit. In fact, a walk will probably do us both some good."

He picked his next words very carefully, drunk-carefully. "It's not that I want exercise. Simply that I don't want to go home."

I shrugged. "Be my guest."

"There's—there's a little place . . . it's not very far. We could sit there."

I thought of the chill and shivered in anticipation.

"We can have a jar. I mean we can have a go at these." He nudged his paper bag containing the two bottles of wine. It sounded a trifle sordid, but I didn't like that resin-flavored Greek wine anyway—we might just as well guzzle it outside as indoors.

The wind was ruffling that white, overhanging lock of his and he kept tossing it back, girl-like. Except effeminate was the last word you'd use to describe Charlie Goldman.

He seemed to pick up a little. "This way then." He led me down a series of alleys so narrow they could be described as footpaths, and past rows of garbage cans. For some reason or other, I thought of *Waiting for Godot*—the ominous light? A couple of pseudo winos?

I must say that it was with something of a shock that after traversing a further narrow passage and climbing some worn stone steps I found myself with Charlie in a small, not very well-tended churchyard.

"This is it. It's very quiet here. No one will disturb us."

"Where the hell is it? Who does it belong to?"

"We are in the graveyard, sweetheart, of Clerkenwell parish church."

He apparently thought that sufficient explanation because he immediately moved ahead, picked his way carefully through the longish grass, found two tombstones close to the far wall, and sat down.

"Come on, come and sit with me here."

I must have faltered, hesitated.

"It's all right, my dear. The churchyard's full up and the services are over for Sunday anyway. I've been coming here since . . . since . . ." He looked up, dazzling false smile revealing dazzling false teeth. "I've never met a soul here. Cross my heart and hope to die."

I sit, lean back against Josiah Perkins, 1779–1843, and prepare to allow my mouth to get dry with resinous Mediterranean wine. My Sunday-suited friend, however, sitting on the mossed edge of another Perkins, seems unaware of any incongruity.

He opens the two bottles with the aid of a penknife corkscrew, revealed with a flourish from a waistcoat pocket, and hands me a bottle. They are the same label, I notice. Perhaps he *did* get both bottles at the Greek delicatessen. I realize he must have left the feta and loaf in the pub, but say nothing . . . We drink a while in silence. Silence? There was a low rumble from invisible afternoon traffic, maybe a plane. No birds.

"I was born near here, you know."

"I know. Bart's Hospital. You told me ages ago."

"Did I? I actually told you that, did I? Funny."

"But you went to Cambridge to live as a child."

"Not for very long. Actually, you could say I grew up in this parish."

"You certainly weren't living here when I knew you. When we were at Ace together."

"No. We moved here shortly after you buggered off to Canada, America, wherever it was."

"We?"

"My mate and I."

"Oh?" I hope that sounded casual, but it was far from what I was feeling. A *mate*, as he called it? Charlie? I was wholly caught by surprise. Shocked is the right word, I suppose. Charlie with a male companion? I just—well, couldn't see it.

"Not in that funny little flat where I am now. Another place."

"I—I didn't know, Charlie, that there was somebody. You never mentioned it."

"I know. Not many people did. He wanted it that way. Right after the war we moved about a lot. Couldn't seem to find the right place. My mate was very fussy, you know. He didn't want to live in his practice."

Charlie swigs at his wine bottle. His is half-empty, mine just started.

"Practice?"

"He was a doctor."

That use of the past tense by Charlie is bugging me. "*Was?*" And attempting a jocularity to quell all the unease churning in me: "Has he been struck off the Medical Register then?"

Charlie takes another gulp. I attempt to match him. I sense I need some extra strength anyway. He looks at the tufty clumps of grass about his feet and his voice goes much softer. I have to strain now to hear.

"It hasn't been easy. Not easy at all." His head turns toward me. I can't help it but I turn away. I can't stand the feigned brightness.

"Thirty years is a long time, don't you know. Thirty years with the same bloke? You know what I mean, Davey? You sort of get used to one another?"

"I—I suppose you would."

I don't think he even heard me. Then his kind of questions, these kind, they don't need answers.

"I—I moved after it happened. I even got someone to do the moving. I didn't want to see it all again, you see, not after my mate was gone."

O Charlie-boy, what on earth are you dredging up? Your face looks terrible, distorted . . .

Charlie stands up. He is agitated. That lock of hair over his face again. But this time he doesn't bother to toss it back. "I had to do it all on my own, you see, Davey. There was no one there." He leans toward me and I smell the wine on his breath, notice little bubbles of spittle at the sides of his mouth. Christ! is he in a state!

"In a hotel room. Málaga . . . Oh, sweetheart, I don't speak a

147

word of Spanish. And there he was, lying there. I was in the bathroom shaving when I heard the crash. I came out and . . . and . . . It wasn't nice. It wasn't nice at all.

He rocks, I notice, as he recollects. I see his bottle is empty. Mutely I hold out my hand, take it from him, and give him my half-finished one. He takes a deep draught, obviously needing it. He kneels, now, in front of me, and I forget to be embarrassed by what I see in his eyes.

"When you've known someone like that—I mean their body, their face, everything, for ever so long, and suddenly it's all *gone* —that's bloody terrifying, Davey. I mean it *scares* you. I ran out of the room but I couldn't find anyone. Imagine that. No waiters, no maid, nothing. No one. And usually they're scampering 'round you like a lot of mice. So I went back in. He hadn't moved. That started to sink in then. He couldn't move. Was never to move of his own will again. 'You're dead, old mate,' that's what I said to his body and that empty room. 'You're dead and you can't move.'"

. . . The wine, the earlier booze, the memories—what are those tears in his eyes made of? Who cares? He is somewhere I have never been, never want to go. Charlie, you are *frightening* me . . .

"Just speaking, talking to him, sort of helped. I realized I had to do something. I mean, he was lying there with only his pajama top. That's how he always slept. I didn't want anyone to see him like that. My mate was funny. Prudish, you might say. I used to twig him about it. But he never altered. Hated dirty jokes, for instance. And I never heard him use the word 'gay' in his life."

Charlie blinks more frantically than ever behind the glasses.

"So I went to work. I mean I had to, there was no one else, see? I got him on the bed, found my pajama trousers and got those on him. Pulled up the sheet. Of course, people came in the end. But I had to do everything. You've no idea, sweetheart, what a *business* death is. I found the will when I got back. He was always tidy. Believed in things properly tied up, my mate did. I went to the bank and there it all was, just as he used to say. Then I arranged the funeral. There was a sister. I wrote to her. But she was even older than he was. Too ill to come. So I was alone at the funeral. I mean, apart from the people that did things. There were a couple of our friends . . . I suppose I should've asked them, but I didn't want to. I didn't want anyone to know, really. He was such a very *private* person, my old mate was."

I swallowed emotion. "I'm sorry," was all I said.

"And since, Davey, there's been nothing. Just a great big hole. Actually, I'm a great big fake. I don't feel anything any more. That going to St. Alban's with you this morning? All a bunch of poppycock for me, you know. All that stuff is outside me. I did it for you, bless you, my old darling. I don't have a belief in a single bone. It all went with him."

"Not nothing," I say. "You have grief, Charlie. I don't know what that is, but surely it isn't nothing."

Charlie's face comes within inches of mine. Only, it's no longer a face but an assembly of grotesque features. "I'll tell you what I have, sweetheart. I've got hatred. Hatred for that old bastard cutting me off from everything and everyone for all those years —and then leaving me like that."

His eyes are red beads, like a white rat's. I move back. Or try to, rather: the headstone of the late Mr. Perkins won't let me go far.

"You're wrong, Charlie. You're wrong," I whisper.

"Hate and emptiness. The wicked old sod. The bit of money he left—that's enough for the booze and the rent. God knows how long that'll last. I hope long enough, that's all."

He makes a feeble grab at me as I scramble to my feet. "Come here, sweetheart. Give us a kiss, my old darling. Don't you just stick with your mate till he cheats on you like mine did."

But I can't take any more. I cannot make a new person out of what had seemed so safe and familiar. I start to run.

Under darkening skies and through the wind-rippling grass of the churchyard, his voice comes to me again and again: "Come back, Davey, come back. Don't let your mate cheat on you like that old bastard did in Málaga."

I ran faster, and still knew the sense of fleeing when I was back home safe in Vancouver.

You bury ever deeper in the sheltered womb of Vancouver, Davey, the place where nerve ends end, where unfortunately, it is so easy for reality to be put on ice. On ice, that is, for David Watmough. Perhaps not for my hero. For Davey Bryant has opened himself to the city beyond all mountains, has decreed the sanctuary of the Lower Mainland of British Columbia, whereas his nervous creator tiptoes regularly back to Europe, afraid that nowhere is solace but that everywhere must be tried. Oh, infinitely more vulnerable Davey, you have established with jutting chin your second nest. And you have found a courage to look down the spectrum of aging flesh and found that the path to the garden is also blocked by skin which has sagged. Indeed, that a gate to the garden is closed . . . I will not face that yet . . .

Chapter Nine

I would have called her anyway. Even though I hadn't seen Nora for years. But there was something about my dingy little room at The Empress, something about the dispiriting sequence of windows filled with tourist junk along Government Street that not only turned me right off Victoria but made the thought of an old friend a truly desirable thing.

Empress Hotel! Mythical but faded hostelry that looked like a château outside and a collection of maids' quarters from within! Perhaps I'm being a little unfair. At any rate, I should perhaps point out that the day I met Nora Duthie after years of just Christmas card contact, was itself back in the 1960s. The Empress has been considerably jazzed up since then. I doubt whether the pokey little room they gave me exists any more—except, maybe, as a closet.

The loud voice when she answered the phone was familiar enough. "Where are you staying then, Davey? Do you still say Davey, or is it 'David' now?"

"Davey's good enough."

"Never said it wasn't. What hotel?"

"The Empress."

"That's a stoopid place to stay! You should've brought a tent. I could've told you a marvelous campground—"

"I shan't see thirty again, Nora. My sleeping-bag days are over."

"I'm double your age, boy! In fact, I'm a tired and worn-out sixty-one—but you'd still not get me into one of those bloody tourist traps. Anyway, when you coming to see an old lady?"

"That's why I called. I assume this address in the phone book's right? And I guess a cab driver can find it without any difficulty?"

"Taxi? Are you kidding? On a day like this and you at The Empress? It'll take you less than an hour and the walk's superb. Besides, buster, if you never get out camping the fresh air will do you the world of good. Now here's the way. It's really very simple."

She showered street names on me, but all I wrote down was the actual address.

"It's eleven o'clock now, so you can have a nice stroll around Oak Bay. Now just get in back of the Parliament Buildings, cross Beacon Hill Park, and start following the coastline around. Get it? That'll make you just in time for lunch."

"Lunch? But I don't want to put you out. I—"

"Grub's all here. Otherwise I wouldn't offer. Nothing fancy, though. Gotten lazy in my old age—though I can still pitch a tent, by God! How's your father and mother? No, don't tell me! Keep it all till we meet. Bye."

I looked at the dead receiver and smiled for the first time that day. Jesus! Didn't even that little bit of telephonically discarnate Nora take me back! I recalled acutely the Cornish cooking smells of saffron and yeast, and remembered a nonshaving self in short pants, as I climbed the slope toward the white-domed weather observatory, and found the open land she had promised.

As I crossed the springy turf, skirted immense clumps of broom almost too yellow to be true, and eventually found as she'd predicted the worn footpath that snaked above the low brown rocks, a strange thing happened to me.

I wanted, you see, to summon up those earlier walks amid equally yellow clumps of Cornish furze that had taken my fifteen-year-old feet from Treworder Farm to her lonely cottage perched on giant cliffs above the Atlantic. Hadn't I spent years wandering North America before settling in Vancouver, finding avenues of memory leading back to that Celtic womb, in a landscape here, a tree there, a bustle of clouds overhead, or one sweet discovery of Cornish pasty stands along the roads of Northern Michigan?

But where I now walked, lit in a March sun, vigorous in the stiff winds of spring, invited no nostalgia for my rugged peninsula or for my childhood and youth spent on it.

"You *must* go to Victoria, you'll love it," they kept telling me in Vancouver. "It's so English it'll remind you of home."

Well, I hadn't loved it. It reminded me more of Sudbury than England—and in any case, I'd never thought of England as my home; just as a place where I had collected some education, been humiliated, and learned that neither the priesthood nor schoolteaching were for me. And downtown Victoria didn't do anything for me at all, except, perhaps, to make me grateful for the broader elbow room of Vancouver and the beaches of Point Grey where I did most of my aching for severed roots from my native, Celtic place.

But this Oak Bay direction was different. It asked not for comparisons—sublime or otherwise. It spoke in languorous terms of middle-class comfort. Englishy? Perhaps for the transplanted English. But for this particular thirty-one-year-old Canadian immigrant feeding appreciatively on funny little stunted oaks, on seaweed and seagulls, and turning every now and then to look inland at beautifully tended gardens alive with clumps of azaleas and camellias, the whole thing was simply Anglo-Saxon: the end-of-the-rainbow quest for many a wandering Celt.

No, not England, but a 1930s cover for *The Saturday Evening Post*—that's what it all spelled for Davey Bryant, who had nervously edged his way up the Pacific coast from San Francisco and on reaching Vancouver had finally decided to call a halt.

So if nostalgia churned in me at all as I passed the regularly spaced park benches with their scattered elderly patrons basking in the morning warmth, it was for another time rather than another place.

I passed a squat lighthouse, boldly white and Mediterranean-looking against its background of blue sea. I looked above at a cormorant, wings stretched and drying as it stood on a water-lapped rock, across to the dazzling peaks of the Olympic

Peninsula. And for the first time since leaving The Empress Hotel I thought of Nora: specifically of those word pictures she had danced before my adolescent farm-rutted mind, of the splendors of the American Northwest and the pristine magnificence of her native British Columbia.

Petulant me, tired of her boasting: "If it's all so marvelous over there, why did you come here to Cornwall?"

Nora in her dark blue slacks (did *they* shock those wartime Cornish matrons!) and sailor's serge jersey, stopping her rhythmic chopping of firewood and staring at me: "Would you know that Mozart is better than Grieg if you hadn't heard both? Comparisons, young man. Until you can make 'em there's not too much to say."

That had shut me up—or at least made me search for a different tack. For at fifteen and still locked into that isolated wartime existence in a remote and rural Cornwall, before my exposure to the Royal Navy and England as well as profound aspects of my own personality, I didn't have very much to compare *with*
. . .

Do I make Nora sound gruff? I do not mean to. She wasn't gruff so much as forthright. Although Nora had opinions—lots of 'em—and was never afraid to express them, she expected an egalitarian response. Unlike any relative I had ever known, she *encouraged* my argumentativeness. That, almost more than anything else, made her so very special for me as I sailed the choppy seas of early adolescence.

"Maybe I wouldn't like Canada. Maybe I should go to Australia and sheep-farm. Lots of Cornishmen have gone there."

"Mebbe. There's only one way to find out, though. And what's that about farming? Yesterday you told me you detested it and wanted to be a veterinarian."

"I suppose I don't know what I want to be."

"That's the most sensible thing you've said all morning. Here, can you carry on chopping while I fix us some lunch?"

There must have been a thousand conversational variants on that. But there was never much discussion of the *other*, though. Only the action itself: the first time between us embedded in my mind and looming up now in misting shapes as my sight traversed the smooth green turf of the clifftop and stopped at a small cove where a few sailboats rode at anchor.

The *other?* Why am I hiding behind euphemism? Because I am on my way to see the very person who had wrested me away from euphemism in taking away my virginity? I suppose I have always been a rather passive person, but as I walked those Oak Bay cliffs that sunny March morning I'm pretty sure I blushed at the recollection of just how pliant, how unresistant as china clay, I had been when in the fold of those other clifftops, in another era, she had taken my shy shape in her arms and moved from a maternal cradling into a questing lover.

I am well aware that I hardly come on as King Kong now, but have I ever been more girlish than when lying there, held in her arms, she gently undressed me, revealing my timorous badge of gender and encouraging it with her work-roughened hand? I had long suppressed the specific details climaxing in my first pouring of seed into the welcome of a woman, but as I walked along Victoria's Oak Bay, or as I write now, over a decade later, I cannot help remembering how I had refused to open my eyes for a single moment: willing but frightened, wanting and not wanting; squirming with untapped lust but so ardently afraid of being embarrassed!

When I *had* opened my eyes, my head cradled in her lap, my sight had followed hers above me. The glistening rocks below, against which the surf boomed and frothed, were invisible. Instead, we had watched a small convoy, scarcely more than black dots on the horizon.

"I may be in one of them—the escorts I mean—in a couple of years. I'm dying to get into the Navy."

She stroked my hair, which was nice, and her voice was dreamy, faraway, when she answered me: "I doubt it, honey. The goddamn war should be all over by then. Then it will be *me* sailing west. In '39 I came via Panama from Vancouver. But this time I'll take the C.P.R. from Halifax. Stop off and see my sister in Toronto. It's been nearly five years already."

"Does looking out there make you homesick, Nora? I think I'll always be homesick for Cornwall, especially these cliffs." I snuggled closer to exposed thighs. "Particularly after—well—just now."

Gently but firmly she eased me up to a sitting position; rearranged her clothing and tossed her hair. "You're a romantic, that's what you are! Too romantic for your own good. It's going to make your emotional life a very choppy affair, Davey lad."

I switched my mind back abruptly to the Oak Bay present and, as I watched a tweedy Victoria matron struggling with two standing Irish setters on their leashes, reflected rapidly on the validity of that wartime prophecy atop Tregardock cliffs. Me romantic? You could just as easily call it emotional heart disease! I thought suddenly of poor Tim from my college days—and continued to wince as I mentally reeled off the forlorn list of collapsed love affairs that had littered my progress into my thirties and which had taken me across four countries and two hemispheres and which even Ken's presence hadn't prevented.

One of the bounding dogs got away from its owner and came gamboling in my direction. I welcomed the diversion; grabbed its trailing lead and returned it to its owner.

"Thanks. Down, Gresham! Now heel! I guess he's friskier than ever today, as I didn't get out with them yesterday."

"They're lovely dogs. Plenty of energy, though!"

"They're mother and son, if you can believe it. To see them fool around out here together you'd think they were from the same litter."

As she spoke she didn't seem quite so "tweedy"—or maybe I had just been uncritically swallowing Victoria myths, like so many people. She was about thirty; rather attractive in a sharp-featured way, with quick dark eyes and a front tooth that was just prominent enough to rest on her lower lip when her mouth was closed.

Was it the trail of reminiscence over Cornwall I had just been following which made me think of Nora as I looked at her? Then I realized in sharp reality that I had no idea of how Nora looked now—and only the haziest recollection of her face as I had known it at fifteen. Her body was another matter . . .

"Well, they'd better get on with trying to pull my arms out of their sockets!"

"Oh, one thing," I said. "Perhaps you can help me. I'm making my way to Newport Avenue. Would it be over there somewhere?"

"It's the turning by the right of that white house. I've just left there. What number do you want?"

"Here, I've written it down." I fumbled in my pocket and drew out the scrap of paper on which I'd written "number 2516."

"Mrs. Duthie's place. It's halfway down on the west side."

"Oh, you know her then?"

"She's my neighbor."

"Really? You must know her quite well then."

"Nora's a great person." She gave me a quick look. "You wouldn't be her grandson, would you?"

The idea seemed so bizarre I couldn't help smiling. "No—no. Just an old friend, that's all. I haven't seen Nora for years. I knew her best when I was growing up in Cornwall."

"You must be Davey then."

"Davey it is. So Nora's been talking!"

"Poor old Nora talks a lot. Trouble is, most of the time she's got no one to talk *to*. Her daughter Kathie is only in Seattle but she never comes over—which means Nora doesn't see the grandchildren. Which *also* means that apart from Mother and me she scarcely sees a soul. Of course, her deafness doesn't help."

"Deafness? I didn't know."

"If she'd only keep wearing the hearing aid it wouldn't be so bad. But saying Nora Duthie is just another way of spelling 'stubborn.' Then her tongue doesn't exactly endear her to other people either. She doesn't hold back her opinions, does Nora, and I'm sure she's managed to put off around ninety per cent of those she's met since she came back to Victoria."

I drew deep breath, a little at a loss for words. "Well, I can try and cheer her up. Nora always knew her own mind, I remember that. But that doesn't bother me. I'm a pretty good listener, I think."

The dogs were still straining—in opposite directions.

"Let me walk over the golf course with you. I think I'll take these two madcaps down on the beach. I can let 'em off there and there's no road for them to fly out into."

157

"Why don't you let me take one?" I offered.

"Okay. Here. Now just tug sharply if she keeps pulling."

"This is really some coincidence," I said, as we crossed the springy turf together. "It's funny, but in school, remember, we were always being told that people like Dickens kept dragging in coincidence for their plots? Yet in real life it happens all the time. I mean, of all the people I should meet out here it would be someone who actually knows Nora."

She made no attempt to reply to that but was silent for a while. When she spoke it was in quite a different vein. "Do you mind if I ask you something personal? It has to do with Nora."

"Not all all. Those things don't bother me." (That wasn't quite true, but what on earth do you say when people start off like that?)

"Are you married?"

I thought immediately of Ken. "No."

"Nor am I. Nora has a bee in her bonnet about that, though. Whenever she's brought your name up—I'm thinking over the past four or five years I've known her—she's always mentioned something about hoping that you were. Then she's usually gone on to make some rather acid remarks about me in the same quarter. 'Can't stand spinsters or bachelors! No one without kids has ever really lived!'—that kind of thing."

"I can imagine," I said slowly. "Yes, I guess she would be a bit like that. But thanks for telling me, all the same. I'll think up the right kind of reply."

At the end of the grass verge I returned the bitch to her and said goodbye. I turned, though, on realizing I didn't even know her name. But her dogs had obviously read her thoughts and were tugging for all they were worth toward the shoreline and their unleashed freedom, which lay below.

In a few seconds I came to the house where Nora Duthie lived. I paused, though, as soon as I saw it, stopping outside where presumably the neighbor with the setters lived, and checking my watch. In spite of stopping to talk, it was still on the early side for lunch. But I knew that wasn't the real reason that made me hesitate. What really made me linger there for a moment, ostensibly eyeing the patches of narcissi and white trumpeter tulips in the front yard before me, was that question as to my marital status. Certainly I knew immense relief in our decision for Ken to stay home in Vancouver and for me to make this trip alone, but that did not prevent old fears of Nora's sharp probing of my intimate life at an unfocused fifteen returning now in a quickening of pulse and perhaps even a faint flush to my cheeks. That aspect of Nora, along with the exact precision of her features, was something else I had forgotten over the blurring track of the years.

I started asking myself mental questions: 'What the hell am I doing here, anyway?' 'What have I come for?' 'Why didn't I insist we meet at The Empress—where at least we would be on neutral ground?'

Not that the location would have had the slightest effect on her propensity to throw questions at me. Hadn't it always been so? Not just the routine questions that adults often feel they have to demand of children: 'What are you doing at school?' 'How did your last test go?' 'What are your plans for later in life?'—things like that.

No, Nora's were more personal—especially after that morning on the clifftop. She often questioned me closely, for instance, over my friendships with Rosemary Pengelly and Audrey Trebilcock.

"Didn't I see you with that Pengelly girl yesterday?"

"You may have done. We all bike home from school together."

"Have you done with her what we do together?"

Then I'd go silent. I *hated* those stabs of hers for information. There were so many things at that time in my life that I didn't dare ask myself, let alone ask anyone else . . .

I guess that makes Nora out as jealous. But I don't really think she was. Indeed, sometimes I had the feeling she was wholly uninterested in my answers—even when I gave them, that is. No, she just liked *asking* questions. And she liked trying to lift the lid off my body secrets all the time.

"I guess you masturbate one hell of a lot. That'ud explain why you can't manage now." (That was in her bed where we'd taken to ending up on Saturday afternoons when I had lied to my mother, saying I was going down to the cinema in Wadebridge.)

"Not all that much."

"What do you think of when you're doing it?"

"I—I've forgotten."

"Think of me sometimes?"

"Perhaps."

"You shouldn't try and hide things from me. I'm the one person you needn't be afraid of, do you know that?"

"I think I like hiding things."

"Secretive little baby, that's what you are. Here, come closer. I want to show you something else. Bet you've never done this before."

Each weekend seemed to be a lesson in nudity with her: some experiences likable, some less so. Her body's knowledge I wanted; it was her talk that ruffled and embarrassed me.

I edged a little toward her house. A few steps, that is. I looked about me. I didn't want to seem some kind of suspicious character hanging about that quiet street. But I was still reluctant to arrive at her front door, which I could now see all too clearly.

I turned the uneasy memory tape on again—to the last time we did it. That, too, was in the open air. But not up on the cliffs. Snuggled, rather, in a nest of tall ferns in the heart of Poltrewirgie Woods. I suppose you could have called it an idyllic setting. A sort of Lady Chatterley and Mellors thing. Only I didn't fool around with garlanding the thick mat of her pubics with woodland flowers. I was always too hungry, panting sweatily with excitement, for any kind of trimmings. Besides, I'd never heard of D. H. Lawrence then, and this business of fucking with Nora, my sexual mother, I kept fiercely from the rest of my life. It wasn't true that I thought of her when jacking off. I *never* thought of her physically, except when we were going at it. I wanted it to be only something that just happened when we were together and I could leave my mind and imagination entirely out of it.

But back to that swansong when we lay on the bruised fern fronds, me half-straddling her as I played with her large, purplish nipples that were almost leathery in their feel. I had already come (maybe she had too, but I didn't know anything about women coming then).

Our bottoms shared a shaft of sunlight, the rest of us lay in shade. A little way off we could hear the gurgle of the trout stream; overhead the cooing of woodpigeons and the occasional harsh scream of a jay which something had disturbed in the woodland thickness.

"Nora?"

"Yes?"

"Are—are you a nymphomaniac?"

She jerked up to a sitting position, sending me sprawling onto damp green grass—cold to the sun-warmed tenderness of my backside.

"Am I *what?*"

It didn't need the tone of her voice added to the abruptness of her action to tell me I'd asked the wrong question. Hastily I tried to make amends. "A boy at school was talking. He said that women—women who liked young boys—well, they were called that."

"What a stupid bunch of— Christ Almighty! Has none of you ever heard of a goddamn dictionary? And how come you were talking about me?"

"I didn't say we were talking about you. I'm sorry I mentioned it."

"Well, let's deal with the birds and bees first. No, Davey, a nymphomaniac is just a woman who likes sex, period. If there's a word for the other, I don't know it. Anyway, I just happen to like you. I'm not in the market for every pimply-faced little asshole in Cornwall! Get it?"

Something in me went very cold. After sex with her I always knew a twinge of guilt, and with it a sense of being trapped: a prisoner, somehow, of her more sophisticated body. Perhaps those ingredients were there now, as we sat confronting each other in the woodland glade. But if so, they were joined by something new—a desire to hurt her for her brusque reaction to my question.

"I know you're not *just* interested in people my age," I said slowly, "'cos I've seen you."

I say I was speaking slowly, but, God, my mind was moving like lightning! In a way I was bluffing, you see. It's true I had seen someone—two or three times, that is—making his way toward Nora's cottage. And not up the front lane where he would have surely been seen by others, too—even though it was invariably dark when I was up Nora's way on my way home from Aunt Jessie's and had taken the clifftop track to our farm.

I had meant to ask Nora about that man, thinking the first Saturday night that it happened that it might have been one of the servicemen from the coastguard station up to no good. But the second time I saw what looked like the same tall figure, it was quite obvious that he knew his way down the gully and up over the stile and past her row of beehives. In any case, I had stopped long enough that second time to see a flare of light as she'd opened the back door (blackout restrictions not withstanding) and realized that whoever it was had been invited in. But *who* it was, and whatever his purpose, of course I had no idea.

However, it wasn't my intention to give her that impression as we sat there amid fern and long grass, under a leaf-fragmented sky.

Her body stiffened. She tilted slightly to one side, and I noticed her knuckles were whitened on the forest floor.

"What in hell do you mean by that?"

I strained for nonchalance. "What I say. I've seen him. I know, that's all." I held my breath. A couple more questions and my bluff would be called.

It was, of course, no generous impulse of hers that got me off the hook—indeed, seconds later I was wishing desperately that she never had. "If—if you saw him—why the hell didn't you tell me?"

As I prepared to lie my way out of that, the soft, fatal words followed from her suddenly trembling lips: "You—you haven't mentioned anything to your mother, have you? She doesn't know anything about me and Frank?"

In the silence between us my stomach churned. From where my words came, let alone the power to think, God only knows! "You needn't worry. And don't worry about Father either. We hardly talk together anyway—let alone about his sex life!"

And with that I jumped up and started to dress. I wouldn't say that Nora was subdued exactly, as we retraced our steps through

Poltrewirgie Woods across the moorland uplands to her house. But apart from suddenly stopping, turning to face me and saying, "Forget about it, do you hear me? Put it out of your mind. It will never happen again," she never made reference to her and my dad again.

Come to that, I haven't brought it up with anyone from that day to—well, this moment. Not even Ken, although he will now read it here. But it certainly filled my head that spring day in Victoria, as I reluctantly left the safety of her neighbor's garden and began my final walk up to her front door.

As I drew deep breath and pressed the small white diamond buzzer, I strove vigorously to obliterate the past and to anticipate what a woman I hadn't seen for all those years would not look like; what a woman I had known intimately (how intimately!) when I was only fifteen would look like now that she was sixty-one, and I was sporting gray hairs at my temples, and lines under my eyes that would never go away.

I forced a vision of white hair instead of soft brown curls, but even though that was to prove correct it hardly softened the blow as, hands sweating freely, I stared at the old lady who opened the door. Nora? Of course it was Nora—but only in the forlorn distinction of the devouring years. She looked more like seventy than sixty!

Is there anything quite like that black vision of recorded mortality, when a once-familiar face and form is seen again after the seemingly innocent passage of days has pitted its remorseless message across a once soft-contoured face? Ask any emigrant returning decades later to the womb of family . . . the shock is icy, removing air from the lungs, forcing a turning away from a grave-beckoning apparition—as I did now on Nora's front step.

"God, Davey! I wouldn't have known you!"

"Nora. Oh, *you* haven't changed that much," I said, looking afresh at her and lying with that ease with which we cloak the trappings of mortality.

"Hair's a little whiter, maybe."

"Whiter? Hell, it wasn't even gray when we last met!"

The voice. Thank God for the voice! Maybe a little less trenchant, even a slight tremble. But essentially the same that had whispered in my ear on Tregardock Cliffs; had reluctantly confessed the liaison with my father . . .

"Well, come on in! We sure look like a couple of idiots gawking at each other out here. Park your fanny somewhere over there. I'll get us some sherry. You're not a teetotaler or anything peculiar, are you?"

"I'd love a sherry," I said, moving into the living room.

As she moved about the kitchen (slow, rather deliberate movements, I noticed, rather than the purposeful, staccato ones I recalled now from her Cornish cottage) I looked about me. A cream-colored sofa and two matching armchairs, a shiny sidetable crammed with photographs; some western lithographs, derivative of Remington's cowboys, on the wall. How shall I put it? All very middle-class—very bland and conveyor-belt. In other words, eons removed from Nora's living room which I had experienced with such profound cultural shock as a boy growing up.

I was looking closely at one of the photos, one of her daughter Karen (in fact, the only object I recalled from my early adolescence as being there, in the cottage) when Nora returned with the two sherries in long, fluted glasses on an ornamented silver platter.

"I *assume* you like it dry. Most of the people around here prefer cat's piss flavored with saccharine!"

That sounded like the old Nora. If only the breezy sentiment didn't have to come out of such a withered and drawn mouth. It was then I realized that Nora had no teeth. She seemed to read my thoughts.

"I've got dentures," she said, "but they click and clack because they don't fit properly. I told that fool dentist right from the start. So most of the time I don't bother to put 'em in. It's like this damn thing." She pointed to her ear, and I recalled the neighbor's remarks about Nora's hearing aid. "Only if I don't bother with this I can't hear a bloody thing! I tell you, getting older is no joke, Davey."

She placed the tray down on the coffee table and straightened. "But you're not here to listen to the complaints of an old woman. Tell me about yourself. What are you doing? I must say you look

164

prosperous enough. Quite the city dandy, eh? Far cry from the farmer's boy when I first knew you."

Behind the brightness I read something else. But I wasn't anxious to have it articulated.

"I'm writing," I told her. "I've been commissioned to do a book on D. H. Lawrence for a New York publisher. I do a certain amount for the C.B.C., too."

I eased myself back in the armchair, crossed my legs, and sipped my sherry. "Well, I must say you've got a very comfortable place here, Nora. Quite different from the old cottage, though! I bet you don't have to chop wood any more!"

She had seated herself opposite me. "I've heard you on the radio. Didn't recognize your voice, though. It was only when the announcer gave your name."

I knew she was talking just for the sake of talking, but at least that kept us from thin ice. "That's Karen's picture, isn't it? How is she?"

"So you remember Karen, do you? Fancy that!"

"She came down to your cottage. She was in the WRENS or WAVES or something."

"WAVES. She became a Yank like her father. She's all right, I guess. Not that I see her that much. Lives in San Francisco playing mother to a bone-idle husband and a son who spends most of his time acting like her daughter."

"San Francisco? I thought it was Seattle."

"That's Kathie—not Karen. Now how in hell did you know that?"

It came very strongly to me that mentioning the meeting with her neighbor might not please her. "I think Mother told me in a letter," I told her.

"Oh yes, your mother. How is she? I get a card at Christmas but she never puts anything on it. I don't know why people bother sending cards without including their news. But look who's talking! I've given up sending any goddamn cards myself."

"Mother's very well. As a matter of fact, she's just gotten back from Palmerston, New Zealand. That's where my younger brother, Harry, now lives. Remember him?"

"Of course, of course. I guess she's a grandmother too. You got kids?"

There was a tiny silence between us.

"No, Nora. I haven't got kids."

"What went wrong?"

I was trying not to be paranoid, but surely her voice was now harsher than even its usual brusque tone?

"I take it you're married?"

Again I suppressed any image of Ken. "Not at present," I parried.

"I see."

'You don't!' I told myself silently.

She seemed, then, to backtrack somewhat. "Well, who in hell wants kids? I have three and in their different ways they're all ingrates. The truth is, I much prefer my grandchildren. But do you know that Kathie hasn't brought her children to see their grandmother since last summer? And, God knows, it's only a ferry trip from Seattle."

"Three? I thought there were just the two girls." (Statistics was a safer subject than her complaining.)

But she took the bait—at least for the moment. "No, there's Derek too. My eldest. But God knows where he is right now. Rio, maybe. His wife's from there. She sent photos of their three kids once—and sort of hinted they needed cash. So I sort of hinted back that I wasn't about to subsidize my son's sexual prowess. And that was that. Like I didn't hear from her again."

"I never met him."

"No, he was a lot older than the girls. I was married at eighteen, don't forget."

I looked down into my drained sherry glass. "So your children are scattered and you're the one that's come home. I remember so well all the things you told me about here. About Victoria and Duncan . . . and Long Beach. Especially Long Beach, and the whales spouting offshore. I thought of you when I first went there two years ago. Your ears should have been burning!"

"Hmmm. Haven't been there for years! Probably overrun by tourists by now. We used to sail up the coast from here. Put in at

Tofino. Some more sherry? Here, give me your glass. Two won't make us drunk."

I watched the back of her faded print dress as she moved once more into the kitchen. Funny, I had only associated her with slacks over all these years. When she got back I was standing, looking out of the window at her sun-washed front lawn. We chinked glasses, though we hadn't the first time, and both murmured, "Cheers." Very formal.

"You really have got a nice place here. You did the right thing coming back, you know that. Cornwall's been ruined. It isn't the same any more. Clogged streets . . . hardtop carparks along the cliffs . . . Mother says it takes them ages to get into Wadebridge for the shopping. In fact, in summertime they hardly go out any more. It's only bearable from September on."

"How's Frank?"

Her gray eyes met mine—really for the first time since I'd arrived. It was the question I'd been waiting for, subconsciously dreading, I suppose. But now that it had come it wasn't as hard as I'd anticipated.

"He's—he's all right," I said slowly. "He had a heart attack a couple of years back—playing at St. Enodoc. But he's recovered quite well. Doesn't do too much now . . . potters around the garden, that kind of thing. You know they retired to a place on the Estuary? Just outside Padstow?"

"I'm glad they didn't split up. Over me, that is. You know that's why I sold up and left?"

"You always said you'd come back to British Columbia, Nora. I remember—"

"I was a frightened woman. Homesick a little, too, perhaps. But only because there was no one to turn to."

"There was me. You could've made me understand, I think."

"You? A kid?"

"Old enough—after what we did together."

"You don't understand. Even now, you don't understand. I was madly in love. Frank was everything. I'd never known anything like it before. Not with my own husband—or with the others. You—you were just a way to be close to him. Crazy, of course! I was quite insane then, I think. I fulfilled a need for you, I guess. But every time I took you, let you explore me, it was really the father of the son I wanted about me."

"Mother told me once that she thought you were very good for Dad. She wasn't a bit jealous, you know."

"Strange woman. I never understood her. I know Frank didn't. She was the last familiar person I saw in England. We went to lunch together. A little place in Chelsea. She told me I should stay, keep the cottage in Cornwall, and that things would work themselves out. I could have taken that from anyone but her. So I came back."

Nora then sighed heavily. "And that, believe me, was a great mistake. I've sat here eating my heart out—and growing old at the same time. I'm a miserable old woman, Davey, and that's the truth."

I immediately tried to cheer her up, of course. Or was I just trying to keep her misery from invading me? Anyway, we progressed from the sherry to soup (tomato) and sardine sandwiches, with her persisting with her raw, sad commentary—counterpointed by my blithely idiotic Hollywood solutions to her problems.

Long before she served us two cups of Nescafé, I was bored to the point of sweating palms, and planning my escape tactics. But it was she who took the initiative, even here. For the umpteenth time I was striving to connect this wrinkled old woman with the firm-fleshed, fortyish matron to whom I had so contentedly surrendered in the folds of the clifftop, when she suddenly let her coffee cup fall heavily back in its saucer.

"I can see the pity on your face. You shouldn't have come. It was wrong for both of us."

"Not pity, Nora. I'm just sorry that—"

She rose. "I've made a fool of myself. Self-pity should only be a private affair. And you should let the past stay buried, Davey Bryant. It's always a mistake to try and resurrect things."

"Especially hard for me, perhaps. Yet I seem to spend my life doing it. Anyway, I'm pleased I've come and seen you, Nora. I can now write home and—"

"I am sure you will. But my writing days are over. No Christmas cards, please. Not even one like your forgiving mother's, without any message."

"You must try not to be bitter. I'm sure your children . . . your next-door neighbor—"

"Goodbye!" she interrupted. "You'll understand, won't you, if I don't see you out."

I don't think she was actually crying, but she turned abruptly and walked quickly toward the kitchen. And that, really, is that. In a way, I'd like to report that things got tidied up. That I called her again when next time in Victoria and that things went better a second time around. But I never did call her again. I got a phone call from Seattle—oh, it must have been a good five or six years later—saying that they had put their mother in an old people's home as she couldn't cope any more.

And there, I suppose, she still is. Maybe I will never know when she actually departs this life. In fact, all I know for sure is that I lack the courage to ever seek her out once more. For I don't think I could stand hearing from such aged lips that life had been a terrible mistake . . .

Why? Why at forty be seduced from the safe choreography of familiar sexual patterns? For the prosaic, dear Davey, you are devoid of choice. Now David Watmough . . . oh, you ask any of those in the Beloved Province who know him and they will tell you quickly enough where he stands! No deviate from sexual heterodoxy is our Watmough! But Davey, my Davey, who is yet your own Davey, you will persist in the freedom from your progenitor and reveal the power of your subjective liberation from me. For in the honesty I have given you which I found denied in me, you can speak of incidents and anecdotes suggested by the ghosts of sexual possibilities. Yes, for you, Davey Bryant, it was not even Victoria but Vancouver (the alternate "V") which suggested a victory from a garden which had become a harvest of threats. But in the California mood of the Okanagan, in the years of accumulated blindness against the blithe youthfulness of your feminine antagonist, you have to learn that Eve is cupid for you, and that nothing but nothing is what it seems! That is something your author knows better than you . . .

Chapter Ten

The external constituents were unlikely for a love affair; even for as brief and abortive a love affair as I want now to get off my chest. I mean, a motel with a ludicrously colored pool, a resort town splashed gaudily across the valley of the Okanagan, and high summer, when the natives stay in their holes or behind their cash desks, and everywhere is inundated with the restless rain refugees from Vancouver . . . not a scene, perhaps, to readily evoke the soft lights and lush violins theme.

But, as I say, this wasn't a normal love affair anyway. Certainly not your usual romance. It started with a timid tap on my motel door. I was lying on my bed wearing only my underpants. It was late afternoon and very hot. I had had a nap and was too lazy to get up and switch the air conditioner on. In any case, when I had summoned up enough energy to do more than sensually stroke my naked belly (it was too hot for anything more vigorous) I had decided I was going to plunge into that revolting green pool.

Another scratch on the door: . . . Slowly it got through to my befuddled self. "Jesus Christ! You can't take a goddamned nap . . ." I was still muttering, zipping pants and buttoning up my shirt, as I opened the door.

"Hi. I'm Joanna."

I must have looked as blank as I felt.

"Remember me? I'm in your Creative Writing class. Well, sort of. I'm taking poetry with Ted Lineham."

Her small, oval face and long encircling hair were familiar, though I had never put a name to her.

"Come on in. Forgive the mess. I was having a nap." I went in front of her and hastily pulled the moss green coverlet back in place.

"Why not sit over there—that's the most comfortable chair. Would you like a drink?"

She sat on the edge of the seat and I realized she was nervous. Not with me. This was 1969 and teen-age girls weren't frightened of me, I liked to think.

"I'm sorry to interrupt but Ted said you were usually here in the afternoons. You'd already gone when we quit this morning."

I'd nipped out smartly at noon to ask a cute kid taking modern dance with my friend Gordon if he'd have lunch with me. But I saw no reason why she should know that. I held up an empty glass inquiringly. "Gin and tonic?"

"That 'ud be great."

Pouring the drinks, the makings of which were behind me on the headshelf beyond my bed, I suddenly felt self-conscious. How old was she? Sixteen or seventeen? She'd probably be happier with pot. I bet she's thinking, here's another middle-aged creep like Mommy and Daddy, tucking into the gin. (That's one thing about your peer group—at least your chosen friends—they don't make you feel somehow unclean about a nice, refreshing g & t in the middle of the afternoon.)

"It's a nice place you've got here. I've never been in this motel before."

"You from here, then?"

Most of the kids at the summer school seemed from the coast, but there were a few locals from the Okanagan.

"Nanaimo."

"Home of the world's only bathtub race and all that, eh?"

"Jesus! *That* crap!"

Which made me glad that I had forborne to say I'd stood shivering on a chilly summer's day in Vancouver waiting for those idiots to come into the shoreline at Kitsilano after braving the cold and choppy straits.

"I always thought it rather silly, but that's what comes, I guess, from having an extrovert mayor. We suffer the same thing in Vancouver. Here's to the downfall of all extrovert mayors." I raised my tumbler and she sipped her drink. I had the feeling she didn't like it.

"Now what's on your mind, Sandra?" I hoped in that dim room, for I had pulled the drapes against the sun's glare, she could see that my eyes twinkled in the prescribed counselor's manner.

"Joanna," she corrected casually—though still making me feel a fool.

"Like I'd like to cut out of Ted's group into yours."

"Why? You and Mr. Lineham not seeing eye to eye, that it?"

"I'm getting too involved with him. He makes me lose my cool. Then—"

"Yes?"

"Well, like I got friends who say with you it's different."

"Different? In what way?" I took a substantial swig at my g & t.

"Like you're different. It's sort of easier with a guy—" She broke off this time, rather than tailed off. I steered quickly away from that one.

"Mr. Lineham takes the poetry class, Joanna,"—getting her name right that time—"because he writes poetry. I don't, so I stick to teaching the fiction."

She didn't answer and we sat there quietly, looking at one another. It wasn't much of an exploration for her, I thought, because she obviously saw me daily when I looked in for a couple of minutes at both Lineham's group and that of George Sills. I had some vague idea of downplaying the fact I was in charge and sought to give the impression that we were just one big family with a general theme of equality running through the whole thing.

But if I was a fairly familiar sight for Joanna, she was quite an unknown phenomenon to me. True, I'd recognized her face at the door. But that was about all. Now, though, I not only took in the trim if immature body under the T-shirt and blue jeans regalia, but tried to read the personality inhabiting that sartorial cliché.

I thought myself back into a fifteen-year-old skin. But that didn't help too much. I saw a pimply pubescent, a rather faggoty farm boy wandering alone across Cornish fields, locked in the distorted womb of World War Two with only Nora as consolation. But all that was more than a little remote from this Canadian-contoured child, touched by the froth of the counter-culture and sitting there, slim thighs boyishly apart, bare feet squeezing and unsqueezing toes on the hard Acrilan carpet.

My mind sped to Nanaimo, where the ferries had so often taken me to temporary freedom from the complexities I had contrived on the Lower Mainland. I never went in summer when the tourists took over, so my images were those of cool sunlight filtering through sentineled cedars, of mist hanging silkily about tangles of alder and arbutus, and wreathing the salmonberry. And always the waveless waters of the sound resolving themselves in thin-lipped tides that created neither sibilance nor foam. An autumnal stillness in January: high gray skies unmoving over flat and steely gray seas. There was something of all this calm, all this quietude, in the girl-woman sitting opposite me. Place and time met in her, I reflected. An island isolation joined congruously in her with the monosyllabic mores of her generation.

"Like another drink?" I asked.

"Okay." But she didn't move an inch, still held the tumbler with the stubby, unringed fingers of both hands—as if she were keeping a coffee mug warm.

I peered down at my own melting ice cubes. Better not rush her, I thought. I didn't want her reeling out pissed from The Greenlawns Inn. There were enough mini-scandals, crises, and tensions going on at the Summer School without old Daddy Davey adding to them . . .

"Have you talked to Ted about quitting his classes? Was it his suggestion you come to me?"

"Like I said, Mr. Bryant, I can't *talk* to him."

"Call me Davey, for Chrissake. This isn't a high school."

"Davey, then. Promise you won't laugh at me?"

"Promise."

"Well, I guess I love him. Only he ignores me. Like it's as if I don't exist for him."

"The classes are too big, that's for sure. If I had my way they'd—"

"That's got nothing to do with it. That's not where it's at between us."

"Look, why don't you tell me *all* about it." I sat back, forgetting my own drink for the moment, as well as hers.

"Like when you all first came up, it was different. There was a party on that first Saturday, remember? He and George Sills threw it. Ted came on real strong then. We balled that night. The next night was groovy too. We screwed down by the lake. He told me I was the best lay he's ever had." She looked from her glass to me. "He hasn't spoken to me since. He's married, isn't he?"

With all that raw truth from her, I didn't feel like lying. "Yes."

"I thought he was. He never said so, though. Do you think—"

"What, Joanna?"

"—that he thought if I knew I wouldn't have done it? I would, you know. It makes no goddamn difference. I've no hangups in that scene, man."

"Don't call me 'man,' sweetheart," I said gently. "It's too demanding."

"I don't mind if you put me down, either."

"I'm not putting you down, Joanna. Just keep that 'man' bit for Ted. After all, he's proved it."

"You're uptight because I told you."

Bugger her for her percipience! Nevertheless, I suppressed irritation.

"It's a free world. What you and Ted do together with your bodies is no concern of mine. But if he's hurt you, made you unhappy, then that's something different again. From the little you've told me, I'd say at the very least he's been bloody selfish."

"I'm not knocking Ted. I just want out of his class, that's all."

There was an abrasion in the room now. Nothing excessive, but I thought I could see that she was pouting slightly. As for me—well, that was quite right, I certainly was pissed off with Ted. Christ! He'd *begged* me to bring him up there so that he could earn a little extra bread. And I'd only agreed because . . .

An image of that quick-smiling mouth, curly hair, and wiry body suddenly sprouted in my head . . .

"What about George Sills?" I asked abruptly. "Maybe you'd be happier with *his* sessions. He digs poetry, even if he is primarily a playwright."

My mental icon changed to Master George's handsome mug. Nothing of aquiline, chisel-featured Ted about him! But there were those startling blue eyes above the broad, rather animal pug nose. His squat, athletic body had been stored up in my memory too, when I'd called him and asked if he'd be interested in summer school work that year.

"George has been shacking up with my friend Tessa McKay. Though I know he's balled with some of the other kids too. He turns me right off 'cause he hasn't leveled with Tessa—even though she won't believe me."

"Give me your glass," I said, getting up. I wanted time and space to digest this fresh piece of information. I had to go into the bathroom for the tub of ice. My thoughts flashed like nervous neon lighting as I physically followed through the liturgy of drink-making. I cursed through clenched teeth. So this is what my brace of handsome heteros had been up to! Fucking minors all over the place! Steadily screwing their way through my female charges with about the discretion of sex-starved apes! And to think I had gone to such special trouble to raise recruits from my straight friends precisely to avoid the kind of scandal they had apparently had two or three years earlier involving some gay idiot with a fellow male instructor!"

I handed Joanna her fresh gin and tonic without speaking. The only difference between that past situation and the present one was a mere matter of irony.

"Creative Writing seems to have turned into Practical Biology," I said, trying to grin but suspecting it looked like a leer, as I sank back on the hideabed.

"Pardon me?"

I had forgotten that a sarcastic tone was lost on this generation. I tried another tack. "Just coming into my class—that really won't solve things for you, will it?"

"It 'ud be a start."

"I should have to discuss it with Ted, of course."

"You can tell him his class is a drag. We all think that!"

"How come?" I am sure my voice must have sounded as uninterested as I now felt.

"He just doesn't turn anyone on. Maybe he's better in the private sessions. But I wouldn't know anything about *that*, of course."

"Of course," I added mechanically.

It was depressing enough to learn that my staff was busy deflowering the young. If they had been brilliant teachers, that might have helped. But now I just thought the whole thing sordid. I sighed, and she obviously noticed.

"I've screwed up your afternoon for you, haven't I? I'm sorry. I guess you've got problems of your own."

I looked quickly at her. She was watching me intently. I realized she meant what she said.

"You know, Joanna, I'm not really a teacher." I thought back to those remote St. Benedict days and my two temptresses: Harriet and Pamela. "It's too dangerous a profession for me. And I am certainly not used to handling staff problems. First time in my life I've ever had to do it, in fact."

"Well, I don't want to be any *trouble*. I'm not knocking Ted. It's all in myself. I just wanted to rap with you, I guess."

I was pleased to see her taking a sip at her drink. I'd finished mine.

"That's what I'm here for. I'm glad you've come. It's the only way I hear things."

"So now I've told you. I guess I oughta split." She didn't sound too convinced.

"Must you?"

"They serve up that crap in the Cafeteria at five."

My mind flicked ahead. "Forget it. You can eat with me. They do a barbecue out there on the lawn. It's not bad."

"Okay. Say, can I use your bathroom?" She was already bouncing back and I envied her that youthful resilience. "Be my guest."

As she sauntered out I enjoyed the slim vulnerability of her shoulders from behind, and in so thinking I felt my whole mood change. This young woman had entered my afternoon as an unwonted rupture of my rest, turned into a mildly pleasant diversion, changed again into an irritating summer school problem, and now—well, what exactly *was* I thinking about Joanna as she closed the bathroom door and I stared, brooding, at her invisible wake.

I know that the twin images of Harriet and Pamela in that distant Aldershot during the closing days of my British self flitted intermittently about the edges of my mind. But they were so much *younger*, I told myself. And they were so seductive in the potential of their femininity. But this girl in her jeans and man's shirt looked and walked as if she had never worn a dress! In any case, I told her absence, this was no classroom, for God's sake!

Actually, a lot of little worms wiggled to make up the mosaic of my mood. For one thing, it occurred sharply to me that her boyish body had lain with the squirting form of attractive Ted Lineham. Then, there was that sense of hurt she exuded that made me feel almost maternal and longing to protect her from all the hurt that she was yet to know.

I got up and moved about the soulless motel room, decided the dim light was a suffocating restriction, so pulled back the drapes and pushed back the sliding glass door leading onto my patio. The sun was no longer overhead, but as yet gave no hint of evening. From the far end of the lawns the motel enclosed I heard a child's voice. The only other sound I was conscious of was the steady swish-swish of the sprinkler system which kept the grass green and ankle-deep.

For a moment I sat on the spikes of the low white wicker fence which bordered the patio area, but decided they pushed too uncomfortably into my bottom, so sank instead into the white garden chair in the shade of the multicolored umbrella. It was still very hot.

It was here Joanna joined me. The first thing I noticed outdoors that I hadn't inside was her marked suntan, that and the magnificent white teeth that seemed to hallmark all today's North American youth. I also realized that the long, straight hair she was constantly pushing away from her eyes was streaked with the blond bleach of the sun. As she sat down and sprawled next to me in the twin wooden chair, my eye stopped its lightning scrutiny at the middle of her fly. 'Jesus!' I thought, 'these girls today even have baskets like the boys.' But I as quickly chided myself for the outrageous fancy. That is what in dirty books would be called the mound of Venus, I told myself, and its interest for you, Davey Bryant, is minus zero!

I shifted my vision to the vicinity of her breasts—a less embarrassing region for me. I was pleased to note that they were modestly unmaternal: no flopping gourds, heavily brazen in female power.

"Finished?"

"Finished?"

"I'm sorry." I realized I must have been staring quite hard. Christ! Whatever must she be thinking!

"It—it was dark in there," I said quickly. "Now I can see you properly."

"Do I pass the test?"

Somehow all this had to be put on an even keel.

"You remind me of a boy I know."

"A boy?"

"He's attractive too."

"Have you ever thought of suicide, Davey?"

That was a pretty desperate way of changing the subject, I thought. But I went along with it.

"When I was your age, I thought about it a lot. Why? Is that how you feel?"

She shook her head and that tawny blond hair swayed prettily. "Not now, I don't. Say, it's neat out here! You've gotten yourself a real groovy place. Better than those goddamn dorms where we are."

Attractive, Miss Joanna might be, but she wasn't going to wriggle out of things *that* quickly! "What made you bring up suicide, then? Do you often get depressed?"

"Everyone does, don't they? I mean, like some days are just bad trips. I guess all you can do then is sweat it out. Like this kid I knew who had a bummer on acid."

"It's—it's hard to command each day, I'll grant you that. But I have to make some effort to redeem the time. After all, I've got less of it before me than you. And if I didn't come up with at least some skeleton of activity I think I'd just drown under all the pointless hours breaking over my head."

Her response was remote from my thinking.

"I like the way you talk. Gee, you really groove on words, don't you?"

"Well, don't embarrass me or I'll dry up."

"You embarrassed? I'd like to see the day!"

"I can be. Easily. And I should say young ladies are the most *potent* form of embarrassment I can think of."

"What's with that 'young ladies' shit? You sound like something out of Jane Austen."

"So you've read Jane Austen. Which? *Pride and Prejudice? Persuasion?*"

"Now you sound like a schoolteacher!"

"Isn't that what I'm supposed to be? At least for these few weeks of my life?"

"You haven't come on like one up to now."

"Really? Tell me how I have come on."

That nonplused her, as I intended. She had to reflect a moment.

"Oh I dunno. Just as a guy, I guess. Like—"

"Yes?" I put a lot of gentleness into that.

"Well, you're sort of sympathetic. You're easy to rap with."

"So let's rap."

"On what?"

"On you, for instance."

"There isn't enough about me. I haven't done enough to be interesting."

The honesty of that simply delivered statement found its way to my stomach. Where in hell did anyone summon up the bleak strength to talk that way? Why, at five I thought I was fascinating, at fifteen a misunderstood genius; at thirty I called myself sui generis, and now at nearly forty I was only prepared to settle for the "misunderstood genius" bit again.

"That's nonsense, Joanna. You interest *me*, for a start."

"That's only because you're bored. And there's no one else here."

Maybe it had started that way when she had first arrived. But it was so no longer, and it was suddenly terribly important to convince her of the fact.

"That's balls. Let me tell you something. I *hate* bores. I'm totally allergic to 'em. I'll run a mile, a hundred miles, to escape them."

"All right, all right—I believe you. You needn't go on."

I read the upturn of amusement at the edges of her mouth and was reassured. "Now tell me why you took creative writing here. You write a lot of poetry, is that it?"

She put her hands behind her, joined her fingers and stretched back on the white wooden slats. "It's crummy stuff. Let's not talk about that."

"Okay. What you going to do when you leave school? What grade you in now?"

"Grade Eleven. I dunno. I was thinking of college."

"U.B.C.?"

"Hell, no! Simon Fraser maybe. But I'm not sure. I'd like to run around for a while. Europe, maybe."

She's a schoolgirl, I told myself secretly. Imagine her back in England . . . at St. Benedict's . . . the Sixth Form probably . . . Dressed in one of those gym slips . . . black stockings . . . a straw hat with a floppy brim . . . She's a *child* I told myself fiercely, a girl-child—keep *that* idea out front. Remember Harriet and Pamela. How close to disaster they had brought me!

"It's a big world out there, Joanna. Ever think of that?"

"It's a big world right here, isn't it?"

"What do you mean?"

"If my dad saw me sitting here with you, he'd be thinking I was sure as hell in a bigger world than *he'd* want me in!"

I looked around frantically. Maybe for some irate father . . .

"What an extraordinary thing to say! I can't think of a smaller world than the Summer School of the Arts."

"Depends where you stand, don't you think? Like Vancouver seems pretty big from over in Nanaimo. But to someone like you, I guess it's kinda small town."

As I seemed to spend far too much time informing Vancouverites that their city represented a bigger time than they ever gave it credit for, I found Joanna's argument not altogether to my liking.

I shrugged. "Everything's relative, I'll grant you that."

"Tell me about you, why don't you? How come *you*'re here?"

That shook me somewhat. I wasn't used to students asking me about myself. Today's kids don't talk much, anyway, and they tend to see the likes of us older ones as "instant person"—ready-mades to listen to them or just frustrate their wants.

"That's a long story, Joanna. I assume you don't want a blow-by-blow account of the Davey Bryant saga? Especially the edited version, which is all you'd get anyway."

"You're not married?"

"You asked me that before. No."

"I wasn't really asking—just thinking, that's all."

"Well, let's give you some food for thought. I suppose you could say, using today's jargon, that I was into animals. Probably a result of frustration of the parental instinct. Though you would have had to come up with a different explanation when I was younger than you are. Anyway, I've two dogs and a cat back in Vancouver. And I've raised fox cubs, a badger, two ferrets, and, more recently, a skunk. Oh, and I had a pony named Tinker who hated drains and pigs. That was back in Cornwall."

"Tell me about Cornwall, why don't you? That's a pretty groovy place, isn't it? I've met kids who've been to St. Ives. They said it was kinda like Long Beach on Vancouver Island. I mean, the kids go there and don't get hassled by the fuzz all the time."

"I'm afraid I've heard it was otherwise. It's an artists' colony as well as a fishing village and those two groups have never gotten on. Then the hippies—sorry—the kids turned up. Now each bunch hates the other two. Not a very happy place at all, they tell me."

"My dad says today's kids are the shits. He works on the logging booms. Got his own towboat. But he won't hire anyone under twenty-five. Says they're unreliable. Do you go along with that?"

"I wouldn't know, would I? I mean, I've never hired anyone and I certainly don't know anything about logging booms except to see 'em floating offshore."

But she wasn't buying my fence-sitting. "Well, do you like kids, then?"

I sat back and tried to be frank with her. "I'm not really sure. I *think* so. But then maybe I'm just chasing the vestige of kid left in me. Either that, or separating myself from the kind of hard-hat attitude your father seems to have. I tell you what, though, I certainly don't like middle-aged men who act and dress like the kids do. That gives me the creeps."

"That's funny. That's really cute." Then she actually chuckled.

"What's so funny?"

"Well, my dad talks all the time like he was still young and here's you, like one half his age, going on like you were a hundred!"

"How old is your father, Joanna?" (Thinking of my upcoming fortieth birthday.)

"Thirty-eight—around in there, I guess."

I swallowed dryness in my mouth. That made me realize my glass was empty again. It also occurred to me that the harsh light in which I was sitting was distinctly unflattering.

"Do you mind if we go in? I could do with a refill for one thing."

She didn't seem to notice the rupture in our line of thought; got up just as if I had made it an order. I thought how passive she was as I followed her through the sliding glass doors. Inside again, the pace quicked. Or, rather, the atmosphere was different from when we had last sat there in the curtained gloom. She was moving about now. Restless. Picking up this object and that and vaguely examining each before sauntering across to something else—a bottle of aftershave, a pocket paper-stapler, a Jane Rule novel which I'd brought with me to read.

"Do you want to borrow something to read? Not that one though, 'cos I haven't finished it myself."

"Yes. Yeah, I would. What do you recommend? I see you got quite a little library over here."

She had crossed over to where I had put some half-dozen paperbacks on the shelf of the headboard behind my bed.

"How about this?" She held up a paperback edition of *Daniel Deronda.* "Jesus! This is one hell of a lot of book, isn't it?" She balanced it in her hand like so much hamburger meat. I smiled at her from my armchair.

"I'm not sure you'd like it. Have you read much George Eliot?"

"Is he Canadian?"

I wanted to hug her then. "*She* was English."

"Gay Lib?"

"*Not* Gay Lib, Joanna. A great nineteenth-century writer. My favorite. That book was the first, I think, to deal with anti-Semitism—or at least an aspect of it."

"Now you sound like a teacher again."

Irritation brushed me. "Christ Almighty! You musn't accuse everyone of pedantry every time information is exchanged. Otherwise we'll all end up fucking ignorant!"

She darted fast from that, though. "Hey! Wait a minute! You're having me on! I've just seen that guy's name. On the other book I picked up." She walked over to where she'd put the Jane Rule novel down and turned to its back cover. "What did I say? Here it is—George P. Elliot."

"No relation, sweetheart. Your one praising the Jane Rule book is contemporary American. And a man. The George Eliot we were talking about was English, Victorian, and a liberal lady."

"Some coincidence, huh? I pick up two books with the name on 'em."

"Let's say the mildest kind of coincidence. Eliot isn't the rarest name. If you discount the different spellings, there are others too. In fact, I think I've got a 'T. S. Eliot' somewhere around here."

"You don't go much on coincidence, then. How about E.S.P.? Say, I don't even know which sign you were born under."

(I knew the jargon of all that stuff. My lover, Ken, brought it back from his students at the university.)

"I'm a Leo."

"You are? I'm a Pisces. I don't think I'd have known you were a Leo, though. They're supposed to be aggressive."

"There's them what would say that's exactly what I am."

"Not with me you're not."

I read the look on her face with perfect comprehension. How well I understood that abrupt lowering of one hip and the corresponding tightening of her bum! Hadn't I done the very same things more times than I cared to remember? 'Silly little flirt,' I told myself, 'you're hardly cut out to seduce a wary old thing like me!'

But the ludicrous, the incredible thing was, I found myself moving slowly up from my chair and toward her. I tried desperately to think of all the off-putting things I associated with womanhood: of messy menstruations, gross hips, enormous buttocks . . . all the misogynistic vocabulary of the gay world flitted through my head . . . yet none of it found lodging. The words . . . hairy snatches, smothering cleavages, and the rest . . . all passed on. The images of hate exploded before they were fully formed. And before I could discover the safe moat of my inversion, my arms were timidly about her, and I found the warmth of her young and sinewy body driving away the prickles of my fear.

"I—I was wondering when," she said. "They said—they said you didn't with girls, I mean."

In spite of her hard body's balm to mine, there was still a space in my head that fought. I addressed her forehead, stared fixedly at the roots of that long, blond hair.

"They—they're right. I—I don't. I'm—"

"You mean you *didn't*. Now—now they're wrong."

"You don't understand, Joanna."

"There's nothing to understand, is there?" Her hands moved about my shoulders and back, ended up pressing gently against the backs of my thighs. And I liked the feel of their presence there.

"I suppose not. But my legs are feeling a little weak. Let's go over there and lie down."

There on the sofa, our manual explorations progressively under way, I felt like some battered old moth fondly seeking solace from a fierce young flame. I remember wincing—just for a second—when the girl's hand first approached that part of me which had not been touched by female hands since those of Harriet Shapiro had fondled me. But shortly after that Joanna drove the old man cold out of me, and some ancient woman sense in her coaxed and encouraged the tentative male lover through the fears of sustaining performance, and made a triumphant youth of me.

And that wasn't the end of it, either! I treasure a cameo of flushed triumph, me panting on top of her, knowing we were linked in fleshly orthodoxy: me dominant, her receiving body all supplication, passive and content with the quickening jerks of my exertions.

However, that brief image soon flickers and fades—into an older icon, perhaps even archetypal. I cannot recall whether we physically changed our positions, but even before the quiet of coital completion, I lay in *her* arms, sucked at her boyish breasts.

No bull-man here . . . no male stud flinging his sperm indifferently into the ordained cradle for masculine pride. Instead, this middle-aged man of me huddled in fetal snugness within the strength of her curves.

And for a long, long time, after the flurry of our spending, it remained that way. We didn't stir, didn't talk—until her arm finally slid off my naked shoulder and her hand went down to tilt my chin and bring it to the level of her own, when she gently kissed me on the lips. Then we got up, showered, and, still without much talk, made our way over the now long-shadowed lawns to the barbecue pit where trestle tables were laid out for dinner.

As we tackled sizzling steak and extracted baked potatoes from their gold-foil jackets, the night rapidly darkened. One by one the other diners departed for their patios, there to sit quietly talking in the dusk. I felt the dew grow heavy about my feet in the grass and, looking beyond the pale frame of Joanna's head, noticed the fresh rash of stars in the Okanagan sky.

I took a long draught at the g & t that I had surreptitiously taken to the table (drinking was still banned out there on the lawn by the archaic B.C. liquor laws) and watched her meticulously separate lean from fat as she tackled her New York cut. Little mounds of rejected meat appeared on the edge of her plate, and her finicky precision mildly irritated me.

"Don't you like that?"

"Sure. It's good steak. Better than the crap I'd have eaten back at the school. Why'd you ask?"

"Just wondered. You're a slow eater."

"No rush, is there? It's groovy out here. Hear those bugs? I thought it was the sprinklers at first."

"Yes, I hear them. They're chirruping . . . they're crickets." (I forbore to add that the naturalist in me hated vague words like "bugs.")

"You look kinda stern. Something eatin' you?"

"No, no. Not at all. I was just thinking. You know, our meat ration was something like half an ounce a week in the war."

"Is that so?" She couldn't have shown greater indifference—especially as she was currently rejecting another portion of her steak on which I could detect no fat whatever.

"You make good love, you know that?"

"I'm glad I pass your test," I said, eyeing her knife and fork. "I don't often get such expert opinion."

She lowered her cutlery onto her plate.

"That wasn't very nice, Davey."

I relented immediately. "I'm sorry. I guess I'm a bit pooped. I don't have your youthful resilence, you know."

"My what?"

"Doesn't matter. Let's just say you look very young sitting there. And I feel very old."

"You should cut out that kinda talk. It's—well, it's stupid. Like it isn't true."

She abandoned the remnants of her meat entirely and picked instead at potato fragments from within the gold-foil shell.

"Say, could I get a sort of reading list out of you?"

I couldn't help smiling. "Sure, I'll make you out a list, Joanna. I'll do it tonight and drop it off at the school in the morning."

I sat back, lit a cigarette, looked up and over her to where the Milky Way twinkled and glowed in the desert sky. Then I looked down again at her oval face framed in that silky straight hair. I probably imagined it, but I thought her eyes shone too, like those stars above.

"Davey?"

"Huh?"

"Do you think I could change into your class? It 'ud be really neat to take playwriting with you."

"No, Joanna. I'll see that you're transferred from Ted Lineham's poetry class to George Sills' though. You'll get all the playwriting experience you want with him."

Then I stood up, the moist grass cool to my sandaled feet. I waited for her to join me as we began to amble slowly back to motel unit. Her hand found mine and I didn't resist. It was only our fingers that were entwined.

"There's another thing, sweetheart . . . Tonight—that was it—I shan't have you back here again. I've thought about it. That's best. Understand?"

Her feet faltered, and we stopped somewhere amid the undulations of the night-darkened grass, under those extravagant stars.

"Sure, sure. I understand. I guess it's too risky. I mean, for you and that."

My own motives lay a thousand miles from thought of risk. But her words brought the cold realization that I no longer had a leg to stand on if I sought to deal with either Lineham or Sills and their philandering. Yet I felt a compulsion to be honest with her.

"Not only that," I said. "But tonight—well, tonight was special. Sort of sealed off. Anything else between us would be imperfection."

I could read her face in spite of the gloaming. On it was the expression of resignation, of bowing to the inevitable, that I see so often on the faces of today's young, and which I had thought, in my own youth, belonged only to such people as Arabs, bent by the rigors of implacable climates and terrains.

"So long, Davey. Sorry it couldn't work out." Her voice was low, muffled. Then she kissed my cheek and walked quickly ahead.

When I reached the room, she had already departed through the farther door. The chain, which she'd taken out of its slot, was still swinging slowly from side to side . . .

*Do we ever stop beating upon the gates of the garden?
Davey, you have not. Maybe I have. Then by these
particular pages I have had the benefit of illumination
from my younger alter ego. But I profess no wisdom but
what I have been taught by my Davey, who is less stiff
in carapace than I am.*

*But between the two of us, author and character,
touching and dividing, through where we have gone,
where we are going, and where we shall end up in the
pages yet to be written, we have learned already
through the blood and hurt of our insect persistence
that there is no more return to the haven of yesterday.
The toys are put away forever. Sigh away as you will,
but Mummy and Daddy are gone.*

Chapter Eleven

Sometimes it isn't that the words themselves are hard to find but that the subject matter—red and angry—is warning to stay away. Rather like those inflamed spots I used to get on my neck as a child: spots that readily invited squeezing as a relief from their tension under the skin, but which I knew would bring eye-watering pain in the act of bursting them.

Such wanting and not-wanting, such approach to a topic intinct with hurt—then flying from it—has haunted me all these endless days of my Vancouver summer as I have sat in the sun on my lonely beach and stared out at anchored ships, and dreamed of a terrible place to which any of them might have sailed.

Terrible because of what occurred there all those years ago; terrible because of the pain and sickness that still afflicts lives affected by a tragedy in which even death was not the culmination but a short cut out of a maze of more horrible things.

For the umpteenth time I start to relate those events as I prop my writing pad upon my bended knee as I sit on the hot, white sand. That smooth and passionless sand, yesterday's experience washed from it by last night's tide, is itself an invitation. So is the recollection that twelve years ago I had also sat somewhere along here—in the privacy of my so-inaccessible cove—gazing out on the same summer water; staring up at the identical ridge of snow-crested peaks at the end of Howe Sound; reading over and over again the pale blue air letter telling me what had happened along a Cornish lane near the lisping edge of another ocean than the one I had recently come to live by.

There is something so *catholic* about the sea: in truth, it is that which bonds me to this Canadian west coast and keeps the vital arteries of time open for me between a Cornish past and a British Columbian present.

I am staring up at the inflamed red trunks of untidy arbutus hanging perilously over the soft-stoned clifftop. And in my turning from vistas of sea and sand the invitation to memory becomes a threat; the longing to run the figures of recollection over the fading face of my cousin Janet (remembered as beautiful before the bloody events of that sunny, Sunday afternoon) turns into an ominous warning.

Under a cloudless sky, in August heat, I shiver. A dog may return to its vomit, a queen may mourn for half a century, but there are incidents beyond sickness, transcendent of death, that we return to at our peril . . .

But the bleeding arbutus, the mournful madrone, is so much more insistent in its exotic particularism than the bland generalities of water and sky. So, fearful but persistent, I determine to lay the ghost that has whispered to me ever since that day, twelve years back, with a telephone conversation hounding my head, a crumpled airletter in my pocket, I wandered, dazed, about the peeling trunks of that arbutus grove which now stands behind me.

TELEPHONE CONVERSATION RECOLLECTED:

(It was—how do they put it?—as clear as if my cousin Miriam were in the next room . . .)

"Davey? Is that you?"

"Yes, it is. Who's that speaking?"

"Your cousin Miriam. I'm over at Uncle Harry's 'cos they've got the phone. Something awful's happened. I thought 'ee ought to know."

(Shock hit me like a kick in the stomach.)

"Is it Mother? Father?"

"None o' they. There've been a terrible accident though—to one'n the family."

(Six thousand miles away I responded in taut irritation to that Cornish voice.)

"Who, then? For God's sake, Miriam, who?"

"'Tis, 'tis Aunt Eileen's girl—your cousin Janet up to Poltinny? Her's, her's *dead*, Davey. It all happened so quick. And you being so close'n that, I thought 'ee'd loike to know."

"Thank you, Cousin Miriam. Of course of course. Now when—where?"

(I didn't know, didn't care, what I was asking. Could think of and see only a laughing little girl, snub-nosed, brown-eyed, pulling at my hair and then running as fast as her chubby, ten-year-old legs would take her, over the stubble of a recently harvested wheatfield.)

"To little Janet, Miriam? What—what could happen to a little girl like that?"

There was a pause, when I thought I could detect my cousin's breathing.

"She weren't a *baby*, no more, Davey. She were a beautiful young girl of eighteen. Beautiful . . . beautiful . . . ask any on 'em—they'll all tell on 'ee the same."

"Yes. Yes, of course. I'm sorry. I've been here in Vancouver so long. I'd forgotten."

"Too long, too long, Davey. But she never forgot 'ee, Davey. Her allus called 'ee her favorite uncle. You know she called on 'ee 'uncle' and not 'cousin' don't 'ee?"

I thought of the ten years or so separating us. Hadn't I introduced her mother to that fair-haired husband of hers, then a sailor with me in Devonport barracks?

"No—no, I didn't know, Miriam. But it's understandable. Miriam?"

"Yes."

"You—you still haven't told me what happened."

"She were out riding—like she always do on Saturdays. She loved that mare—jest like you did that colt, Rob Roy, when you was growing up, Davey. There b'aint been another so fond of the animals in the family since you, as our Janet."

"Miriam—don't cry."

"Tryin' not to. Well, she was up Blisland way, they say. On the road comin' in off the moor. Some lorry come up behind her quickly. They reckon neither she nor the horse heard'n coming. You know how the wind do blow up there in the moor? Anyways, the mare shied, and Janet come off. They reckon her head hit the roadway and—and—"

"All right, Miriam. You needn't— Don't upset yourself any more."

"Oi got you telephone number from your mother. I knew'd you'd want to know. That's why Oi'm phoning, loike. You and Janet was allus so close. Loike your mother says, 'twere loike older brother and little sister. Then you was always closer to Janet's mother than most on us."

"How is she? How is Eileen taking it?"

"Carryin' on something terrible she was. Then the doctor give her something. You remember what a one she were for grieving when Great-Aunt Eileen went."

I did indeed. I had, in fact, been staying with my aunt Eileen (who happened to be my own age and therefore never referred to by me as other than plain Eileen) when her mother had died. (Oh, this intricate mesh of Cornish relationships, all so carefully designated with second and third cousinships titled accordingly, and all so meticulously traced and explained to the inquiring stranger!)

Yes, I did most certainly remember Eileen's strange wailing when she had taken that cup of early morning tea upstairs which the old lady lying stiffly there would never drink.

"What about Frank, Miriam? It must be hard for him with his little girl gone and Eileen to take care of."

Miriam didn't answer. Not for a long time, that is.

"That's another reason I telephoned, Davey. Frank's gone."

"What do you mean, gone?"

"He hadn' come back. He were there, see. At the accident."

"You mean he saw—"

"Everything."

"Oh my God!"

"He stayed for the police and the ambulance and all that. But he never did go home, and no one's seen of 'un since."

"I can imagine he might well want to be on his own."

Imagine? What the hell was I saying! As if I could possibly imagine a father's thoughts as he witnessed the violent death of his beautiful eighteen-year-old child. An only child. Father and daughter . . . And quiet, gentle Frank of so few words, who never responded to Eileen's somewhat neurotic goading save with smiles and patient explanations of why they could not as yet afford this or that. Of *course* Frank would flee the articulate grief of our lachrymose clan, just as a wounded animal would retreat to a private place to lick its wounds and succumb to its sorrow.

"Were they the pips?"

"Pips?" But even as I queried her I remembered the British term for the end of a telephone time period.

"It doesn't matter, cousin Miriam. I'll send you the money for this phone call. Don't worry about it."

"You'll write to poor Eileen, then? I know she'd love a letter from you more'n anyone else in the world, Davey."

"Of course I will. And, Miriam?"

"Yes?"

"Don't do anything about Frank. Let him handle it in his own way. But when he does turn up, will you give him a message from me?"

"What would that be then?"

"Just tell him—oh, tell him I'll get over just as soon as I can."

We said our goodbyes and I heard a click at her end of the line. For a moment I stood there, staring out at the cultivated effulgence of my August garden, then let the phone fall heavily back in its cradle. I even recall glancing down and noticing that the receiver was crooked—not snug in its berth. But somehow I lacked the energy to straighten it. With the breath all gone from me as the result of Miriam's news, I continued to stand there, staring unblinking at the late spikes of pale blue lupine, the masses of golden shower roses, and at the mobile sprinkler flip-flopping rhythmically in the center of the green expanse of lawn.

"Why can't they all leave me alone?" I said aloud to the jumble of floral color that Ken and I had created around ourselves.

"Why the hell did they think I left to come here if it wasn't to escape *all that?*"

When Ken came back later that afternoon it was to find me stripped to the waist, immersed in the process of tearing out the old and woody hydrangea clump at the foot of the back steps, where we had vaguely talked of planting a crimson camellia as relief from daffodil yellow the following March.

I remember letters, or rather fragment of letters:

. . . And so, Eileen, I return to what I said at the outset: this is truly the hardest letter I have ever had to write. If there are answers, then I do not know them. I wouldn't for a moment presume to suggest reasons why a beautiful young girl should be taken while people like me endure. When Grandpa Bryant died I knew a sense of loss, even of guilt for those times I had been quite unnecessarily rude to him. But I cannot honestly say I have ever experienced the grief which you must be suffering at this very moment. I have never mourned as I watched you mourn the passing of your mother that bleak winter we shared together. So, out of a great sense of frustration and powerlessness, Eileen, let me offer my love for you and Frank, and the thought from all these miles apart that, since Miriam's phone call, there has been scarcely a moment when the two of you, in your tragic bereavement, have been out of my consciousness.

Your cousin-cum-nephew, but more importantly your friend, lovingly—Davey . . .

Tregellis,
St. Teath,
nr. Camelford,
Cornwall.
August 22, 1962

Dear Son,

Your mother's been tellin' me to write this to you ever since the accident. Little Janet, I mean. I know Miriam didn't mention it when she telephoned you, 'cos she knew nothing of it. Nor does Eileen know. She's in enough state as 'tis. But if she knew she'd go right out of her mind, I don't mind tellin' 'ee, Son. Poor Frank knows—'cos he's the one that saw it all happen. It could not have been more horrible, Davey. When the mare shied and she fell off, lying in the road and that. The truck come back in reverse to see what had happened, and went over her. Her father saw it all. Just imagine that. No wonder he looks like a dead man himself.

Why am I telling you this? Because your mother and I fear for that couple. And you was closest to both of them, you know that. There's few their age 'round here. I know there's your cousin Miriam, but she and Eileen were never that close, were they? That's why if you could come over, Son, you would be doing your Christian duty, believe me. I know you've been out there in Canada for nigh on six year, and that you left memories behind you'd rather not re-live, I dare say. But we are not getting any younger, and of course we'd love to see you . . .

That was the contents, in part at least, of the crumpled air letter which arrived a few days after the phone conversation with Miriam and which I took with me to the arbutus grove. That was the letter which I did not answer and whose request I denied until it was too late . . .

Oh yes, I went back to Cornwall. But that was not until several years later, and there is something I have to explain first. Maybe "explain" is the wrong word. In any case, how do you "explain" Vancouver? How do you explain the realities of the unreality which is so much of my west coast life?

There was first, of course, the weather. On the very evening that my father's letter came, a depression moved in off the Pacific and for the first time in many weeks the mountains on the north shore were hid from view, and day and night the foghorn at Port Atkinson moaned steadily. With a September rawness prematurely in the air, the heavy gray clouds seemed to sink lower and lower upon us, until it took little effort of the imagination to believe that only the high-rise buildings of the downtown were holding the skies off our heads.

Roses in the garden that had been about to bloom refused to do so—and in consequence grew sodden and waterlogged, and even mildewed, as they hung unhappy on their stems. For piled clouds soon turned to rain, and on August 28, my diary records, we lit a fire in the living room, squatted on the floor before the flames of the blazing alder, and listened to the phonograph.

We talked a lot, of course, about what had happened in Cornwall, and several times Ken asked me if I was considering a visit. I told him that I was certainly thinking about it, but that perhaps it would be better to wait until the fall, off-season fares, and time to finish off such magazine and C.B.C. commissions I had scheduled to complete that summer.

But we had no sooner returned to an "r" in the month when the clouds blew onward to Alberta, and the Lower Mainland stood revealed in that clarity of light—green softness of mood—when it is at its most truly seductive. It was not the same sunshine we had known before. The days were once more hot, the sky, if anything, a fiercer blue. But the mood of it all was different. The lawn, for example, no longer needed the sprinkler to sparkle. The dew did that each night. Dahlias and daisies now set the dominant tones in the flowerbeds. And with the coming of darkness came the chill breath of autumn, while the ripples of the bay stepped up their sibilance as they met the shingle of the shore and awaited the return of the waves that the fall equinox would bring on the wings of the wind.

How then could I fly away and leave all this—knowing that these golden days were but a ration from the North Pacific, soon to be followed by the cold, the gray, the wet? How could I? Easily enough! And so Ken told me more than once, as September crept into October and still the benign days did not break. But I shunned him as I shunned a rereading of my father's letter. Even so, the solitary walks along Kitsilano beach with only waterfowl warily watching, the visits to my isolated stretch of sand where one was unlikely to encounter anyone else, even before Labor Day, all proved insufficient anodyne. For there was always Ken, you see, when I returned home, to inquire gently of a decision and to suggest duties where I saw only grotesque dread.

So I took the ferry to Saltspring and stayed with Hilda for a few days—Hilda being a thirty-year-old divorcee whom I knew to be so full of herself and her marital melodramas that she would never stop to press and probe at my Cornish wound. I returned to the mainland and Ken with my mind and feelings happily without focus. I had gone to Saltspring deliberately seeking distraction and the island did not let me down. I came home utterly distracted—to the point that my roommate found himself having to shout at me to get my attention.

There was one letter awaiting me, though, that I could not ignore. It was from Frank, the dead girl's father.

Dear Davey,

If Eileen knew I was writing this letter I'm sure she'd want me to thank you for your letter of condolence. But she does not and I shall not tell her. You see, Cousin Miriam has gone and told her that your parents have said you were planning to come over here on account of us and our tragedy. And this has upset Eileen something proper, I don't mind telling you.

I cannot write of our affliction except to say we are managing as best we can. But we are not seeing no one at present and it would be a waste of time your coming here as neither Eileen nor I feel up to it.

Cousin Miriam caught Eileen on Fore Street, the first time Eileen was out shopping since our tragedy. It will be a long time, I am feeling, afore Eileen will go out again, and I reckon then we shall go down St. Columb for our shopping.

Eileen is still under the Doctor and I have been having nightmares something terrible. I can't remember when I last had a proper night's sleep. I sometimes wonder whether we shall pull through, but people's pity would be even worse than this what we are going through, and have since the jaws of hell opened for us.

I would rather you not answer this letter, Davey. And, like I said, do not come over here to the farm as it would only upset Eileen and me and we can do without that, I don't mind telling you.

> Hoping you understand,
> As ever,
> Frank.

Well, I didn't ignore *that* letter—indeed, was only too keen to take it at its face value. So Frank didn't want me to return to

Cornwall to see them? He need not have worried! Never had my life in Vancouver seemed more attractive, harder to leave . . . Never had the heavy Celtic immersion in death seemed more alien to my exiled spirit. So Frank and Eileen would switch their shopping patronage from Wadebridge (pop. 10,000) to St. Columb Major (pop. 4,000), and just nine miles down the road over the moors. Big deal! *I* should be impressed? I, who had switched my own mores thousands of miles? Had yielded a whole ocean for another? Had made a commitment to a whole new country whose inhabitants not only spoke with different accents from mine, but, if I used my Cornish ways of speech, would regard me as either incomprehensible or a figure of mild mirth; as something faintly rustic, something "provincial" in the British sense?

(Strange, that. I mean, that the soft-burred sounds of my childhood and youth, the language in which I learned of love and lust, of illness and death, and of the awesome probings of religion, should become just a party turn of my Canadian life. The costs of emigration can be subtle as well as severe, at least for the likes of me . . .)

But don't misunderstand me. I had made my choice, and as the days of my Pacific-girt life grew into years, as I began slowly to forget talk of rocks and of wrens, of furze and of swayling, and to acquire a vocabulary of salal and salmonberry, of grackles swaying precariously on the slim branches of broom, so did the mountains at the head of the Fraser Valley become, not a wall of isolation, but a screen of protection.

It was just a matter of days after reading Frank's letter, but I can recall so vividly the return of the snows to the peaks of the north shore and the sense of immense relief that for us of Vancouver the white shutters of winter were up once more.

As the rains sloshed and sluiced around the gurgling gutters of Granville Street, or pitted the deserted sand in front of the flaking bathhouse at English Bay, I sortied out into the leaden light of November, wearing just a raincoat over a sweater, loving the water streaming down my face, and hysterically glad that my life was free from aching eastern cold and green-obliterating snow . . .

But it was more than beguilement of climate that further softened my will to leave my wet west coast that fall and winter. Something happened one November Saturday that led to a chain of events which persuaded the weird illogic of my emotions that Vancouver must be my moist and mild fortress until I was strong enough to look the anguish of others in the eyes again.

Parking Ken's car on a grass verge of Southwest Marine Drive, I took a quiet-looking lane that eventualy broke free of the dripping firs and descended steeply to the flat of the Southlands that stretched to the delta of the Fraser, and to the edge of the ocean, over to my right. This was an area I had not explored before and I remain puzzled to this day as to why I should have persisted in walking across that dun, somewhat waterlogged landscape where farms and sundry buildings seemed littered rather than built and where the overall flavor was of the ramshackle and unkempt.

All I know is that as the road degenerated into mere track, the evergreen stands on either side, petering out into clumps of still-red-berried mountain ash, I grew conscious of a smell I had known since childhood. Not that at first, as I skillfully skirted the plenteous puddles (there had been lots of rain for several days previous), I was able to identify it. Not until the lane curved sharply and I saw in front of me a pile of horse manure, steaming.

Strange that something as prosaic as horseshit should prove such a vigorous conduit to memories of youthful bliss. But there it was—a few shattered balls of equine turds on the stony ground and I was away down memory lane to that moment of ecstasy when a father had led his unsuspecting nine-year-old son up through the farmyard to the field we called Grandma's Meadow.

"Whose horse is that, Father? B'aint seen him before."

"Yours, boy. That is, if 'ee grooms on 'im proper, keeps his stall clean, and feeds of 'un regular."

"Mine? O gosh, Dad, thanks! You didn't forget . . . All that time . . ."

"I said when 'ee were nine. That's only next month. Your mother and Oi seen of 'un down to Wadebridge market yesterday. 'Twere too good a bargain to pass up. Welsh pony he is. Bred by Trebilcock up to Delabole."

At which point the object of our attention stopped munching and came directly toward us. Quickly I stooped and plucked a clump of grass. I lay it flat on my hand as the soft muzzle brushed my palm, sniffed, and then started to eat. I tell you, I almost peed my pants in the excitement of it all.

"What—what's his name?"

"Whatever you do call of 'un, boy."

"Then it's Rob Roy."

"Rob Roy. What koind of name's that, you!"

"It's a horse in *Black Beauty,* the book I'm reading."

"You and your books! Well, Rob Roy here will get 'ee out of the granary and all that readin' into the fresh air. That's what Oi do hope, anyways. On the other hand, your mother's scared 'tis goin' interfere with your school work."

"I want to ride of 'un roight away! Did 'er come wi' a bridle and saddle and that?"

"Bridle's in the stables, along with the others for the work horses. You'll have a saddle when Oi've taught 'ee to ride proper, bareback and not a day before. That's 'ow Oi learned, and so shall you. 'Tis the best way, Davey, mark my words."

And that's how I did learn; doing everything with my knees and legs about the sides of Rob Roy before I ever had use of saddle or stirrup.

Now, as I walked on down the track, it was the recollected smell of horse sweat and the memory of chafed bare legs that unfurled in me, and when I turned a corner to see a cluster of buildings with the faded sign: McGovern's Riding Stables on the wall of one of them, I had a strange feeling of past and present brought abruptly together.

As if in a trance I entered the straw-strewn courtyard and asked a plump girl in dirty jeans and navy-blue turtleneck about hiring a horse. My voice must have been dreamy or unusually soft, as I remember having to repeat my request several times. Then again, I may have lapsed back into that Cornish dialect which was my only speech at the age of nine and the acquisition of Rob Roy.

"You used to ridin'?"

"I reckon."

"Well, there's Daisy in there. Most of 'em's out. Like Saturday afternoon and that."

"I'll take her then."

"Five bucks an hour, okay? Don't give her too much rein—that mare's got some will of her own."

"So had Rob Roy."

"I beg your pardon?"

"Nothing. He could be a hellion, though, when 'er was moinded."

"What's that? 'Fraid I don' getcha."

"Eh? I'm sorry. Thinking out loud. I'll take Rob Roy then."

"Daisy. By the way, I've got a western up on her, but with that accent of yours, maybe you want an English saddle?"

"No, no. Not at all. Western's great."

(I'd never ridden "western," but what the hell! 'Jesus,' I reflected, 'I haven't been on *any* kind of saddle for nearly twenty years!')

As the fat-bottomed girl led Daisy out of the gloom of the galvanized makeshift shed, I looked somewhat apprehensively at the big, raw-boned mare of dappled gray. Her black mane was short and the thick, well-muscled neck was held low. She didn't look at all pleased about having her Saturday afternoon interrupted this way. However, after a loud snort, exposing bright red nostrils, her head came up somewhat—the better to inspect me.

"That's a girl, Daisy. The exercise'll do ya good. Here, let me fix them stirrups for ya. They're fit for a midget the way they is."

While she fiddled with that, I tried to get to know Daisy better. I patted the white blaze between her eyes and then let my hand touch the velvety softness of her mottled muzzle. That, and her hay-scented breath so close to my own, etched Rob Roy's memory even sharper than the earlier smell of manure.

It was the same when I finally mounted her. In spite of the oddity of that phallic stump in front of me, of the western saddle, and the clumsy and heavy stirrups that would have looked more congruous on a carthorse, there was the same magic of feeling as my thighs and legs beneath my jeans took the pulsation of the horseflesh, the ripple of Daisy's muscles. I closed my eyes in the nostalgia of it, then leaned forward to pat the straining neck and say the soft-silly words of affection I had once used on Rob Roy.

As we started off, back through the gate I'd entered which the girl now held open, and back along the lane, it vaguely occurred to me that I had no idea where to go on horseback. But Daisy seemed to have it all worked out. At one intersection I made a feeble attempt to take a muddied path leading west, but I learned at one and the same moment that my mount had a mouth as sensitive as old leather and that she was quite confirmed in her itinerary. Up the steep hill we climbed sedately. (Daisy, as I also discovered about that time, was a horse who was not in a rush.)

It wasn't long before she brought me to the complex of bridle paths that cut deep into the forested areas of the University Endowment Lands of Point Grey. And it was here, as we slowly meandered past dripping bushes, over the soft, brown floor below giant Douglas firs, and along the crumbling clay banks of rush-whispering ponds, that the inevitable vision of young cousin Janet confronted me with all the force of that Pauline phenomenon along the Damascus Road. What had been vague, seemingly undirected, now became clear and cruelly meticulous in detail. Although Daisy, in reality, just plodded on, slowing as much as she dared every now and then to pluck at some foliage, I heard the sudden squeal of brakes, the murderous racket of the truck's engine; felt my horse shy under me and whinny in pain and fear. I let the reins droop, put my suddenly cold hands on the warm neck of the mare as I shivered and felt the sweat break out on my forehead.

'Oh dear, dead Janet . . . this is the closest I can get . . . this way I can speed the route of the mind's eye . . . look at the bloody destruction of your youth and beauty. Because Janet, my child, my broken-winged angel, I am *safe*. I am *not* on your trim young mare but this tired old nag. And I ride through the screened green trails of these soft woodlands where no traffic rumbles: anonymous in an anonymous vegetation, where all are alien.

'Yes, *now* I can look at your bloodied body—child companion of my young manhood; *now* the lament of your grief-crazed loved ones can sing freely in my ears. For now, up here on Daisy —stubborn, humble, contented old Daisy—looking preposterous on a western saddle, city-shoed feet in these gigantic stirrups, I can face the fact of my cowardice, learn the dimensions of my limitations.'

On and on, then, that November afternoon, Daisy took me. And as we crossed and recrossed our tracks the face of little Janet turned into the wild-eyed one of her mother, then the clenched-teethed one of Frank. I saw the patient but anxious expressions of my parents, the worried look of dear, fat Miriam, who had picked up the phone to plug me into their pain.

But it was the warmth and strength of plodding old Daisy which sustained me. And when she finally returned me to the stables, although my mind was made up (firmer in resolution than it had been since that black day in August), my legs were so weak I thought for a moment I was about to totter and fall.

"Hey! Be careful! Guess you're feeling a bit stiff, huh? Long time no ride, that it?"

"Not really. I had a great time. As a matter of fact, I'd like to book her for next week."

"You can have something better, you know. 'Specially if you reserve. Daisy ain't the greatest, I gotta admit that."

"No. It's Daisy I want."

"It's Daisy you got then."

"In fact, *every* Saturday. Right through the winter."

"That ain't necessary. Pay every time. Then there ain't no bookkeeping. Besides, you never know with the weather, do ya?"

"See you next week, then."

"Surely. I'll have her nice and ready—won't we, Daisy?"

But Daisy was already staring toward her stall with its hay-stuffed manger.

Well, there's not much for me to add. I did go nearly every Saturday—right through to late spring, when I left for Toronto for a couple of weeks. As for Cornwall, it was nearly four years before I got there.

The reason for that was my dad's funeral, which is really another story. Neither Frank nor Eileen were in the packed little church, nor at the burial. Miriam told me apologetically afterward that they were both suffering from very bad colds. I didn't go over to see them and, as luck would have it, I didn't bump into either of them in Wadebridge or St. Columb. The closest I got to them, I guess, was that laughing April afternoon when, with the rooks cawing incessantly in the elms overhead, and the blackthorn foaming prettily in the spring-green hedges, I walked up to the upper churchyard and stood for a long time amid the primroses that surrounded Janet's excessively neat and cared-for grave.

The grass may be a coverlet, the grave a final bed. But from here there is only rest, the circle being completed. Davey and David are not yet ordered to sleep. But in the wandering of us both, one thing is certain . . .

. . . *NO MORE INTO THE GARDEN.*